THE

Mark Haddon writer and playwright who has written ...... books for children and won two BAFTAs. His bestselling novel, *The Curious Incident of the Dog in the Night-time*, was published simultaneously by Jonathan Cape and David Fickling in 2003. It won seventeen literary prizes, including the Whitbread Award. His poetry collection, *The Talking Horse and the Sad Girl and the Village Under the Sea*, was published by Picador in 2005, and his last novel, *A Spot of Bother*, was published by Jonathan Cape in 2006. His play, *Polar Bears*, ran at the Donmar Warehouse in 2010. He lives in Oxford.

MARK HADDON

The Red House

VINTAGE BOOKS
London

Published by Vintage 2013

2 4 6 8 10 9 7 5 3 1

Copyright © Mark Haddon 2012

Mark Haddon has asserted his right under the Copyright, Designs
and Patents Act 1988 to be identified as the author of this work

First published in Great Britain in 2012 by
Jonathan Cape

Vintage
Random House, 20 Vauxhall Bridge Road,
London SW1V 2SA

www.vintage-books.co.uk

Addresses for companies within The Random House Group Limited
can be found at: www.randomhouse.co.uk/offices.htm

The Random House Group Limited Reg. No. 954009

A CIP catalogue record for this book
is available from the British Library

ISBN 9780099570172

The Random House Group Limited supports The Forest
Stewardship Council (FSC®), the leading international forest
certification organisation. Our books carrying the FSC label are
printed on FSC® certified paper. FSC is the only forest certification
scheme endorsed by the leading environmental organisations,
including Greenpeace. Our paper procurement policy can be found
at www.randomhouse.co.uk/environment

Typeset by Palimpsest Book Production Ltd,
Falkirk, Stirlingshire

Printed and bound in Great Britain by Clays Ltd, St Ives PLC

To Clare

with thanks to Mary Gawne-Cain

Friday

Cooling towers and sewage farms. Finstock, Charlbury, Ascott-under-Wychwood. Seventy miles per hour, the train unzips the fields. Two gun-grey lines beside the river's meander. Flashes of sun on the hammered metal. Something of steam about it, even now. Hogwarts and Adlestrop. The night mail crossing the border. Cheyenne sweeping down from the ridge. Delta blues from the boxcar. Somewhere, those secret points that might just switch and send you curving into a world of uniformed porters and great-aunts and summers at the lake.

Angela leant against the cold window, hypnotised by the power lines as they sagged and were scooped up by the next gantry, over and over and over. Polytunnels like silver mattresses, indecipherable swirls of graffiti on a brick siding. She'd buried her mother six weeks ago. A bearded man in a suit with shiny elbows playing 'Danny Boy' on Northumbrian pipes. Everything out of kilter, the bandage on the vicar's hand, that woman chasing her windblown hat between the headstones, the dog that belonged to no one. She thought her mother had left the world a long way back, the weekly visits mostly for Angela's own benefit. Boiled mutton, Classic FM and a commode in flesh-coloured plastic. Her death should have been a relief. Then the first spade of earth hit the coffin, a bubble rose in her chest and she realised her mother had been . . . what? a cornerstone? a breakwater?

The week after the funeral Dominic had been standing at the sink bottle-brushing the green vase. The last of the freak snow was still packed down the side of the shed and the rotary washing line was turning in the wind. Angela came in holding the phone as if it was a mystery object she'd found on the hall table. *That was Richard.*

Dominic upended the vase on the wire rack. *And what did he want?*

He's offered to take us on holiday.

He dried his hands on the tea towel. *Are we talking about your brother, or some entirely different Richard?*

We are indeed talking about my brother.

He really had no idea what to say. Angela and Richard had spent no more than an afternoon in each other's company over the last fifteen years and their meeting at the funeral had seemed perfunctory at best. *Where's the exotic location?*

He's rented a house on the Welsh border. Near Hay-on-Wye.

The fine sandy beaches of Herefordshire. He halved the tea towel and hung it over the radiator.

I said yes.

Well, thanks for the consultation.

Angela paused and held his eye. *Richard knows we can't afford a holiday of our own. I'm not looking forward to it any more than you, but I didn't have a great deal of choice.*

He held up his hands. *Point taken.* They'd had this argument way too many times. *Herefordshire it is, then.*

Ordnance Survey 161. The Black Mountains / Y Mynyddoedd Duon. Dominic flipped up the pink cover and unfolded the big paper concertina. He had loved maps since he was a boy. Here be monsters. X marks the spot. The edges of the paper browned and scalloped with a burning match, messages flashed from peak to peak using triangles of broken mirror.

He looked sideways at Angela. So hard to remember that girl on the far side of the union bar, her shoulders in that blue summer dress. She disgusted him now, the size and sag of her, the veins on her calves, almost a grandmother. He dreamt of her dying unexpectedly, rediscovering all those freedoms he'd lost twenty years ago. Then he had the same dream five minutes later and he remembered what poor use he'd made of those freedoms first time round and he heard the squeak of trolley wheels and saw the bags of fluid. All those other lives. You never did get to lead them.

He gazed out of the window and saw a narrowboat on the adjacent canal, some bearded pillock at the tiller, pipe, mug of tea. *Ahoy there, matey.* Stupid way to spend a holiday, banging your head every time you stood up. A week in a boat with Richard. Think of that. They were in the middle of nowhere, thank goodness. If it all got too much he could walk up into the hills and yell at the sky. To be honest, it was Angela he was worried about. All that hard-wired sibling friction. Do not return once lit and so forth.

Richard's hair, yes. Now that he thought about it that was where the evil was located, this luxuriant black crest, like the tusks of a bull walrus, a warning to beta males. Or like a separate creature entirely, some alien life form that had pushed suckers into his skull and was using him as a vehicle.

The children sat opposite. Alex, seventeen, was reading *Main Force* by Andy McNab. Daisy, sixteen, was reading a book called *The Art of Daily Prayer*. Benjy, eight, had swivelled so that his feet were on the headrest and his head was hanging over the edge of the seat, eyes closed. Angela poked his shoulder with the toe of her shoe. *What on earth are you doing?*

I'm on horseback beheading Nazi zombies.

They looked like children from three separate families, Alex the athlete, all shoulders and biceps, off into the wide blue yonder every other weekend, canoeing, mountain-biking, Benjy a kind of boy-liquid which had been poured into whatever space he happened to be occupying, and Daisy . . . Angela wondered if something dreadful had happened to her daughter over the past year, something that might explain the arrogant humility, the way she'd made herself so ostentatiously plain.

They plunged into a tunnel and the windows thumped

6

and clattered. She saw an overweight, middle-aged woman floating out there in the dark for several seconds before she vanished in a blast of sunlight and poplars, and she was back in her body again, dress pinching at the waist, beads of sweat in the small of her back, that train smell, burning dust, hot brakes, the dull reek of the toilets.

Carter placed his boot on the man's shoulder and rolled him over. This couldn't be happening. He'd killed Bunny O'Neil. They'd trained together in the Cairngorms ten years ago. What was an ex-SAS captain doing in the middle of Afghanistan, armed with a black-market Soviet rifle, trying to assassinate a billionaire head of an international construction company?

Further down the carriage the ticket collector was squatting beside a bird-frail woman with long grey hair and spectacles on a red string. *So you've come on the train with no ticket and no means of payment?* Shaved head, cloudy blue tattoo on his meaty forearm.

Angela wanted to pay for her ticket and save her from this bullying man.

She was trying to pick something invisible from the air with her tiny liver-spotted hands. *I can't . . .*

Is someone meeting you at Hereford? A tenderness in his voice which she hadn't heard the first time. He touched the woman's arm gently to get her attention. *A son, maybe, or a daughter?*

The woman clawed at the air. *I can't quite . . .*

Angela felt a prickle at the corner of her eye and turned away.

Richard had remarried six months ago, acquiring a step-daughter into the bargain. Angela hadn't gone to the wedding. Edinburgh was a long way, it was term time and they'd never felt like brother and sister, just two people who spoke briefly on the phone every few weeks or so to manage the stages of their mother's decline. She'd met Louisa and Melissa for the first time at the funeral. They looked as if they had been purchased from an exclusive catalogue at some exorbitant price, flawless skin and matching black leather boots. The girl stared at her and didn't look away when Angela caught her eye. Bobbed chestnut hair, black denim skirt almost but not quite too short for a funeral. So much sheen and sneer at sixteen. *Melissa's directing a play at school.* A Midsummer Night's Dream.

Something slightly footballer's wife about Louisa. Angela couldn't picture her going to the theatre or reading a serious book, couldn't imagine the conversations she and Richard might have when they were alone. But his judgement of other people had always been a little wobbly. Ten years married to the Ginger Witch. The presents he bought for the kids when he last visited, so much effort aimed in the wrong direction. Benjy's football annual, Daisy's bracelet. She wondered if he was making a new version of the same mistake, whether she was simply not-Jennifer, and he was another rung on the social ladder.

I'm going to the loo. Benjy stood up. *My bladder is so awesomely full.*

Don't get lost. She touched his sleeve.

You can't get lost on a train.

A sick pervert could strangle you, said Alex, *and throw your body out of a window.*

I'll punch him in the crutch.

Crotch, said Alex.

Critch, crotch, cratch . . . sang Benjy as he made his way up the carriage.

Eventually we find that we no longer need silence. We no longer need solitude. We no longer even need words. We can make all our actions holy. We can cook a meal for our family and it becomes prayer. We can go for a walk in the park and it becomes prayer.

Alex photographed a herd of cows. What was the point of being black and white, evolutionarily? He hated real violence. He could still hear the snap of Callum's leg that night in Crouch End. He felt sick when he saw footage from Iraq or Afghanistan. He didn't tell anyone about this. But Andy McNab tamed it by turning it into a cartoon. And now he was thinking about Melissa unzipping that black denim skirt. The word *unzipping* gave him an erection which he covered with the novel. But was it OK fancying your uncle's step-daughter? Some people married their cousins and that was acceptable, unless you both had recessive genes for something bad and your babies came out really fucked up. But girls who went to private school were secretly gagging for it, with their tans and their white knickers that smelt of fabric conditioner. Except she probably wouldn't speak to him, would she, because girls only spoke to twats with floppy hair and skinny jeans. On the other hand, normal service was kind of suspended on holiday and maybe they'd be sharing a bathroom and he'd go in and open the shower cubicle door and squeeze her soapy tits so she moaned.

A man is trapped in a hot flat above the shipyard, caring for a wife who will live out her days in this bed, watching this television. Twin sisters are separated at seven weeks and know nothing of one another, only an absence that walks beside them always on the road. A girl is raped by her mother's boyfriend. A child dies and doesn't die. *Family*, that slippery word, a star to every wandering bark, and everyone sailing under a different sky.

And then there was her fourth child, the child no one else could see. Karen, her loved and secret ghost, stillborn all those years ago. Holoprosencephaly. Hox genes failing along the midline of the head. Her little monster, features melted into the centre of her face. They'd told her not to look but she'd looked and screamed at them to take the thing away. Then in the small hours, while Dominic slept and the ward was still, she wanted that tiny damaged body in her arms again, because she could learn to love her, she really could, but the points had switched and Karen had swerved away into the parallel world she glimpsed sometimes from cars and trains, the spiderweb sheds and the gypsy camps, the sidings and the breakers' yards, the world she visited in dreams, stumbling through dogshit and nettles, the air treacly with heat, lured by a girl's voice and the flash of a summer dress. And this coming Thursday would be Karen's eighteenth birthday. Which was what she hated about the countryside, no distraction from the dirty messed-up workings of the heart. *You'll love it*, Dominic had said. *Inbred locals surrounding the house at night with pitchforks and flaming brands*. Not understanding, in the way that he failed to understand so many things these days.

Dominic wiped the sandwich crumbs from his lip and looked over at Daisy who smiled briefly before returning to her book. She was so much calmer these days, none of the unpredictable tears which spilt out of her last year, making him feel clumsy and useless. It was bollocks, of course, the Jesus stuff, and some of the church people made his flesh crawl. Bad clothes and false cheer. But he was oddly proud, the strength of her conviction, the way she swam so doggedly against the current. If only her real friends hadn't drifted away. But Alex wouldn't look up however long you stared. If he was reading he was reading, if he was running he was running. He'd expected more from having a son. That Oedipal rage between two and four. *Stop hugging Mummy*. Then, from seven to ten, a golden time, filling a buried cashbox with baby teeth and Pokémon cards, camping in the New Forest, that night the pony opened the zip of their tent and stole their biscuits. He taught Alex how to play the piano, theme tunes arranged in C Major with a single finger in the left hand. *Star Wars*, *Raiders of the Lost Ark*. But he grew bored of the piano and gave Benjy the key to the cashbox and went camping with his friends. Devon, the Peak District.

He wondered sometimes if he loved Daisy not because of the strength of her belief but because of her loneliness, the mess she was making of her life, the way it rhymed with his own.

Behind everything there is a house. Behind everything there is always a house, compared to which every other house is larger or colder or more luxurious. Cladding over thirties brick, a broken greenhouse, rhubarb and rusted cans of Castrol for the mower. At the far end you can peel back the corner of the chicken-wire fence and slip down into the cutting where the trains run to Sheffield every half-hour. The tarry sleepers, the locked junction box where they keep the electricity. If you leave pennies on the rail the trains hammer them into long bronze tongues, the queen's face flattened to nothing.

Pan back and you're kneeling at the pond's edge because your brother says there are tadpoles. You reach into the soup of stems and slime, he shoves you and you're still screaming when you hit the surface. Your mouth fills with water. Fear and loneliness will always taste like this. You run up the garden, sodden, trailing weed, shouting, *Dad . . . Dad . . .*

Dad . . . And you can see him standing at the kitchen door, but he starts to evaporate as you reach the cracked patio, thinning in waves like Captain Kirk in the transporter room, that same high buzzing sound, and the door is empty, and the kitchen is empty, and the house is empty and you realise he's never coming back.

Have you not got anything else to read? asked Angela.

Yep, said Daisy, *but right now this is the book I would like to read if that's all right by you.*

There's no need to be sarcastic.

Ladies . . . said Alex, which would have escalated the row to flashpoint if they hadn't been interrupted by Benjy running down the carriage and pinballing off the seat backs. He'd been standing in the toilet when he remembered the werewolf from the Queen Victoria episode of *Doctor Who.* Eyes like black billiard balls, the heat of its breath on his neck. He squirrelled himself under Dad's arm and rubbed the silky cuff of Dad's special shirt against his upper lip. Dad said, *You all right, Captain?* and he said, *Yeh,* because he was now, so he took out his Natural History Museum notebook and the pen that wrote in eight colours and drew the zombies.

When he re-entered the world they were changing trains at high speed, sprinting to another platform to catch a connecting train which left in two minutes. Halfway across the footbridge he remembered that he'd forgotten to pick up the metal thing. *What metal thing?* said Mum. *The metal thing,* he said, because he hadn't given it a name. It was a hinge from a briefcase and later on Mum would call it *a piece of rubbish* but he loved the strength of the spring and the smell it left on his fingers.

Dad said, *I'll get it* because when he was a child he kept a horse's tooth in a Golden Virginia tobacco tin, and Mum said, *For Christ's sake*. But Dad came back carrying the metal thing with seconds to spare and gave it to Benjy and said, *Guard it with your life*. And as they were pulling out of the station Benjy saw an old lady with long grey hair being arrested by two policemen in fluorescent yellow jackets. One of the policemen had a gun. Then there was another train travelling beside them at almost exactly the same speed and Benjy remembered the story about Albert Einstein doing a thought experiment, sitting on a tram in Vienna going at the speed of light and shining a torch straight ahead so the light just sat there like candyfloss.

You hate Richard because he swans around his spacious Georgian apartment on Moray Place four hundred miles away while you perch on that scuffed olive chair listening to Mum roar in the cage of her broken mind. *The nurses burn my hands. There was an air raid last night.* You hate him because he pays for all of it, the long lawn, the low-rent cabaret on Friday nights, *Magic Memories: The Stars of Yesteryear.* You hate him for marrying that woman who expected your children to eat lamb curry and forced you to stay in a hotel. You hate him for replacing her so efficiently, as if an event which destroyed other people's lives were merely one more medical procedure, the tumour sliced out, wound stitched and swabbed. You hate him because he is the prodigal son. *When will Richard come to see me? Do you know Richard? He's such a lovely boy.*

In spite of which, deep down, you like being the good child, the one who cares. Deep down you are still waiting for a definitive judgement in which you are finally raised above your relentlessly achieving brother, though the only person who could make that kind of judgement was drifting in and out of their final sleep, the mask misting and clearing, the low hiss of the cylinder under the bed. And then they were gone.

M6 southbound, the sprawl of Birmingham finally behind them. Richard dropped a gear and eased the Mercedes round a Belgian chemical tanker. *Frankley Services 2 miles*. He imagined pulling over in the corner of the car park to watch Louisa sleeping, that spill of butter-coloured hair, the pink of her ear, the mystery of it, why a man was aroused by the sight of one woman and not another, something deep in the midbrain like a sweet tooth or a fear of snakes. He looked in the rear-view mirror. Melissa was listening to her iPod. She gave him a deadpan comedy wave. He slid the Eliot Gardiner *Dido and Aeneas* into the CD player and turned up the volume.

Melissa stared out of the window and pictured herself in a film. She was walking across a cobbled square. Pigeons, cathedral. She was wearing the red leather jacket Dad had bought her in Madrid. Fifteen years old. She walked into that room, heads turned and suddenly she understood.

But they'd want her to be friends with the girl, wouldn't they, just because they were the same age. Like Mum wanted to be friends with some woman on the till in Tesco's because they were both forty-four. The girl could have made herself look all right but she hadn't got a clue. Maybe she was a lesbian. Seven days in the countryside with someone else's relatives. *It's a big thing for Richard.* Because keeping Richard happy was obviously their Function in Life. Right.

Shake the cloud from off your brow,
Fate your wishes does allow;
Empires growing,
Pleasures flowing,
Fortune smiles and so should you.

Some idiot came past on a motorbike at Mach 4. Richard pictured a slick of spilt oil, sparks fantailing from the sliding tank, massive head trauma and the parents agreeing to the transplant of all the major organs so that some good might come of a short life so cheaply spent, though Sod's Law would doubtless apply and some poor bastard would spend the next thirty years emptying his catheter bag and wiping scrambled egg off his chin.

Dido and Aeneas. Groper Roper made them listen to it at school. *Pearls before swine.* Probably in prison by now. *Don't let him get you in the instrument cupboard*. It was a joke back then. *Interfering with children*. Looking back, though, it's Roper who feels like the victim, the taunts, those damp eyes, the kind of man who hanged himself in isolated woodland.

Louisa was slowly coming round. Classical music and the smell of the cardboard fir tree on the rear-view mirror. She was in the car with Richard, wasn't she. So often these days she seemed to hover between worlds, none of them wholly real. Her brothers, Carl and Dougie, worked in a car factory and lived six doors away from each other on the Blackthorn Estate. Not quite cars on bricks and fridges in the grass, not in their own gardens at least. When she visited they faked a pride in the sister who had bettered herself but what they really felt was disdain, and while she tried to return it she could feel the pull of a world in which you didn't have to think constantly of how others saw you. Craig had revelled in it. The two worlds thing, Jaguar outside the chip shop, donkey jacket at parents' evening.

Wales. She'd forgotten. God. She'd only met Richard's family once. *They liked you and you liked them*. Had they? Had she? She'd trumped them by wearing too much black. Benjamin, the little boy, was wearing a *Simpsons* T-shirt of all things. She overheard him asking his father what would happen to his grandmother's body *in the coming months*. And the way the girl sang the hymns. As if there might be something wrong with her.

★   ★   ★

Richard had been seated next to Louisa at Tony Caborn's wedding, on what she correctly referred to as *the divorcees' table* in the corner of the marquee, presumably to quarantine the bad voodoo. Someone's discarded trophy wife, he thought. He introduced himself and she said, *Don't chat me up, OK?* She was visibly drunk. *I seem to be giving off some kind of vibes today.* He explained that he had no plans in that particular direction and she laughed, quite clearly at him rather than with him.

He turned and listened to a portly GP bemoaning the number of heroin users his practice was obliged to deal with, but his attention kept slipping to the conversation happening over his shoulder. Celebrity gossip and the short-comings of Louisa's ex-husband, the wealthy builder. She was clearly not his kind of person, but the GP was his kind of person and was boring him to death. Later on he watched her stand and cross the dance floor, big hips but firm, some-thing Nordic about her, comfortable in her body in a way that Jennifer had never been. *No plans in that particular direc-tion.* He'd been a pompous arse. When she sat down he apologised for his earlier rudeness and she said, *Tell me about yourself*, and he realised how long it had been since someone had said this.

Mum was smiling at Richard and doing the flirty thing where she hooked her hair behind her ear. It made Melissa think of them having sex, which disgusted her. They were in a traffic jam and Mika was singing 'Grace Kelly'. She took out a black biro and doodled a horse on the flyleaf of the Ian McEwan. How bizarre that your hand was part of your body, like one of those mechanical grabbers that picked up furry toys in a glass case at a fair. You could imagine it having a mind of its own and strangling you at night.

Mine with storms of care opprest
Is taught to pity the distrest.
Mean wretches' grief can touch,
So soft, so sensible my breast,
But ah! I fear, I pity his too much.

He was thinking about that girl who'd turned up in casualty last week. Nikki Fallon? Hallam? Nine years old, jewel-green eyes and greasy blonde hair. He knew even before he'd done the X-rays. Something too malleable about her, too flat, one of those kids who had never been given the opportunity to disagree and had given up trying. Six old fractures and no hospital record. He went to tell the stepfather they'd be keeping her in. The man was slumped in one of the plastic chairs looking bored mostly, tracksuit trousers and a dirty black T-shirt with the word BENCH on it. The man who'd abused her, or let others abuse her. He stank of cigarettes and aftershave. Richard wanted to knock him down and punch him and keep on punching him. *We need to talk.*

Yeh?

Richard's anger draining away. Because he was hardly more

than a teenager. Too stupid to know he'd end up in prison. Sugar and boiling water thrown in his face on kitchen duty. *If you could come with me, please.*

Melissa rolled up the sleeves of Dad's lumberjack shirt. Still, after all this time, the faintest smell of him. Plaster dust and Hugo Boss. He was an arsehole, but, God, she looked at Richard sometimes, the racing bike, the way he did the crossword in pencil first. There were evenings when she wanted Dad to ride in off the plains, all dust and sweat and tumbleweed, kick open the saloon doors and stick some bullet holes in those fucking art books.

Land of hope and glory, sang Mika. *Mother of the free ride, I'm leaving Kansas, baby. God save the queen.*

Hereford, home of the SAS. Richard could imagine doing that, given a Just War. Not the killing so much as the derring-do, like building dams when he was a boy, though it might be thrilling to kill another man if one were absolved in advance. Because people thought you wanted to help others whereas most of his colleagues loved the risk. That glint in Steven's eye when he moved to paediatrics. *They die quicker.*

Louisa had squeezed his hand at the graveside. Drizzle and a police helicopter overhead. That ownerless dog standing between the trees like some presiding spirit, his father's ghost, perhaps. He looked around the grave. These people. Louisa, Melissa, Angela and Dominic and their children, this was his family now. They had spent twenty years avoiding one another and he couldn't remember why.

Melissa pressed *pause* and gazed out of the window. Bright sun was falling on the road but there was rain far off, like someone had tried to rub out the horizon. That underwater glow. There'd be Scrabble, wouldn't there, a tatty box in some drawer, a pack of fifty-one playing cards, a pamphlet from a goat farm.

Real countryside now, the land buckled and rucked. *A sense sublime of something far more deeply interfused.* Blustery wind, trees dancing, flurries of orange leaves, a black plastic sack flapping on a gate. The road a series of bends and switchbacks. Richard driving too fast. Low pearly cloud. Turnastone. Upper Maescoed. Llanveynoe. They broached the top of a hill and the view was suddenly enormous. *Offa's Dyke*, said Richard. A dark ridge halfway up the sky. They made their way into the valley on a single-track road sunk between grassy banks like a bobsleigh run. Richard still driving too fast and Mum gripping the edge of the seat but not saying anything and . . . *Shit!* yelled Louisa, and *Fuck!* yelled Melissa, and the Mercedes skidded to a crunchy halt, but it was just a flock of sheep and an old man in a dirty jumper waving a stick.

Two gliders ride the freezing grey air that pours over the ridge, so low you could lean a ladder against the fuselage and climb up to talk to the pilot. Spits of horizontal rain,

Hay Bluff, Lord Hereford's Knob. Heather and purple moor-grass and little craters of rippling peaty water. By the trig point a red kite weaves through the holes in the wind then glides into the valley, eyes scanning the ground for rats and rabbits.

This was shallow coastal waters once, before the great plates crushed and raised it. Limestone and millstone grit. The valleys gouged out by glaciers with their cargo of rubble. Upper Blaen, Firs Farm, Olchon Court. Roads and footpaths following the same routes they did in the Middle Ages. Everyone walking in the steps of those who walked before them. The Red House, a Romano-British farmstead abandoned, ruined, plundered for stone, built over, burnt and rebuilt. Tenant farmers, underlings of Marcher lords, a pregnant daughter hidden in the hills, a man who put a musket in his mouth in front of his wife and sprayed half his head across the kitchen wall, a drunken priest who lost the house in a bet over a horse race, or so they said, though *they* are long gone. Two brass spoons under the floorboards. A twenty-thousand-mark Reichsbanknote. Letters from Florence cross-written to save paper, now brown and frail and crumpled to pack a wall. *Brother, my Lungs are not Goode.* The sons of the family cut down at Flers-Courcelette and Morval. Two ageing sisters hanging on through the Second World War, one succumbing to cancer of the liver, the other shipped off to a nursing home in Builth Wells. Cream paint and stripped pine. The fire blanket in its red holster. *The Shentons – 22nd to 29th March – We saw a deer in the garden . . .* Framed watercolours of mallow and campion. Biodegradable washing-up liquid. A random selection of elderly, second-hand hardbacks. A pamphlet from a goat farm.

Dominic had asked for a people carrier but a Viking with an earring and a scar appeared in a metallic green Vauxhall Insignia. They had bags on their laps and the windows were steamed up and spattery with rain. Benjy was squashed between Mum and Daisy which he enjoyed because it made him feel safe and warm. He had been lonely at home because he wasn't allowed to play with Pavel for a week after the fight and getting blood all over Pavel's trousers, but he enjoyed being on holiday, not least because you were allowed pudding every night. He had never spoken to Uncle Richard but he knew that he was a radiologist who put tubes into people's groins and pushed them up into their brains to clear blockages like chimney sweeps did and this was a glorious idea. An articulated lorry came past riding a wave of spray and for a few seconds the car seemed to be underwater, so he imagined being in the shark submarine from *Red Rackham's Treasure*.

Alex totted up how much the holiday was going to cost him. Two missed shifts at the video shop, two dog walks. A hundred and twenty-three quid down. But the hills would be good. Lots of kids thought he was boring. He couldn't give a fuck. If you didn't earn money you were screwed. He'd get through college without a loan at this rate. He rubbed his forehead.

Tightness behind his left eye and that sour taste in the back of his throat. Fifteen minutes and the pain would arrive, flurries of lime-green snow sweeping across his field of vision. He opened the window a crack and breathed in the cold air. He needed darkness. He needed quiet.

Oi, said Dad, but when he turned he saw the expression on Alex's face. *Do we need to pull over?*

Alex shook his head.

Ten minutes, OK?

They turned off the main road and suddenly they were out of the rain, the world cleaned and glittering. They roller-coastered over a little summit and Offa's Dyke hove into view, a gash of gold along the ridge, as if the sky had been ripped open and the light from beyond was pouring through.

Holy shit, Batman, said Benjy, and no one told him off.

Beeswax and fresh linen. Louisa stood in the centre of the bedroom. A hum from deep underground, just on the limit of hearing, a chill in the air. Hairs stood up on the back of her neck. Someone had suffered in this room. She'd felt it since childhood, in this house, in that corridor. Then Craig bought Danes Barn and she couldn't bear to be in there for more than five minutes. He told her she was being ridiculous. A week later she heard about the little boy who'd hidden in the chest freezer.

Melissa walked down the cold tiles of the hall and into the bright rectangle of the day. She took her earphones out. That silence, like a noise all by itself, with all these other noises inside it, grass rubbing together, a dog yapping far off. She dried the rain from the bench with a tea towel and sat down with *Enduring Love*, but she couldn't hang on to the words because she'd never spent more than five consecutive days in the countryside before. Kellmore in Year 11. Ziplines and Bacardi Breezers. Kasha's epileptic fit in the showers. There really was absolutely nothing to do here. She had two joints at the bottom of her bag but she'd have to smoke them up there with the sheep. Richard stoned. Jesus. Imagine that. *Goodness, I don't think I've realised how amazing this Mozart Piano Concerto is. We haven't got any more biscuits, have we?* But it *was* beautiful, when you thought about it, this huge green bowl, clouds changing shape as they moved, the smell of woodsmoke. A banana-yellow caterpillar reared up like a tiny question mark on the arm of the bench. She was about to flick it away when she imagined it having a name in a children's book, but suddenly there was a green taxi bumping through the gate and Alex and his little brother spilt from the door like clowns from a circus car.

. . . stunning views of the Olchon Valley . . . Grade 2 listed . . . sympathetically restored . . . a second bathroom added . . . large private garden . . . shrubbery, mature trees . . . drowning hazard . . . mixer taps . . . a tumble dryer . . . no TV reception . . . £1,200 per week . . . all reasonable breakages . . . American Express . . . the septic tank . . .

★   ★   ★

Dominic helped the driver unload while Benjy retrieved the briefcase hinge from a crumb-filled recess. Richard hugged Angela with one arm, his mug of tea at arm's length. Post-rain sparkle and the dog still yapping far off. Daisy shook Richard's hand and unnerved him slightly by saying, *It's good to see you again*, as if she was a colleague, so he turned to Benjamin. *And how are you doing, young man?*

Melissa held Alex's eye for two seconds and he forgot briefly about the nausea. *Unzipping*. Maybe normal service really was being suspended. But Melissa saw how much he wanted her and how naïve he was and the week seemed no longer empty. She walked slowly towards the front door, his gaze like sun on her back. *Bitch*, thought Angela, but Alex could see the first flurries of green snow and had to get to the bathroom. She had that glossy, thoroughbred look, thought Daisy. Hair you shook in slow motion. Leader of some icy little coven at school. But being fashionable and popular were shallow things which passed away. Daisy had to remember that. Shallow people were people nevertheless, and equally deserving of love.

The Vauxhall Insignia did a four-point turn and drove off scraping its manifold on the ruts and there was silence in the garden so that the red kite, looking down, saw only a large square of mown grass tilted towards the opposite side of the valley and, sitting confidently at its geometric centre, a house, stately and severe and adamantly not a farmhouse. Tall sash windows, grey stone laid in long, thin blocks, a house where Eliot or Austen might have lodged a vicar and his fierce teetotal sisters. A drystone wall ran round the boundary of the property, broken by two gates, one for walkers, one for carriages, both of ornate cast iron now thick with rust. A weathervane in the shape of a running fox. There were rhododendrons and a shallow ornamental pond thick with frogspawn. There was the skull of a horse in the woodshed.

Alex sluiced his mouth under the cold tap and felt his way back across the landing with his eyes closed. He lowered himself onto the bed, put the pillow over his head to cut out light and noise and curled into a ball.

Angela had been trapped by Louisa in the kitchen with a glass of red wine. That expensive mildew taste. *Melissa's vegetarian. I'd happily give up meat as well, but Richard is a bit of a caveman.*

Why did she dislike this woman? The cream rollneck, the way she held the measuring jug up to the light, for example, as if it were a syringe and a life hung in the balance. Onions fizzed in the pan. She thought about Carl Butcher killing that cat last term. *They were swinging it against a wall, Miss.* She'd recognised the policeman from Cycle Proficiency. Carl's hard little face. All those boys, they knew the world didn't want them, bad behaviour their only way of making some small mark. *But people eat cows.* Most intelligent thing he'd said all year.

God alone knows how she's going to survive here, said Louisa. *A hundred miles from the nearest branch of Jack Wills.*

A yellow tractor and the sun setting over Offa's Dyke, tumbledown barns with corrugated iron roofs, the hill so steep

Daisy felt as if she were looking out of a plane window, no noise but the wind. She could have reached out and picked that tractor up between her thumb and forefinger. This was Eden. It wasn't a fairy story, it was happening right now. This was the place we were banished from. A bird of prey floated up the valley until it was swallowed by the green distance. The fizzy tingle of vertigo in the arches of her feet. The centuries would swallow us like the sky swallowing that bird. She and Melissa had passed one another on the landing earlier. She said hello but Melissa just stared at her as they moved around one another, spaghetti western-style, everything in slo-mo.

A red Volvo was zigzagging slowly up from Longtown, vanishing and reappearing with the kinks in the road. Down the hill she could see Benjy in the walled garden doing Ninja moves with a stick. *Oof . . .! Yah . . .!* No one could see her out here, no one could judge her. She looked at herself in the mirror and saw the animal that she was trapped inside, that grew and fed and wanted. She wished above all else to look ordinary so that people's eyes just slid over her. Because Mum was wrong. It wasn't about believing this or that, it wasn't about good and evil and right and wrong, it was about finding the strength to bear the discomfort that came with being in the world.

Clouds scrolled high up. She couldn't get Melissa out of her head. Something magnetic about her, the possibility of a softness inside, the challenge of peeling back those layers.

★ ★ ★

Beers in hand, Dominic and Richard stood looking over the garden wall, gentlemen on the foredeck, a calm, green sea beyond. *Angela tells me you've got yourself a job in a bookshop.* Dominic had been unemployed for nine months, apparently. *Bespoke or chain?*

Waterstone's, said Dominic. *Best job I've ever done, to be honest.* He looked up. No contrails because of the volcanic ash. The way the fields stopped halfway up the hill and gave way to gorse and bracken and scree, that darkness where the summit met the sky, Mordor and The Shire within fifty yards of one another.

Really? asked Richard. But how did one lose one's job if one was self-employed? Surely one simply had more or less work coming in. A talented musician, too. Richard remembered visiting their house some years back and Dominic entertaining the children with a jazz version of 'Twinkle, Twinkle, Little Star' and the *Blue Peter* theme tune in the style of Beethoven. But he made his living composing music for adverts, washing powder and chocolate bars. Richard found it hard to comprehend anyone embarking upon a career without aiming for the top. Which applied to Angela as well, though she was a woman with children, which was different. And now he'd let it all slip through his fingers.

Amazing place, said Dominic, rotating slowly to take in the whole panorama.

You're welcome, said Richard.

*　　*　　*

Benjy pauses by the hall table and leafs idly through the *Guardian*. He is fascinated by newspapers. Sometimes he stumbles on things that terrify him, things he wishes he could undiscover. Rape, suicide bombers. But the pull of adult secrets is too strong. *Four thousand square miles of oil drifting from the Deepwater Horizon rig . . . Thirty people killed by bombs in Mogadishu . . . Fifty tonnes of litter found in a whale's stomach* . . . He has been thinking a lot about death lately. Carly's dad from school who had a heart attack aged forty-three. Granny's funeral. There was a woman on the television who had anal cancer.

He puts the paper down and begins exploring the house, entering every room in turn and making a mental map of escape routes and places where enemies might be hiding. He can't go into the bedroom because Alex is having a migraine so he heads downstairs in search of a knife to make a spear but Auntie Louisa is in the kitchen so he goes outside and finds a big stick in the log shed. He hacks off a zombie's head and blood sprays from the neck stump and the head lies on the ground shouting in German until it is crushed under one of his horse's hooves.

Alex slid his legs over the edge of the bed and sat up slowly, shirt soaked in sweat. His head felt bruised and the colour of everything was off-key, as if he were trapped inside a film from the sixties. At least Melissa hadn't seen him like this. When it happened at school he had to go and lie down in the sickbay. He tried to pass it off as an aggressive adversary he overcame by being tough and stoical, but he knew that some kids thought it was a spazzy thing like epilepsy or really thick glasses. He rubbed his face. He could smell onion frying downstairs and hear Benjy battling imaginary foes outside. *Oof . . .! Yah . . .!*

Melissa popped open the clattery little Rotring tin. Pencils, putty rubber, scalpel. She sharpened a 3B, letting the curly shavings fall into the wicker bin, then paused for a few seconds, finding a little place of stillness before starting to draw the flowers. Art didn't count at school because it didn't get you into law or banking or medicine. It was just a fluffy thing stuck to the side of Design and Technology, a free A level for kids who could do it, like a second language, but she loved charcoal and really good gouache, she loved rolling sticky black ink on to a lino plate and heaving on the big black arm of the Cope press, the quiet and those big white walls.

Daisy walked into the living room and found Alex sitting on the sofa drinking a pint of iced water and staring at the empty fireplace. *How are you doing?*

Top of the world. He held up his glass in a fake toast. The ice jiggled and clinked.

Always these stilted conversations, like strangers at a cocktail party. *I went for a walk up the hill. It's, like, Alex World up there.*

He seemed confused for a moment, as if trying to remember where he was. *Yeh, I guess so.*

A couple of years back he'd been a puppy, unable to sit down for a whole meal, falling off the trampoline and using his plastered arm as a baseball bat. They'd played chase and snakes and ladders and hide and seek with Benjy and watched TV lying on top of one another like sleeping lions. He seemed like another species now, so unimpressed by life. Dad's breakdown hardly touched him. She'd read one of his history essays once, something about the economic problems in Germany before the Second World War and the Jews being used as scapegoats, and she was amazed to realise that there was a person in there who thought and felt. *What do you reckon to Melissa?*

She's all right.

He was talking rubbish. He obviously fancied her because boys couldn't think about anything else. She wanted to laugh and grab his hair, start one of the play fights they used to have, but there was a forcefield, and the rules had changed. She reached out to touch the back of his neck but stopped a couple of centimetres short. *See you at supper.*

You will indeed.

Richard opened the squeaky iron door of the stove. Ash flakes rose and settled on the knees of his trousers. He scrunched a newspaper from the big basket. *PORT-AU-PRINCE DEVASTATED.* A grainy photo of a small boy being pulled from the rubble. No one really cared until there were cute children suffering. All those little blonde girls with leukaemia while black teenagers in London were being stabbed every day of the week. He flirted with the possibility of a firelighter but it seemed unmanly, so he built a tepee of kindling around the crumpled paper. An image of the Sharne girl passed through his mind. *She rowed for Upper Thames.* Think of something else. He struck a match. Swan Vesta. The way they lay in the box reminded him of the stacked trunks by Thorpe sawmill. The paper caught and the flame was an orange banner in a gale. He closed the door and opened the vent. Air roared in. His knees hurt. He needed to do more exercise. He imagined making love with Louisa later on, the cleanness of her skin after a shower, the cocoa butter body wash that made her taste like cake.

They're hiding in the trees, said Daisy, *with bows and arrows. And we've got the secret plans.*

Secret plans for what?

She peeled a lump of moss off the edge of the bench. *For a moon rocket.*

This is boring, said Benjy.

She thought about the men with bows and arrows. They were really here, weren't they, once upon a time. And mammoths and ladies in crinolines and Spitfires overhead. Places remained and time flowed through them like wind through the grass. Right now. This was the future turning into the past. One thing becoming another thing. Like a flame on the end of a match. Wood turning into smoke. If only we could burn brighter. A barn roaring in the night.

★   ★   ★

Angela looked out of the bedroom window. Dominic and Richard chatting at the edge of the garden, the way men did, beer in one hand, the other hand thrust into a trouser pocket, both staring straight ahead. She wondered what they were talking about and what they were avoiding talking about. Forty-seven years old and she still felt a fifteen-year-old girl's anger at the younger brother who had teamed up with Mum and frozen her out after Dad died. She took the Dairy Milk from the bottom of her case, tore back the paper and the purple foil, snapped off the top row of chunks and put them into her mouth. That nursery rush. Mum and Richard had visited Dad in hospital the day before he died. Angela wasn't allowed to go and she was haunted for months afterwards by a recurring nightmare in which they had conspired somehow to cause his death. Someone banged a large pan downstairs and shouted, *Dinner*, like they were guests in a country house. Flunkeys and silver salvers. She'd better go and join the fray.

Daisy, please. Angela reached out to grab her sleeve. *Not now.* But Dominic was standing in the way and she couldn't reach.

What were you going to say? asked Richard.

Grace, replied Daisy. *I was going to say grace.*

The room snapped into focus, wine bottles green as boiled sweets, galleons on the table mats. Melissa let her mouth hang open comically.

Fire away, said Richard, who was accustomed to situations where other people felt uncomfortable.

Oh Lord . . . People drifted through life with their eyes closed. You had to wake them up. *We thank You for this food, we thank You for this family and we ask You to provide for those who have no food, and to watch over those who have no family.*

Amen and a-women, said Benjy.

Excellent. Richard rubbed his hands together, Melissa said, *Fucking Nora,* under her breath and the scrape of chairs on the flagstones was like a brace of firecrackers. Louisa lifted the red enamelled lid of the big pot and steam spilt upwards.

Alex looked over at Daisy and gave her a thumbs-up. *Nice one, sister.*

Dominic poured two centimetres of wine into Benjy's wine glass.

Is this place not wonderful? asked Richard, widening his arms to indicate the house, the valley, the countryside, perhaps life itself.

Louisa was frightened of talking to Daisy. She didn't know any proper Christians, but Daisy said, *I love that sweater,* and suddenly it wasn't so bad after all.

Richard raised his glass. *To us,* and everyone raised their glasses. *To us.* Benjy drank his wine in one gulp.

Melissa saw Daisy and Mum laughing together. She wanted to force them apart, but there was something steely about the girl. She wouldn't back down easily, would she?

Alex couldn't stop looking at Melissa. That terrible yearning in his stomach. He was imagining her in the shower, foam in her pubes.

Angela looked at Richard and thought, *We have nothing*

in common, nothing, but Richard eased back into his chair. *You remember that dead squirrel we found on the roundabout in the park?* He swung the wine around his glass like a man in a bad advert for wine. *We thought it was a miracle.*

How do you remember this stuff? But why had she forgotten? That was the real question.

He closed his eyes as if running a slideshow in his mind's eye. *The tapestry cushion covers. God Almighty. Cats, roses, angels . . .*

She felt obscurely violated. This was her past too, but he had stolen it and made it his own.

Fuck. Melissa leapt to her feet, tomato sauce all over her trousers. *You little shit.*

Hey, hey, hey. Louisa raised her hands but Melissa swept out.

I'm sorry, said Benjy. *I'm really really sorry.* He was crying.

Come here, little man. Dominic hugged him. *You didn't mean to do it.*

But Alex felt a weight lift. No more sexual interference messing with his head.

Teenage girls, said Richard to the table in general, his tone neutral, as if he were opening the subject up for discussion.

Yes, she remembered now. The dead squirrel. So perfect, the tiny claws, as if it had simply lain down to sleep.

Can I have some more wine? asked Benjy.

This tastes good.

Morrisons in Ross-on-Wye, amazingly.

Nine weeks we had the builders in.
He went to Eton.
Ouch.
There's plasters in my toilet bag.
Twenty stone at least.
You got blood in the Parmesan.
She had a fractured skull.
Fifty press-ups.
Apple crumble.
A quarter of a million people.
Brandy? Cigars?
Dizzee with a double E . . .
And then the Hoover blew up. Literally blew up.
Sit down. I'll do the washing-up.
I'm stuffed.
Bedtime, young man.
Up in them thar hills.
Goodnight, Benjy.
Daisy, will you read to him?
Teeth. Remember what the lady said.
Night, Benjy.
Night-night.

She sat on the floor between the bedside table and the wall. Laughter downstairs. She pushed the point of the scalpel into the palm of her hand but she couldn't puncture the skin. She was a coward. She would never amount to anything. That fuckwit little boy. She should walk off into the night and get hypothermia and end up in hospital. That would teach them a lesson. God. Friday night. Megan and Cally would be tanking up on vodka and Red Bull before hitting the ice rink. The dizzy spin of the room and Lady Gaga on repeat, Henry and his mates having races and getting chucked out, pineapple fritters at the Chinky afterwards. Christ, she was hungry.

Paolo's father died and he went back to Italy. Dominic handed Louisa a wet plate. *And I discovered that I wasn't very good at selling myself.* He tipped the dirty water out of the bowl and refilled it from the hot tap. *I was in a band at college. I thought I'd be famous. Sounds ridiculous now. We were into Pink Floyd. Everyone else was listening to The Clash.*

I was listening to Michael Jackson. She held up her hands, begging forgiveness.

Eventually you realise you're ordinary.

Melissa appeared at the door and Louisa pressed the start button on the microwave. Dominic saw that there was a bowl of apple crumble already in there, waiting. While it turned and hummed in the little window Louisa laid her hand on Melissa's forearm for three or four seconds as if performing some kind of low-grade spiritual healing. She took a pot of yoghurt from the fridge, a spoon from the drawer and laid them neatly beside one another on the worktop. *Thanks*, said Melissa quietly and for a fraction of a second Dominic saw the little girl under the veneer.

★   ★   ★

The trees were thinning up ahead and Joseph could see gashes of sunlight between the trunks. He picked up speed and ten seconds later he stumbled out from between the pines into a space so big and bright that he stood on the little beach, stunned, trying to taking it in (Daisy shifted position to make her back more comfortable). *They were looking at a lake, rippled and silver under the grey sky. They had been living underground for so long it felt like the ocean. Mellor opened the map. 'We've arrived,' he said.*

'What do you mean?' asked Joseph.

(Benjy's eyelids were getting heavy.)

Mellor pointed out across the water. 'The house is out there.'

Joseph's heart sank. 'The map has to be wrong.'

'Ssshh . . .' Mellor put his finger to his lips.

In the distance Joseph could hear the faint barking of dogs. The Smoke Men were coming.

(Benjy closed his eyes and turned over.)

Mellor stuffed the map hurriedly into his rucksack. 'Quick. Take off your boots.'

Richard pulled his shirt over his head. *She has to learn some manners.*

She's sixteen.

I don't care how old she is.

You can't force children to do anything.

So you let them do exactly what they want?

Richard, you are not her father. Sorry. I didn't mean that . . .

No, I'm sorry. He shook his head like a dog coming out of water. *It's the Sharne case. It's getting to me.*

You did nothing wrong.
Being innocent is not always enough.
Come here.
But he wouldn't come. *I'm going outside to clear my head.*

Dominic stared at the black grid of the uncurtained window. If only he could fly away. How had he not seen the danger when Amy came into the shop that day? Blonde eyebrows, albino almost. They'd talked in the playground six years before. Two boys a couple of years above Daisy. She lingered at the till and he wondered if she was flirting but it had been so long that he found it hard to be certain. Then she mentioned her address in a way that was clearly an invitation which could be ignored without embarrassment and he dreamt that night of her long pale body with a vividness he had not felt since he was twenty. They slept together three weeks later in the middle of the afternoon, something he and Angela had never done, and this in itself was thrilling. She made a great deal of noise so that he wondered, briefly, if she were in actual pain. They lay afterwards looking up at the big Japanese paper lantern turning in the dusty curtained glow and Amy said, *Thank you, kind sir.* He turned onto his side and ran his fingers over her hip bones and her little breasts and into deep dints above her collarbones and realised there was a secret door in the house where he had been trapped for so long.

Angela was two hundred miles and thirty-five years away, trying to conjure the hallway of the house where she'd grown up, the newel post they called The Pineapple, the china tramp that lay on the carpet smashed one morning as if a ghost had brushed past in the night, the Oscar Peterson Trio on the gramophone. Dominic climbed into bed and the bounce of the mattress woke her briefly. She listened to the silence and thought of Benjy and felt the old fear. Was he still breathing? A cracked wooden beam ran across the ceiling, splinted with a rusty iron spar. She was slipping away a little now. Sherbet Dabs and Slade singing 'Cum on Feel the Noize'. Briefly she saw Karen sitting in the darkness some-where further up the hill, looking down on the sleeping house, like a rabbit or an owl. Then she let go.

Daisy opened the book and put the Monet postcard to one side.

I sat down beside her, and presently she moved uneasily. At the same moment there came a sort of dull flapping or buffeting at the window. I went over to it softly, and peeped out by the corner of the blind. There was a full moonlight, and I could see that the noise was made by a great bat, which wheeled around, doubtless attracted by the light, although so dim, and every now and again struck the window with its wings.

Fingernail moon. The Bay of Rainbows. The Sea of Tranquillity. Richard had never really got the space thing. It worried him, the possibility that his imagination wasn't strong enough to get past the earth's atmosphere. Neil Armstrong's heart rate staying under seventy during take-off. *All brave men are slightly stupid*. He and Mohan had sat opposite one another at the table by the window. He can see it as clear as day. Mohan was eating a container of M&S salad with a white plastic fork. *It could be an abscess*. Of course he should have put it in the report, that was precisely why he had tracked Mohan down, to make sure. Now the girl was in a wheelchair and Mohan was pretending the conversation never happened. Everyone knew the man was a shit, sleeping with two nurses and his poor bloody wife without a clue, which counted for nothing in a court of law, of course, just gossip and hearsay. The way the lawyer stared at him during that meeting. He half expected his eyelids to slide in from the side. Bloody hell, it was freezing out here.

With a little grunt, Alex came messily into the cone of toilet tissue in his right hand then leant back against the door, breathing heavily. That sudden disinterest, pictures of Melissa naked blowing away like mist. He wiped the splash from the wooden floor with the toe of his sock. He was thinking about canoeing on Llyn Gwynant. Then he was thinking about how quiet the house was and whether anyone had heard him. Richard's shaving brush glared from the window sill. He imagined it containing a little camera. Richard sitting at the dining table replaying the grainy footage, saying, *Angela, I think you should see this*. He dropped the tissue into the toilet bowl, pulled the flush and smelt his fingers. Seasidey. Nice.

★　　★　　★

You run your hand along the bumpy, magnolia wall. Paint over paint over plaster over stone, smooth, like the flank of a horse. Something alive in the fabric of the house. Earlier today, in Café Ritazza at Southport, Richard had put his hands behind his head and stretched out as if he owned the place. Polo shirt, TAG Heuer watch. A young mum was staring from a nearby table, pink tracksuit, scraped-back hair. He looked through her like she was furniture. But Melissa does have to learn some manners, and maybe you haven't been strict enough. You remember yourself at fourteen. The Hanwell flat. You and Penny standing on the outside of the balcony rail, seven floors up, one Sunday afternoon, leaning over that woozy drop, hearts pounding and the scary tickle in the back of your knees. Dogs in the park, the traffic on the ring road, a scale model of the world. You whoop as loud as you can and your voice bounces off the block opposite. There's a little crowd gathering now. Someone shouts, *Jump.* You look around and it occurs to you that this isn't real, this is only a memory, that you could let go and topple into that great windy nothing and it wouldn't matter. What frightens you is that for a couple of seconds you can't remember where the present is and how to get back there.

The click of the Mercedes cooling. A barn owl on top of a telegraph pole, eyeballs so big they rub against one another as they revolve. Bats slice the air above the garden. Limestone freakishly white under the moon. The sheep lie beside an old bath, still gathered against the wolves which haven't hunted them for two hundred years. The deep quiet under the human hum. Bootes, Hercules, Draco. Eight thousand man-made objects orbiting the earth. Dead satellites and space junk. The asteroid belt. Puck, Miranda, Oberon. To every moon a fairy story. The Mars Rover squatting near the Husband Hills. The Huygens probe beside a methane lake on Titan. The Kuiper belt. Comets and Centaurs. The Scattered Disc. The Oort Cloud. The Local Bubble. Barnard's Star. The utter cold warmed only by starlight.

Richard made his way down the dark stairs. He couldn't use the bathroom on the landing because of the tangled pipes under the sink. Tubing, plumbing, large-bore wiring. *Phobia* never quite described it. *A discrete period of intense fear or discomfort in which at least 4 of the following 13 symptoms develop abruptly* . . . The four in his case being a choking sensation, feelings of unreality, abdominal distress and a fear of going insane. He couldn't use Car Park E at work because it meant walking past the ducts at the back of the heating block. Last year he'd been standing on the Circle Line platform at Edgware Road en route to a conference in Reading. The brickwork on the far side of the tracks invisible behind a great rolling wave of sooty cables. He came round with a gash on his head looking up at a ring of people who seemed to have gathered to watch a fight in the playground.

He unbuttoned his pyjama fly and aimed just left of the water to minimise the noise. He should get his prostate checked. The floor was cobbled and cold and the walls smelt of damp but the sink down here was enclosed in a wooden cabinet and the ribbed white shower flex was single and therefore benign. He flushed the toilet and washed his hands. Bed.

Saturday

Daisy made herself a mug of sugary tea then went outside in her coat and scarf to watch the dawn come up. A great see-saw of light balanced on the fulcrum of Black Hill, the sun rising on one end, the other end sweeping down the flank of Offa's Dyke and switching the colours on as it went. The beauty kept slipping through her fingers. The world was so far away and the mind kept saying, *Me, me, me*. Petty worries rose and nagged, Benjy so distant, Mum angry with her all the time, the horrible graffiti in the changing rooms at school. But the valley . . . wasn't this amazing? *Look*, you had to say to yourself, *Look*.

The truth was that she hadn't been able to sleep. She'd tried reading *Dracula* but what seemed ridiculous in the daylight seemed like documentary before dawn. She felt so lost. You changed at sixteen everyone said, and changing was hard. But this wasn't normal, it came out of the blue, the unshakeable conviction that while she looked like a human being and acted like a human being there was nothing inside, just slime and circuitry.

Eighteen months ago she found herself talking to Wendy Rogan, the science TA from Year 12. She can't remember why. Providence, perhaps. Wendy suggested a coffee after school over which she listened in a way that no one else had, not friends, not Mum, not Dad. The following weekend she was having supper in Wendy's flat when Wendy suggested putting a video on. Daisy thought for several horrified seconds that it was going to be something pornographic, so when it turned out to be a promotional video for the Alpha Course she was initially relieved. A footballer scoring a goal, a model sashaying down the catwalk, a mountaineer climbing a cliff-face, each of them turning to the camera and saying, *Is there more to life than this?* All camera sparkle and soft rock. She felt ambushed and soiled.

A week later she remembered why the mountaineer seemed familiar. He was Bear Grylls, the guy Alex loved, who climbed Everest and ate maggots and drank his own urine on television. She Googled him and found herself watching, with a sickly mix of fascination and disgust, a video on YouTube in which he was stuck on a tropical island. *When you get the chance to be saved, you have to take it.* He swung on vines and swam across a bay and built a fire on the beach and signalled to a helicopter using the silver cross on the front of his Bible. It was laughable. But she was crying.

The valley almost full of light now, dew drying, everything washed in our absence. Melissa hated her. There was a kind of reassurance in that. Nothing to lose. No chance of feeling pleased with herself.

Be patient, David had said. *The spirit will come.* And there was a warmth in that room that she felt nowhere else, being lifted by those soaring voices, but the spirit hadn't come, only that constant sniping voice. *I'm more intelligent than these people.* Which was what it meant to be tested, of course, the pressure always at your weakest point. Faith was a belief in the impossible. Of course it looked ridiculous from the outside. *Jesus loves you, bitch.* Scratched into the metal of her locker door so it couldn't be washed off.

Suddenly there was a fox. Real orange, not the dirty brown of urban foxes, trotting through the gate, cocksure and proprietorial, like the ghost of a previous owner. Two different times were flowing through the garden. The fox stopped. Had it seen her? Had it smelt her? She didn't breathe. The gap closed between herself and the world. She was the grass, she was the sunlight, she was the fox. Then she wondered if it was some kind of sign and the spell broke and the fox trotted off round the far side of the house and she was shivering.

Dominic stands under the shower, eyes closed, water pouring onto the crown of his head. Hot water. How amazing to be alive this late in human history. Miners in their tin baths, a kettle on the coals, Queen Elizabeth the First taking three baths a year. But showers were never quite hot enough or strong enough on holiday, were they? That crappy plastic box. Down the corridor Benjy unlocks the mini-kit on the second Captain Brickbeard level and gets the wizard, while

Melissa rises through that turbulent region of half-sleep, part of her still at primary school, everything in slo-mo, a tiger padding slowly between the desks. Beams creak and pipes rattle as the house comes to life. A scurry in the roofspace, the same dog far off. Alex pees noisily. The whirr of an electric toothbrush. A cockerel. Daisy pours a small portion of Marks & Spencer's Deliciously Nutty Crunch into a bowl.

Alex squatted on the flagstones by the front door to lace his trainers then stretched his hamstrings on the ivy-covered sill. The faintest smell of manure on the bright damp air. He set his watch then jogged along the track to the main road, stones crunching and slipping under his trainers. He loved wild places. He felt at ease among lakes and mountains in a way he never did at home or school. Every other weekend he and Jamie would pile into Jamie's brother's Transit, bikes on the back, canoes on top, and Josh would drive them to the South Downs, Pembrokeshire, Snowdonia. Put up the tent in darkness and wake in that igloo glow. He climbed the stile and began the long haul to Red Darren, his mind shrinking with the effort and the altitude, this precious trick he had learnt, doubts and worries falling away at four, five, six miles, the fretting self reduced to almost nothing, only the body working like an engine. Dominic and Daisy asked him about it sometimes and assumed his inability to explain was evidence of an inability to feel, but on Llyn Gwynant, on Nine Barrow Down, he experienced a kind of swelling contentment for which they yearned but never quite attained, and the fact that Alex couldn't explain it, the fact that it was beyond words, was part of the secret.

Because you'll burn yourself. Angela handed him two eggs. *Crack these into the bowl.*

What would happen if you and Dad died at the same time?

What would you like to happen? She scraped mushrooms into the pan.

I'd like to go and live with Pavel.

I'd have to check that with Pavel's mum.

But what will happen to my toys?

She handed him a fork. *You'd take them with you.* She thought how small Pavel's house was. *Now add some milk and whisk it.*

What about the television?

Hasn't Pavel already got a television?

But what about our television? He was on the verge of tears.

You can have the television.

I've changed my mind. I want to go and live with Daisy. Something broke inside him and he was choking back the sobs.

She turned the ring down and wrapped him in her arms.

Benjamin was crying and Richard didn't want to intrude so he poured a mug of coffee from the cafetière and walked outside where he found Alex doing press-ups on the lawn, proper press-ups, knees and back rigid, locking his elbows, touching the grass with his nose, a great eagle of sweat on his back. *Deltoids, teres major, rotator cuff.* He still thought of himself as a sportsman, cross-country at school, 400 metres at college, but in the last year he'd done nothing more than play a few games of squash with Gerhardt and cycle to work for a fortnight after the car was stolen. Alex stood up. *Wondering if I should have a go myself.*

Alex put a foot on the bench to unlace his trainer. *It's a big hill.*

Daisy had very nearly done it with her friend Jack. She was never quite sure whether they were going out or not. He had three earrings and a pet snake and some invisible barrier that only Daisy was allowed to cross. They'd drunk two large glasses of some poisonous green liqueur his dad had bought in Italy. He put a hand under the hem of her knickers and she was suddenly aware of how angular he was, all bones and corners, and she was going to let him do it because she couldn't think of an alternative, because this was the door everyone had to pass through. But with this thought came a scrabbling panic. She didn't want to go through that door, she didn't want to be like everyone else and she was having real trouble breathing. She pushed him away, and he seemed relieved mostly, but the near miss had scared them both, so they finished the bottle and the embarrassment was obscured by the memory of a hangover so bad that its retelling became a party piece. For six months they were best friends, then Daisy joined the church and he called her a *fucking traitor* and vanished from her life.

★   ★   ★

Alex wasn't trying to put Richard down. It was a stab at friendliness he failed to pitch quite right. He had always rather admired his uncle and felt that Mum's complaints were unjustified. Or perhaps admiration was the wrong word, more a kind of genetic bond. He recognised nothing of himself in Mum and Dad, her distractedness, the lack of care she took of herself, his father sitting around the house feeling sorry for himself, doing the cleaning and the shopping and Benjy's school pick-ups like it was the most natural thing in the world. When friends visited he felt embarrassed by the air of defeat which hung around him and part of the attraction of mountains and lakes was their distance from both of them. But the way Richard carried himself, his air of efficiency and self-possession . . .

Why did you do that last night? asked Angela.

Do what?

You know exactly what I'm talking about. Saying grace. Making everyone feel uncomfortable.

I think we all should be more grateful for the things we have.

I think we should also be more considerate of other people's feelings.

Oh, like you're considerate of my feelings?

Don't answer me back.

So, what? Just be quiet and do what you say?

You were showing off, and you were patronising people. I don't care what you believe in private . . .

That's rubbish. You hate what I believe in private.

I don't care what you believe in private but I don't think you should force it down other people's throats.

You're just jealous because I'm happy.

I'm not jealous, Daisy. And you're not happy.

Well, maybe you're not the expert when it comes to what I'm actually feeling.

We'll buy some second-hand books, said Richard. *Get some lunch. Stop for a walk on the way back.*

That sounds like the most excellent fun, said Melissa.

Then it's your lucky day. He remained poker-faced. *We can only fit seven in the car.*

Good.

Will you be all right on your own? asked Louisa.

Melissa flopped her head to one side and rolled her eyes.

Can we walk up Lord Hereford's Knob? asked Benjy.

He'll stop finding it funny eventually.

I'll duck out, too, said Dominic. *If that's OK.*

Angela briefly wondered if he had arranged some kind of liaison with Melissa and came close to making a joke about it before realising how tasteless and bizarre it would have been.

Melissa was coming up the stairs when Alex emerged from the bathroom, a sky-blue towel around his waist. Post-exercise fatigue. He made her think of a tiger, that slinky muscular shamble. There was a V of blond hairs on the small of his back. She wanted to touch him. The feeling scared her, the way it rose up with no warning, the body's hunger. Because she loved the game, the tension in the air, but she found the act itself vaguely disgusting, André's eyes rolling back like he was having a seizure, the greasy condom on the carpet like a piece of mouse intestine. Alex turned and looked at her. She smiled. *Hello, sailor.* Then turned away.

Dominic sat beside Angela on the bench. There was a scattering of crumbs on the lawn, a couple of sparrows picking at them, and another bird he didn't recognise. *This'll be good for us, I think. Being here.*

It's a lovely place.

That's not what I meant.

I know.

He remembered a time when they really talked, sitting by the river, lying in that tiny bedroom naked after making love, faded psychedelic wallpaper and the Billie Holiday poster. Both eager to know more about this other life of which they'd become a part. But now? They weren't even friends any more, just co-parents. He wanted to tell her about Amy, to relieve the pressure in his chest, because he was scared, because he had begun to notice the frayed curtains and the smell of cigarettes in Amy's house and the need in her voice. He had assumed at first that the whole thing was no more than a distraction from lives lived elsewhere, but this wasn't a distraction for her, was it? This was her life, this dimly lit bedroom in the middle of the afternoon, and the secret door was in truth the entrance to a darker dirtier world from which he wouldn't be able to return without paying a considerable price. But was it really so bad to have looked for affection elsewhere? They had both been unfaithful in their way. To have and to hold, to love and to cherish. When had they last done these things? He wouldn't tell Angela, would he? He would live with it until the discomfort faded and lying became normal.

Poor Benjy. She examined the inside of her mug. *He was talking about us dying. You know, who would get all the stuff in the house.*

He seems to like it here, though. Because this was what they did. They acted like a real family. Perhaps it was what most people did. *How are you and your brother bonding?*

He remembers everything. She threw the dregs of her coffee into the grass. The birds flew away. *It scares me. Makes me wonder if I'm losing my mind. Like Mum.*

Who's the prime minister?

I'm being serious . . . He could be making it up for all I know.

Don't we always make them up, our childhood memories? His own mother had slept with another man, the dapper little dentist with the soft-top Mini. Or was it just a spiteful rumour?

They sat for several minutes looking at the view. They had this at least, the ability to sit beside one another in silence.

I have difficulty believing that Richard and I are actually related. The birds were reconvening around the crumbs.

Maybe you were adopted. That might solve a problem or two.

Another of his jokeless punchlines. But Richard was calling, *Wagons roll*.

Countryside like an advert on TV, for antiperspirant, for butter, for broadband, a place to make us feel good inside, where everything is slower and more noble, cows and hayricks and honest labour. Somewhere out there, hard by a stand of beech, commanding an enviable prospect of the valley, the house where the book will be written and the marriage mended and the children will build dens and the rain when it comes is good honest rain. How strange this yearning for being elsewhere doing nothing. The gift of princes once, its sweet poison spreading. Lady Furlough surveying the desert of the deer park, the monsters coiling in the ornamental lake, that terrible weight of hours, laudanum and cross-stitch. What every child knows and every adult forgets, the glacial movement of the watched clock, pluperfects turning slowly into cosines turning slowly into the feeding of the five thousand. School holidays of which we remember only mending bikes and Gary Holler killing the frog, the featureless hours between gone forever.

And now you must do nothing for a week and enjoy it. Days of rest long past the point when we're rested, holidays without the holy, pilgrimage become mere travel, the destination handed to us on a plate, the idleness of the empire in its final days.

Melissa had been sitting at the dining-room table reading when Dominic walked through and said he was going for a walk. The door banged and she became aware of how quiet the house was. She stuck her iPod on. 'Monkey Business', Black Eyed Peas, but the inability to hear someone approaching from behind made her feel vulnerable so she took the earphones out again. She stepped into the garden, wanting the minimal reassurance of Dominic's shrinking silhouette, but he was gone and the valley was empty. She went back into the living room and rifled through the stack of DVDs. *Monsters Inc.*, *Ice Age 2*, *Harry Potter and the Prisoner of Azkaban*. There was a *Simpsons* case but it contained a PlayStation disc for *Star Wars: Battlefront*.

A whirr and clang behind her. She spun round. The grandfather clock chimed again. *Fuck.* She needed to talk to a normal human being. Megan, Cally, Henry, anyone. She grabbed her phone and headed for the hills.

He'd been looking forward to it for the last couple of weeks. A town of books. All this learning gathered in and offered up. *Trawling, browsing, leafing.* But now that he was standing in the bowels of The Cinema Bookshop . . . That smell. What was it, precisely? Glue? Paper? The spores of some bibliophile lichen? Catacombs of yellowing paper. Every book unwanted, sold for pennies or carted from the houses of the dead. Battersea Books Home. The authors earned nothing from the transaction. Salaries less than binmen, he'd read somewhere. He thought about their lives. No colleagues, no timetable, no security, the constant lure of daytime television. The formlessness of it all made him feel slightly ill, going to work in their dressing gowns. So much risk and so little adventure.

He laid his hand on the bumpy wall of frayed spines and brittle slip covers. His mother had arranged them according to their height, as a kind of subsidiary furniture. Airport novels and Hollywood biographies. He wished he were better at embracing the chaos, loosening up a little. But the journey was always a circle. You thought you were on the other side of the world then you turned a corner and found yourself in the kitchen with the green melamine bowls and the clown calendar. His neatness, his love of order, the need to keep himself constantly busy, these things weren't a measure of the distance he'd put between them, these were the things they had in common.

The Golden Ocean. Anglo-Saxon Attitudes. The House of Sixty Fathers. They Call Me Carpenter. Tom Swift and His Electric Locomotive. The Velveteen Rabbit. The Chessmen of Mars. The Eagle of the Ninth. Tarzan and the Forbidden City. The Man Who Could Not Shudder. Typewriter in the Sky. The Naughtiest Girl in the School. Black Hunting Whip. The Secret of the Wooden Lady. Five Go to Mystery Moor. The Drowning Pool. The Courage of Sarah Noble. My Life in the Bush of Ghosts. Bonjour Tristesse. The Sky Is Falling. The Sound of Waves.

Holy shit. There was a naked woman tied up. Then another naked woman tied up. Then a naked woman tied up and hanging from the ceiling. Then a naked tattooed woman with her arse in the air and a dildo sitting on a record player in the background. Then a naked woman with an Egyptian hairstyle on an old-fashioned hospital bed tied up with rubber tubing that actually went into her cunt. And it was, like, actual art that you were allowed to look at. Or was it? Alex flipped the cover shut. Nobuyoshi Araki. Phaidon. £85. So it *was* art. Holy shit. You could have it on a coffee table. He imagined being the photographer. Actually being there in the room. There was a close-up of a big veiny penis in black and white which was gross, then two naked women on a bed.

Excuse me.

There were other human beings in the room. The man squeezed past and disappeared into Architecture. Alex stared at the photograph of the two women. He wanted to buy the book. He wanted to steal the book. He wanted to stay here forever. He had to put it down. He couldn't put it down.

Dominic was thinking of the opening of the second Two-Part Invention, that little canon. When the work stopped he couldn't bear to listen to music. Sentimental songs were the worst, 'The Power of Love', 'Wonderful Tonight' . . . He had to leave shops sometimes. Just like Coward said. *Extraordinary how potent* . . . etc. After a couple of months he started listening to Steve Reich and suddenly saw the point of those cool, evolving lines. *Music for Eighteen Musicians*, *Electric Guitar Phase*. Moving gingerly on to Bach. Another kind of coolness. He ran through the fingering of the Two-Part Invention in his head. Who was the guy on that classical music quiz show when he was a kid? He played a dummy keyboard and you had to guess the piece from the thumping. Joseph Cooper. That was it. *Face the Music.*

He looked across the valley and heard *The Lark Ascending* in his mind's ear, that skirling violin, four semiquavers then up and up, pentatonic scale, no audible root, no bar lines even . . . Melissa. Jesus. Was that Melissa? He started to jog down through the bracken. What in God's name was she doing? Vomiting? He tripped and fell and got up again. She was on all fours. He slowed, panting. *Melissa?* He touched her shoulder and she sprang up and screamed, waving her hands like a frightened woman in silent film. *Whoa, sorry. I didn't mean . . .*

It's . . . It's . . . She stroked the air in front of her. Angela's husband. She'd forgotten where she was. She felt naked. Was he going to attack her?

Are you all right?

She mustn't cry. She held out her mobile. It refused to explain the situation. *I couldn't get any signal.*

Have you hurt yourself?

No, I haven't fucking hurt myself. Deep breath.

You were trying to ring someone.

I've got to . . . She turned and walked away and her knees buckled and she tried very hard to make it look like she was sitting down on purpose.

He came over and sat beside her. They said nothing. It

was uncomfortable, then it was comfortable, then it was uncomfortable. *So I guess you're not having a fun time.*

She started crying. *Shit.* She wiped her eyes.

You want to talk about it?

No, I do not want to talk about it. Unsurprisingly.

He picked two daisies and started making a chain. *I had a stepfather. I still have a stepfather.*

What the hell was he talking about?

He was a really nice guy, which only made me hate him more, of course.

Yeh, well, thanks for the advice. She took a packet of Silk Cut from her jacket pocket.

One going spare?

She'd meant to piss him off but things were going a bit off-piste. His cupped hand touched her hand. The scratch and pop of the lighter. Was he going to try and feel her up? She imagined hanging on to the story like a fat cheque she could spend whenever she wanted.

Ooh. He blew a rubbish smoke ring. *Haven't had one of these in a while.*

A sheep trotted past, bleating.

Actually, Richard's all right. He kind of makes Mum happy, which is good. But it was a lie. She hated him for the same reasons Dominic had hated his stepfather.

They finished their cigarettes. Then Dominic turned and stared at her. She wondered if he was going to put a hand on her breast. *Be nicer to Daisy, OK?*

Which caught her totally on the hop.

You'll look back and realise you're not that different.

She laughed. *We are so different.* He held her eye and didn't laugh. She'd lost her bearings now. The fear was coming back. She got to her feet and threw her cigarette stub into the long grass. *I need to make a phone call.*

Don't walk over a precipice.

Was he being, like, metaphorical, or was there actually a precipice?

He watched her stumble up the hill. Town shoes. He imagined getting points for the way he'd handled the conversation. Six out of ten? He'd definitely got the better of her. Seven? The sheep bleated again. He felt a little nauseous. The cigarette, probably.

Benjy was doing a kind of boneless gymnastics on the leather armchair at the side of the shop.

Look at this encyclopedia. Daisy heaved him aside and sat down. *It's from 1938.*

His eyes were fixed on the Nintendo.

Back before computers, when they thought there might be people on Mars.

He didn't look up. *I want to find the Encyclopedia of Torturing Barbie.*

She turned the page. *And what is this thing,* she read, *which the savage coaxes into being by rubbing one stick against another, and the civilised man conjures in a moment by striking a match?* His breath wasn't good. Had anyone made him brush his teeth this morning?

Louisa appeared suddenly. *Benjy . . . Daisy . . .* She had peeled herself away from Richard and set off in search of a sunny book-free location, but there was something cosy about the two of them in the chair. *What have you got there?*

Pictorial Knowledge, Volume 5. Daisy handed it to her.

Woven brick-red cover, the title indented and beneath it an oil lamp radiating beams of wisdom. She glanced at the contents page. How Steam and Petrol Work for Man. A Children's Guide to Good Manners. Folding Model. She was suddenly back in her grandparents' house, chicken-wire window in the larder, Walnut Whips and buttered white bread with fish and chips, the stilts Grandad made her from an old door frame.

Daisy shifted a little to get more comfortable. Louisa had sat herself on the arm of the chair, Daisy sandwiched between her and Benjy. Louisa's leg was very close. Red cords tight around her thighs. The smell of cocoa butter.

Louisa turned a page. Arch, suspension, cantilever, girder. How strange that she should be reminded of them here, of all places, when they didn't have a single book in the house. The fear of getting above yourself. She closed the book and ran her hand gently down the spine. You thought it was all gone, the house demolished, the furniture sold, photos eaten away by mildew and damp. Then you opened a tin of sardines with that little metal key.

He sat on the steps of the town clock, the bag from Richard Booth angled against his calf (*Stalingrad* by Antony Beevor, *The Odyssey* translated by John Hannah, *Fighting Fit: The*

Complete SAS Fitness Training Handbook). There was a trailer containing two sheep, and three local teenagers standing round a scooter, smoking. The Sharne case was nagging at him again. Breathe in, two, three . . . Breathe out, two, three . . . One of the boys revved the scooter and his concentration broke. How restless the mind was. He should run, like Alex, clear it with activity instead of willpower. Breathe in . . . He noticed an attractive woman going into The Granary and heard that tiny sexual alarm sounding in his head. Oh, but it was Louisa. Then she was gone. How disorienting to see her as other men saw her. He remembered meeting her ex-husband that first time, when Craig came round to fit a new pump in the boiler. Absurdly hairy, as if he was wearing a black mohair vest under his T-shirt. *Louisa tells me you're a doctor.* A muscular handshake that went on for just a little too long.

Consultant. Neuroradiology.

Eventually he came to understand that it was a kind of kryptonite, the degrees, the books, the music, though he remembered Louisa shaking her head and laughing and saying, *He wanted it all the time*, and he was never quite able to shake that picture.

There wasn't a precipice, just a huge hill from which you could see Russia probably. An old couple walked past dressed like Boy Scouts. Then her phone made contact with civilisation and a string of texts pinged in, one from Dad in France followed by a stack of messages saying *ring me* and *got 2 talk 2 u* and *need to talk urgent* as if an actual war had broken out.

She called Cally who didn't even say hello, just, *Michelle tried to kill herself.*

How?

Sleeping pills. She told her mum we were bullying her.

Fucking cow.

Thing is, her mum went to see Avison, so now it's official.

Well, it wasn't me who sent that picture to everyone.

Don't fucking dump me in it, said Cally. *You took the photo.*

Stop blaming me, all right. We've got to sort this out. Christ. Two weeks in a sleeping bag in a half-renovated French farmhouse with Dad didn't seem such a bad idea now. She let it all sink in. Michelle being a slag as per usual. Michelle playing the victim as per usual. She should have seen this coming a long way back. *Who else did you send it to?*

Not that many people.

Just tell me, OK?

Jake, Donny, KC . . .

Fucking great. They'd save it, wouldn't they, so they could stab her in the back. All those idiotic little vendettas. If she was only there, in person, to grab the phones out of their stupid hands.

I didn't think I'd be so upset when she died. Angela took a final forkful of Tibetan roast. Benjy was sitting next to her reading a tattered second-hand encyclopedia. She brushed the crumbs from his hair.

Ghastly way to go, said Richard. He'd arranged his cutlery at half past six. *Your mind dying, your body left behind for other people to look after.*

Other people? Meaning *her*.

God forbid that I go like that. He poured the last of his tea through the metal strainer. Over his shoulder a gaggle of nut-brown cyclists gathered at the counter, little black shoes clacking on the stone floor. *Give me a massive cardiac arrest.*

Hang on, said Angela. *Hang on.* Why was she doing this? *I visited her every week for five years.*

I'm not sure what you're trying to say. He could hear the resentment in her voice but was genuinely confused. Surely the gift of the holiday itself had removed any residual bad feelings.

I know you paid for her to be in Acorn House, said Angela. *And maybe that was more important than anything else. I'm grateful, I am, but . . .* She was walking on cracked ice. *Every week for five years.* What good had it done, though? Her mother didn't recognise her at the end.

I know, said Richard tonelessly.

And the person she really wanted was you. She could see the disbelief in his face. He'd expected this to be easy, hadn't he? Rebuilding the family now the troublesome parent had been removed. Bruises and broken bones. She felt a childish desire to make it as difficult as she could. *And you came, what? five times? six?* She knew the exact number but she wasn't going to admit to having kept score.

Richard was drawing little shapes on the tabletop with his index finger. She wondered if he was working out his reply on imaginary notepaper.

She's dead, Angela. We can't change anything now. Perhaps we should just leave it alone.

Benjy turned a page, oblivious to their conversation. Angela glanced over. *The Romance of the Iron Road.* A picture of the *Flying Scotsman. I just wanted to hear you say thank you.* There. It was out.

He laughed. Quiet and wry, but actual laughter.

Richard . . . ? She felt as if she were talking to a child who had made some dreadful faux pas.

I was thirteen when she started drinking.

And I was fourteen.

But you left.

What? She really did have no idea what he was talking about.

When you moved in with Juliette.

The idea was so crazy that she wondered for the first time if he had some less pleasant motive for bringing them on holiday. *I never left. I never moved in with Juliette.*

OK, maybe not moved in. He hadn't meant to bring this up. It was like contaminated earth; if you didn't dig there was no problem. *But you spent most nights there.* He didn't want to settle scores. He simply wanted things to be neatly folded and put to sleep. *For the best part of two years if I remember correctly.*

That's simply not true. The couple at the nearby table had paused to listen.

Perhaps if I'd been better at making friends I would have done the same thing. He laughed again but more warmly this time.

That's not the point. They had to stop this right now or

God alone knew where it would go. She sat back and deep-breathed. *Let's call a truce.*

A truce? said Richard. *Is this a war?*

Maybe now is the time for cake.

Without taking his eyes off the book, Benjy said, *Yes, please. Can I have the chocolate one, please, with the white icing?*

Motor lorries carry heavy goods long distances; motor vans deliver parcels at our doors. Motor charabancs transport tens of thousands of pleasure-seekers daily from place to place, and motor coaches make regular daily journeys between towns hundreds of miles apart. We no longer see the horse-drawn fire-engine, with smoke belching from its funnel, dashing down the street.

Ariel Gel Nimbus 11. Ridiculous names they gave these things. Richard loved the smell, though, plasticky and factory-clean. He laced the left shoe up and leant round to take the right from its tissued box. He felt bruised by the conversation with Angela, less by her feelings than by his failure to predict them. It had never occurred to him that she would feel embittered. His mother had hated him for looking after her, then hated him for leaving. Five years living with an alcoholic woman and no one had thanked him. If there was such a thing as the moral high ground it was surely he who occupied it. From the corner of his eye he saw, through the shop's front window, a rat's nest of black downpipes emerging from the upper storey of the house opposite. He rotated his body a little further towards the rear of the shop.

How much?

£79.99.

Reassuringly expensive.

The assistant seemed oblivious to his irony. But you had to have the best. Save £20 now and you regretted it later. He stood up and examined himself in the mirror.

How do they feel? The young man was ginger and plump and ill nourished with one of those increasingly popular asymmetrical fringes so that he was forced to lean his head to one side in order to see properly.

Good. They feel good. He squatted and stood up again. He remembered the day he left for Bristol, his mother yelling at him as he walked down the street with his rucksack, curtains twitching, like a scene from a cheap melodrama. Ideally he should have gone outside and run up and down but he wasn't sure he had the confidence to carry it off. He jogged on the spot for ten seconds. *I'll take them.*

Angela stayed in the car. She needed time away from Richard and she couldn't imagine another two hundred feet improving the view. A young Indian woman was fighting an orange cagoule. A little further away a man and two teenage boys were tinkering with an amateur rocket, three, four foot high, red nose cone, fins. The man knelt briefly beside it then stepped backwards and . . . *Jesus Christ.* A fizz like Velcro and the thing just vanished upwards. The boys whooped and waited but it simply didn't come down. They swivelled, scanning the distance. Carried off by the wind, no doubt, but something magical about it still, a story for later. She looked back up the hill. Her family were dots.

Was he lying about Juliette? Or had he misremembered to alleviate his guilt? If only she could retort with hard facts, bang, bang, bang, but she had never really looked back, never thought these details might need preserving.

God, she wanted something to eat. Toffee, sweets, biscuits. She opened the glove compartment and a strip of passport photos fell out. She picked them up and turned them over. Melissa smouldering, Melissa blowing a kiss, Melissa flicking her hair. They were oddly touching. She thought of all those pictures of Karen. Two years old, playing with wooden blocks on a sheepskin rug. Nine years old, in front of a rainbow-coloured windbreak. Fourteen years old, in a green duffel coat at some steam fair, the word *OGDENS* in Victorian funhouse lettering on a green boiler behind her head. And for a few giddy seconds they were real, in a leather album on the shelf above the telly. Then the wind shook the car and she was in the world again.

Alex looked back and saw Daisy and Benjy throwing lumps of sheep shit at one another. *Only the dry ones*, shouted Daisy. At school he got the piss ripped for being her brother, Eddie Chan singing 'Like a Virgin' forty thousand times. Nastier stuff, too, especially after the anti-drug assembly, like she wanted people to hate her. He could shut most things out but not this. Was she fucked up or just being a smug twat? Should he protect her or leave her to get what she deserved?

It was a puzzle and it bugged the hell out of him that he couldn't solve it.

That went in my hair, you little . . .

He wondered if she might flip back sometime. Not that they'd be friends or anything. But still.

Louisa moved out of range. A teenage girl playing a little boy's game. It didn't quite compute. Maybe if she'd had boys, if she'd had the brood she'd once dreamt of. Though sometimes, when Melissa was really tired and Richard was out, she curled up on the sofa and laid her head on Louisa's leg and sucked her thumb, which was what one wanted ultimately, wasn't it, that connection.

Goal. Benjy pulled his shirt over his head and ran around in circles.

Daisy shook a wet lump off her jeans. *You are so going to die.*

Richard felt a hand tighten round his heart. He had never done this. He would never do this.

Daisy wrestled Benjy onto the grass. He yelled, *That's cheating*, but it wasn't a serious protest because he loved this. No one gave him piggy-back rides or picked him up any more. You could ask for hugs if you were feeling sad or you'd hurt yourself, but when it happened spontaneously it made you feel so warm inside.

Is Angela all right? Louisa was looking down the hill to the higgledy-piggledly cars.

He loved her for thinking about these things. *The funeral hit her harder than I expected.*

You bought some running shoes.
I saw Alex coming back this morning.
Don't break an ankle.
Trust me, I'm a doctor.

She laughed and he remembered when he'd first said those words to her and how she'd laughed that time too. He wanted suddenly to be on holiday alone, just the two of them, making love in the middle of the day, seeing her body in sunlight through the curtains.

And Daisy and Benjy were lying on their backs. *Look. You can see the sky moving.* And Alex was further up the hill, shouting, *Come on.*

Two crows abandoned something dead in the road as they drove past. A postbox in a wall. Ruinsford Farm. Three Oaks Farm. Upper House Farm. A crazy dog chased them for half a mile. Being in the back of the car made Alex twitchy, too far from the steering wheel, being taken somewhere by someone else. Next year he'd arrange his own holiday. Dolomites, maybe. Next year he'd start to arrange everything. Economics, History, Business Studies. Brighton, Leeds, Glasgow. Travel for a couple of years. Start his own business. Not ambitions, just facts about the world. You knew where you wanted to go, you worked out the route and set off. He didn't understand why so many people made such a bloody hash of it. Then they were pulling in through the gate and Melissa was sitting reading on the low wall at the back of the house and he felt that little surge of panic, like at the beginning of a race, or when you were about to do some stupid vertical drop on the bike. But you couldn't turn back.

He got out of the car and walked over. She was wearing tight jeans and boots and a little black jacket over a lacy Victorian dress. She didn't acknowledge his presence until he was really close and when she turned to him her face was blank. She hooked her hair behind her ear like her mum did.

Here it comes, she thought. Because this was what she liked, this tension in the air, the way you could play someone.

What's the book?

She flipped it over.

Good? He sat and swung his legs like a little boy.

Uh-huh. You had to say as little as possible and let the other person fill the gaps.

So. He looked down at his swinging feet. Did he look casual and relaxed? It was hard to see yourself from the outside. *How do you like it here?*

About one out of ten.

So what's the one?

He wanted her to say it was him. *Peace and quiet, time to think.* She lifted the fizzy little glass of gin and tonic. *No lemon. But needs must, right?*

I bet you don't really like peace and quiet.

He wasn't bad at this.

I love it here. You know, the space, the view from up there.

Or from down here. She raised an eyebrow.

They were silent for a while. Then he reached out and

put a hand on her thigh. The warmth of her skin under her jeans. They looked at the hand, like a bird they didn't want to scare away. He turned and kissed her. She tasted so good. She put her hand on his chest but he couldn't stop because sometimes girls pretended they didn't want to and it was so hard to turn back. His hand was on one of her breasts. But he smelt faintly of sweat and he was pushing his tongue into her mouth and she was surprised by how strong he was. She grabbed one of his fingers and bent it back. *Just fucking stop, OK?*

He sat back. *Sorry.*

Christ.

I got carried away.

I noticed.

They sat beside one another, saying nothing. A helicopter buzzed over Black Hill like a housefly. The taste of her mouth. He still had an erection. Melissa got down off the wall. *Anyway. Things to do. People to see.* She walked off towards the door carrying her book and Alex had absolutely no idea what to think.

There was a random collection of Victorian engravings in the house, purchased as a job lot from the dump-bin of a gallery-cum-junkshop in Gloucester. The North Gable of Whitby Abbey, a dog baiting a bear, Walter Devereux, Earl of Essex, the Brampton hunt at full pelt, a baroque faux-temple of indeterminate location, Mount Serbál from Wády Feirán . . .

★   ★   ★

Louisa slotted her iPhone into the dock and pressed *play*. She squeezed the handles of the tin opener and the sharp little wheel popped through the metal lid. U2. 'Where the Streets Have No Name'. She poured the beans into the colander and rinsed off the gluey purple juice. There was no food processor so she used the potato masher, banging it on the rim when the holes became clogged. It made her think of her mother in the kitchen, beef dripping and hand-mixers. *What are you doing?*

I'm selecting a snack, said Benjy. He loved standing in the golden light and the cold air that poured out of the fridge with its treasure hoard of food.

Well, if you could select quickly I would be really grateful.

He selected and shut the fridge door. That thump and tinkle. Then he was gone. The pepper grinder was empty so she took the little plastic tub off the shelf, ridges round the lid like a fat white coin. She took it off and smelt the contents. Absolutely nothing. Like house dust.

Benjy walked into the dining room, peeling back the little plastic cover then licking the yoghurty patch on his trousers where it had spilt. He put the pot to one side and then folded a sheet of A4 paper into eight so that it formed a little book. He took out the pen that wrote in eight colours. It would be called *A Hundred Horrible Ways to Die* and it would include torture and killing but not cancer. But Mum was standing beside him. *Who said you could have that yoghurt, young man?*

Auntie Louisa did.

Is that a lie?
Only slightly.

οἱ δ᾽ εἰς ὀρχηστύν τε καὶ ἱμερόεσσαν ἀοιδὴν τρεψάμενοι
τέρποντο, μένον δ᾽ ἐπὶ ἕσπερον ἐλθεῖν... *Now the suitors*
waited for evening to come by entertaining themselves with dances
and happy songs ... But Richard was falling asleep.

To be honest, said Angela, *it's not just the Richard thing.*
    Go on.
    It's Karen's birthday on Thursday. She levered a pistachio
shell open.
    Wasn't that in February?
    Not the day she died. The day she was meant to be born.
    What do you mean, the day she was meant to be born?
    5th May. It was my due date.
    You've never talked about this before.
    She'd cracked a nail. *I think I might be going a little crazy.*

Sayid follows the twisted metal cable into the jungle. Marimba
and harp, the sky a scattered blue jigsaw in the canopy,
spiderweb glimmer at ankle height. He crouches and sees
the single tripwire. High dissonant violins. He steps carefully
over. The whip-slither of a rope snapping tight as a sharpened
stake is fired into his thigh. He screams, his legs are yanked
from under him and he's hoisted like a pig for slaughter.

    Alex fast-forwards through the beach section because he
needs dramatic tension to stop himself thinking about Melissa.

Over the last year he has become something of a film buff. Two, maybe three full-length features every shift at Moving Pictures, just a weather eye on the screen during the busy times. Best of all he likes TV box sets. *Lost*, *24*, *Battlestar Galactica*. The consistency mostly. You enjoyed episode 3? You'll probably enjoy episode 4. Less hassle all round.

Night-time. Sayid is lying on the ground. The blur of semi-consciousness. Someone approaches wearing military fatigues. Moonlight on a jagged knife. Sayid's eye fills the screen, then flickers, then closes.

I poured myself another glass of the Monbazillac. As I raised it to my lips something moved in the darkened hallway. Was it the white shoe? My heart hammered, the stimulus rushing through my sensory cortex and hypothalamus to the brainstem, flooding my body with adrenaline. I walked over and found that my coat had slipped off its hook. I breathed deeply trying to slow my racing pulse. Fight or flight, the loyal guard dog that has sat by our side for a million years, alerting us to every sign of danger. But how could one fight an imaginary threat? How could one flee the pictures in one's head? As Hecht had written in his article for Nature, *we had tamed the outside world but not the weapons we possessed for dealing with it . . .*

Melissa put the soggy paperback face down on the edge of the bath, the pages turning slowly into a great damp ruff. Avison would ask Michelle how they'd been bullying her. What was she going to say? She couldn't show him the picture, could she. But if the police were involved they'd look at everything. Shit. She'd always managed to tread the line. You could smoke as long as you did *A Midsummer Night's Dream*. You could skip the odd class as long as you got the grades. But if she got expelled Dad would go fucking ballistic. Goodbye allowance for starters. She didn't even want to think what shitty school she'd end up going to.

There was a print of a robin above the toilet and an air freshener in a crappy pink holster thing on the side of the cistern. Alex groping her. God, she hated this place.

Benjy had a special dispensation to play his Nintendo at the table because he was bored of grown-up talk. Daisy tried to prise him away by asking him about school but he wanted to talk about his ongoing fantasy in which Mrs Wallis killed and ate children in her class which Daisy found tiresome and distasteful so she admitted defeat. She tried talking to Alex but he kept stealing glances at Melissa who was studiously ignoring him. She felt oddly protective and wanted to apologise for her brother's behaviour though she was pretty sure it was Alex who'd come off worst. She stared at her willow-patterned plate. She must have seen the picture a thousand times but she'd never really looked at it, the ship, the temple garden, the figures on the bridge. What was happening?

Mum and Dad were sitting at opposite corners of the table. Why didn't they love each other? It was easier being here with Louisa and Richard and Melissa who acted as a kind of padding. At home the temperature was always a little cooler when the two of them were together. She'd been at Bella's house one day when she was eleven. Bella's father slipped an arm round her mum's waist and kissed her for way too long. Daisy was horrified at first, then she realised and it made her sad.

It's good for Richard being here. Louisa poured herself another glass. *Stop him worrying about things.*

I can't imagine Richard worrying, said Dominic. He could feel something stuck between his front teeth. *Not like the rest of us worry.*

Oh, there's this case at work, said Louisa. *Some legal thing.* Had she said too much?

What kind of legal thing?

We're going to have the stage near the trees at the edge of the playing field, said Melissa. She closed her eyes in order to see the plan more clearly. *The sun will be out at the beginning of the play, which is when we're in the city, and it'll set during the play, which is when everything moves to the wild forest. Cool, no?*

That sounds really interesting, said Angela. Melissa was just a child, wasn't she? Queen of the castle and dirty rascals. *So tell me about being vegetarian.*

I just think it's ridiculous eating animals.

No, said Angela. *Give me a reasoned argument. Imagine you're trying to convert me.*

Well . . . Melissa paused and gathered herself.

It was so easy. Get them on their own and treat them like adults. Except you couldn't do it with your own family, could you? You crossed your own doorstep and took off the cape and you were Clark Kent again.

So, what happens if you're not cleared? asked Dominic.

I think that's highly unlikely.

But hypothetically. Dominic could see that he was making Richard uncomfortable but he was slightly drunk and the opportunities for enjoying this kind of advantage were few and far between.

I suppose ultimately, if one had been grossly negligent, one could be struck off. Richard could think of no way of ending the conversation without giving the impression that he was avoiding the subject.

I suppose most of these cases are settled out of court. Dominic mopped up the last of the sauce with a folded piece of bread.

I would much rather be publicly exonerated. Sadly, it will be the word of an honest man against that of a liar and a hypocrite.

Louisa reappeared with an apple tart in one hand and a tub of vanilla ice cream in the other. Richard got slowly to his feet. *Let me fetch the bowls.*

Angela placed a stack of dirty plates in front of Benjy because she was determined that at least one of her sons would leave home with a few domestic skills. *Put these in the dishwasher. Carefully and one at a time, OK?*

I'll do the greasy stuff in this sink, said Daisy. *You can do the glasses in that one.*

Let's play the story game, said Benjy.

Concentrate, said Angela. *If you drop any it'll be coming out of your pocket money.*

Which story game? said Daisy.

The one where you say a word and I say a word then Mum says a word and we have to make up a silly story.

So long as it doesn't have poo in it, all right?

But I like stories with poo in.

We know, said Angela, patting his head, *but that's a personal problem and I really do think you should keep it to yourself.*

OK, then, but I start.

Go on then.

Once . . .

There . . .

Was . . .

Tangerines . . .

You can't have 'was tangerines'.

Why not?

Because it's grammatically incorrect.

OK. Once there was a . . .

Grapefruit . . .

But I wanted 'tangerine'.

It's not your go. You have to wait till your next turn and then add something ridiculous. So . . . Once there was a grapefruit . . .

Whose . . .

Trousers . . .

Were . . .

Made . . .

By . . .

A . . .
Squirrel . . .
Who . . .
Lived . . .
In . . .
A . . .
Handbag . . .
Made . . .
Of . . .
Poo . . .
Benjy . . .

Melissa popped open the second Rotring tin, took one of the joints out and smelt it. Resin. Like the stuff you used on violin bows in its little velvet handkerchief. It was a kind of amber, wasn't it? Rebuilding dinosaurs from mosquito blood. God, the *T. rex* should have eaten those whiny kids. She got stoned with Mum once and Mum told her how Dad tied her to the bed with the dressing-gown cord sometimes, which was really funny at the time and so deeply not funny the following morning. And when Megan tried it for the first time . . . *This is totally fucking freaking me out*, all snot and mascara, so Melissa spent the whole night feeding her mugs of black coffee and letting her win at Pictionary. But Melissa liked being stoned, the way everything backed off and time went rubbery.

She checked the landing was clear. Downstairs the clatter of plates. There was a door at the end leading to a flight of stone steps into the garden. She opened the Yale lock and left it on the latch and stepped out into the dark. The moon was almost full, ragged clouds were racing high up, but the air in the valley was completely still. The dog was still barking. God, she was going to be hearing it in her sleep for the next month. Faint voices from the yellow windows, everyone drinking coffee and talking bollocks about schools and house prices. She sat on the rusted lawn roller just inside the woodshed and took the joint out of her pocket. She spun the rough little wheel of the lighter. Sparks like a tiny blue thornbush in her hands.

Once upon a time there was a beautiful woman, Koong-se, who fell in love with her father's clerk, Chang. But her father had promised Koong-se to a wealthy duke, so he sacked Chang and built a high wall around the palace to keep the lovers apart. The duke arrived bearing a casket of jewels and the wedding was set for the day on which the willow blossom fell. The day before the wedding Chang slipped into the palace disguised as a servant and the two lovers ran away with the casket of jewels. Koong-se's father saw them and chased them over the bridge brandishing a whip. Luckily they managed to escape by stealing the duke's ship and sailing it to a deserted island where they lived happily together.

Years later, however, Koong-se's father discovered the whereabouts of this deserted island and dispatched soldiers who caught the two lovers and killed them. The gods saw this and took pity on Koong-se and Chang and transformed them into the pair of doves who hover permanently in the sky above the water and the willow trees and the temple garden.

Society has become far too materialistic, said Daisy. *We've lost sight of the important things.*

For an intelligent young woman, said Richard, *you really are incredibly naïve.*

Richard . . . said Louisa.

I am not naïve, said Daisy. She didn't want to be protected, she wanted to win the argument on Richard's terms.

Alex stretched out his legs and knitted his fingers together as if he was settling down to watch a good film.

You want to live in the Middle Ages? said Richard. He knew the conversation with Dominic had upset him and that he was taking it out on Daisy, but he disliked being lectured, especially by someone who thought the rest of them would burn in hell. *You want kids to die of cholera and dysentery? You want your teeth to fall out? No radio, no television, no central heating?*

Richard . . . said Louisa, more insistently this time.

That's not the point, said Daisy. She hadn't drunk alcohol for eight months whereas Richard had downed a bottle of wine. It should have given her an advantage but it seemed to work the other way round.

It is precisely the point, said Richard. *You need money. You need big business. You need competition. You need people to want more, to want better, to want faster. Materialism is not some evil tumour in the body of society. Materialism is the reason why most of us in this room are actually alive.*

Angela had rather enjoyed it at first, these two opinionated people locking horns, but something more was at stake now and she could hear the malice in Richard's voice. She remembered their conversation in The Granary. She was beginning to realise that he was not a very nice man.

Just because you're more intelligent, said Daisy, *you think that makes you right.*

One-nil, said Alex, who had drunk several beers himself. *Straight through the keeper's legs.*

Richard didn't take his eyes off Daisy. *And you've got some growing up to do, young lady.*

I think that's probably enough, Louisa said quietly to Richard, as if he was a small boy, and Angela thought, Yes, that's exactly what he is.

You all right? asked Dominic.

I'm OK. Benjy was sitting on the edge of the bath in his Tarzan pants and his skateboard top. *I'm just a bit sad.*

You're tired, that's what you are. I'll do your teeth for you.

Ouch.

Well, keep your mouth open.

There were bottles and boxes arranged along the window sill like a little alien city. Moisturiser, dental floss, an electric toothbrush, cyber-man bubble bath. He slalomed between them in his space scooter.

Spit and swill.

What's a tampon?

You don't want to know.

Are they like condoms?

Seriously, you do not want to know.

Is it a sex thing?

No, it's a lady thing.

Dominic shepherded him to the bedroom. Benjy got under the duvet and fidgeted himself into a comfortable position while Dominic picked up *The Gate Between Worlds* from the carpet. *So . . . They took off their boots.*

'*Jacket, too,*' *said Mellor.*

'*But I'll get cold.*'

'*You can be cold or you can be dead,*' *said Mellor.* '*Now take it off and leave it on the ground next to the boots.*'

Joseph shivered. The dogs were getting louder. '*Are we going to swim?*'

'*We walk through the shallows,*' *said Mellor,* '*over to the rocks. The dogs will lose our scent and the Smoke Men will think we've drowned or swum to the other side. Quickly. Into the water.*'

Did I miss something? Dominic paused in the doorway.

Daisy and Richard had an argument about religion, said Angela.

He was showing off, said Louisa. *The way men do.*

I resent that, said Alex.

You'll be exactly the same, said Louisa. It sounded almost flirtatious.

Dominic touched Daisy's shoulder. *You OK?*

I'm fine. Though in truth she felt a little unsteady, like when you sliced a finger chopping vegetables.

Benjy all right? asked Angela.

Out like the proverbial. He surveyed the room. *Where's Richard?*

He thought, for a moment, that it was a minor hallucination, an orange firefly in the dark of the woodshed that vanished almost as soon as he saw it. He froze. That breathless adrenaline clarity. Someone was in there. The moonlight dimmed and brightened with the passage of clouds. A wisp of smoke trailed from the gable. He did a rapid calculation. Melissa. He should have let it go. Don't ask, don't tell. But his control over various things had slipped during the day and he disliked the idea of backing down. He walked round to the open side of the woodshed. He expected to see where she was sitting but the interior was filled with a sheer and impenetrable darkness. *Melissa?*

Hello, Richard. Her voice made him jump. *Fancy meeting you here.* Disembodied completely.

The orange firefly appeared. *You're smoking.*

No shit, Sherlock.

Smoking is not good for you. He should have planned this better. But the smell . . . *What's in that cigarette?*

She blew smoke towards him and it bloomed into the moonlight. *Want a drag?*

Put it out.

Go on. That knowing voice, sexual almost. *Help you relax.*

I said . . .

Richard, said Melissa, with amused patience. The effect of the marijuana, perhaps. *You are not in charge of me.*

It was obvious to both of them that he had already lost both the battle and any means of honourable retreat. *Let's see what your mother says about this.* He turned away.

Oh, come on, said Melissa, *she's smoked enough of the stuff.*

I sincerely doubt that.

Melissa laughed. *Jesus, Richard, there are so many things you do not know about my mother.*

He wanted to step into the dark and slap her face. The thought scared him. He moved slowly backwards as if he were carrying a tray stacked with glasses. *We shall talk about this later.*

They have two orchestras, said Louisa. *Swimming pool, climbing wall. But her friends live miles away. She needs a chauffeur, basically.*

The front door thumped shut and Richard walked into the room. He looked punch-drunk. *Melissa is smoking marijuana in the garden and there is absolutely nothing I can do about it, apparently.*

Louisa closed her eyes and breathed deeply. Angela and Dominic looked at one another. Were they allowed to find this funny?

So, anyway . . . He had expected a bigger reaction. Then he saw Daisy and realised how dishonourably he had treated her and how this mattered more. He deflated visibly. Angela poured a coffee from the cafetière and slid it towards the space on the bench he had vacated ten minutes earlier. He sat down. *I apologise for my behaviour earlier.*

That's all right, said Daisy, though she was thinking mostly about Melissa, the drugs, the rudeness, how symbolic it was that she was sitting outside in a cold dark place. If only she were able to look up to the light then Daisy could reach down and take her hand.

It was very bad manners. I'm sorry.

The front door clicked and thumped again. Melissa passed across the yellow rectangle of the lit hallway waving at them. *Nighty-night, campers.*

Louisa got to her feet. *I'm going to have words with that girl.* And she was gone.

Dominic patted Richard on the shoulder. *She's a teenager. Your job is to be completely and utterly in the wrong.*

The Smoke Man ran towards him, roaring and swinging the spiked mace around his head. Benjamin pulled the flintlock out of his pocket and fired. The Smoke Man's mask cracked and the brown gas hissed into the cold air. He screamed and fell to his knees. *Nizh . . . Nizh . . .* He grabbed the pipe from the breathing tank and shoved it directly into his mouth, sucking furiously.

No, Melissa, you listen to me. I know I can't tell you what to do. You have made that abundantly clear. But if you try to drive Richard away . . . I was treated like a doormat by my parents. I was treated like a doormat by my brothers. I was treated like a doormat by your father. I am happy for the first time in my life. Richard loves me. Richard respects me. Richard is kind to me. If you destroy this, I swear to God . . .

> *My fairy lord, this must be done with haste,*
> *For night's swift dragons cut the clouds full fast;*
> *And yonder shines Aurora's harbinger,*
> *At whose approach ghosts, wand'ring here and there,*
> *Troop home to churchyards. Damned spirits all*
> *That in cross-ways and floods have burial,*
> *Already to their wormy beds are gone,*
> *For fear lest day should look their shames upon;*
> *They wilfully themselves exil'd from light,*
> *And must for aye consort with black-brow'd night.*

He rolled over and lay there, watching her sleeping. The butter-coloured hair, the pink of her ear. He touched her shoulder gently so that she didn't wake. *There are so many things you do not know about my mother.*

Lord, said Daisy, *make me an instrument of your peace; where there is hatred, let me sow love; where there is injury, pardon; where there is doubt, faith; where there is despair, hope; where there is darkness, light; where there is sadness, joy . . .*

The witching hour. Deep in the watches of the night, when the old and the weak and the sick let go and the membrane between this world and the other stretches almost to nothing. The moon white, the valley blue. She stands on the hill. The animals sense something out of kilter and move away. Rabbits, mice, nightjars. She gazes down towards the house. The porch light comes on and goes off again. A lamp burns in a bedroom window. Stone walls still holding the heat of the sun. She begins to walk, the grass wet under her bare feet. She climbs a stile over a drystone wall and cuts diagonally across the field below. The lamp in the bedroom window goes out.

She pushes through a low stand of gorse to reach the track which curls around the house. Thorns rip her dress and when she steps onto the broken limestone there are gashes on her thighs and calves that drip and glitter. Someone turns and settles in their shallow sleep.

The lure of human things. She circles the house anti-clockwise then steps under the porch. The door means nothing to her. She stands on the cold flags of the hallway, coats like bats on their brass hooks, the mess of shoes. She can feel it all, centuries of habitation, paint over paint over plaster over stone.

Her mother and father are sleeping in the room to her left. She moves down the corridor, puts her hand on the little metal dog's head of the newel post and makes her way upstairs. The old planks are silent under her feet. Beeswax and camphor, little bouquets of lavender hung in wardrobes. At the top of the stairs there is a print of a bear and a dog fighting. That human smell. Musk, sweetness, rot. She walks along the landing and into the bedroom.

The Art of Daily Prayer. Neutrogena hand cream. Jeans, knickers and navy smock folded on the seat of the chair. The girl turns on her pillow, hands fighting their way through imaginary cobwebs. She knows someone is in the room. She moans something that is not a word.

Does she hate this girl or love her? Perhaps everyone thinks that about their sister. Is this the girl who stole her life? Or is this the girl she would have been? She reaches down and lays her hand against the side of Daisy's head. She struggles but Karen doesn't take her hand away.

Sunday

Alex was running back along the ridge from Hatterall Hill, the ruins of Llanthony below, scattered tents in blue and orange. The map showed a path snaking down the other side so you didn't have to turn back at the cairn, but it was invisible from up here. Fuck it. He headed down through the bracken and long grass. Two weeks and he'd be mountain-biking in Coed-y-Brenin. He'd made a tit of himself with Melissa, he could see that now. Slow learner, or what. He'd only had sex two times, like actually getting his cock in. He avoided Kelly Robinson for two weeks afterwards because they were pissed out of their heads and she was obese, though he thought about it quite often when he was having a wank. But there was someone walking along the road, down there where it flattened out on the way to Longtown, a girl with a bag over her shoulder.

Louisa came round dreaming of *Honk the Moose*, thinking it was 1969 and her mother was sitting on the end of the bed reading to her, but it was Richard and he was wearing the stripy Boden pyjama bottoms that made him look like a pirate, except he wasn't smiling and she wondered if he was about to deliver some bad news. *I'm sorry about last night.*

She hoisted herself up on to her elbows. It was her daughter who should apologise, surely.

She told me you smoked marijuana. And I just wanted to say . . . He slowed and redirected himself. *You don't have to keep secrets.* A little laugh. *Lower dependence and physical harm than alcohol or cigarettes according to Professor Nutt's infamous* Lancet *paper. Oh dear.* He rubbed his face. *I do sound like the most awful prig.*

She brushed the hair out of her eyes. Her mind was fuzzy. She could feel a pillow crease running down her cheek.

Anyway. He stood up. *I shall keep my distance on the Melissa front.*

She sat and swivelled her feet over the edge of the bed and distinctly heard a small boy, standing very close to her, saying, *Dad . . .?*

'I want to cut off her head and take out her heart. Ah! You a surgeon, and so shocked! You, whom I have seen with no tremble of hand or heart, do operations of life and death that make the rest shudder . . .' But the words had stopped making sense, so Daisy closed the book and read the back of the Corn Flakes packet. *Thiamin (B_1) 1.2mg, Riboflavin (B_2) 1.3mg.* Did anyone ever ring the customer care line? Lonely old ladies making friends with young men in Calcutta.

The world felt fuzzy this morning, so hard to cling to.

That nervous bubbling in her abdomen. She wanted her things around her, the battered life-sized cardboard Princess Leia Dad stole from a cinema when he was a student, the enamel signs from Great-Grandad's shop in Manchester, Keener's Kola and broken biscuits.

They'd made a film at school, *Gemma's Choice*, about a girl getting pregnant at fourteen. Daisy played the mother. The thrill of putting on that lime-green cardigan, her own self vanishing, thinking, *I could kiss anyone, I could kill anyone*. She didn't recognise herself on screen. She looked possessed. Now she was doing A-level economics. Adam Smith and production transformation curves. She reopened the book. *'The girl is dead. Why mutilate her poor body without need?'*

Alex appeared at the door, in his socks, sweating. *I think Melissa's jumped ship.*

In what sense?

Walking down the road with a bag over her shoulder.

She suddenly saw it all from Alex's point of view. *Oh, I'm sorry.*

He was still getting his breath back. *Bit of a relief, to be honest.*

And she realised that it was her own heart that was sinking.

Angela is dreaming. The creature is lying in a clean white towel, being offered up to her by a nurse who is unaware that anything is wrong. *Mermaid Syndrome.* Though what dark fairy tale would this monster inhabit? Eyes no more than slits in a head of wet clay, a ragged fin running across the top of the skull, wasted arms, the two legs fused into a stump. *Sirenomelia.*

Those sweet voices calling from the jagged rocks. The thing is screeching. It wants to be held but she can't touch it. She is terrified that it will cling and bite and rip. She has the dream every couple of weeks but never remembers it on waking. Baby birds make her cry, certain cuts of meat, the crippled fragment of Voldemort's soul in *The Deathly Hallows*. She has no idea why this is. She never had amniocentesis, never even had a scan. She missed appointments, said there was a family crisis, she lied to the health visitor, to the GP, to Dominic. Her body knew something was wrong but she was going to be a good mother and a good mother would never reject a child.

Melissa walked for twenty minutes, then her bag started to feel really heavy and there was no way she was turning back so she stuck her thumb out hoping an actual human being stopped and not some weird inbred rapist farmer. A tractor came past, a Post Office van, a removals lorry, a rusty Datsun, then a polished black Alfa Romeo slowed down and pulled over. *Where are you going?* The woman was wearing leather trousers and spoke with a Spanish accent, which was totally not what Melissa was expecting.

I'll go anywhere, said Melissa, as if she were in a film.

Throw your bag into the back seat.

Stuck on the dashboard there was a toy camel with rubber legs which wobbled when the car went round corners. There was a diamanté cat collar in the footwell. *So . . .* The woman lit a cigarette. *Are you running away from home?*

★　　★　　★

. . . ἀλλ' ὅτε τόσσον ἀπῆν ὅσσον τε γέγωνε βοήσας,
ρ'ίμφα διώκοντες, τὰς δ' ου' λάθεν ὠκύαλος νηῦς ἐγγύθεν
ὀρνυμένη, λιγυρὴν δ' ἔντυνον ἀοιδὴν.
Ἀεῦρ' ἄγ' ἰών, πολύαιν' Ὀδυσεῦ, μέγα κῦδος Ἀχαιῶν . . .
*But when we were as far away as a man can shout, pushing rapidly
onward, the Sirens saw our speeding ship and sang their high songs:
'Come here, famous Odysseus, great glory of the Achaeans, tie up
your ship and listen to our voices, for no one has ever rowed past this
island in his black ship without listening to our honeyed mouths . . .'*

Angela walked into the kitchen and found Louisa making
coffee and toast. A sudden memory of the shared house at
college. Dahl and joss sticks, Carol getting scabies at the
hostel. *Are you all right?*

Of course, said Louisa. *Why?*

Last night. Richard and Melissa.

It was nothing.

No fun stuck in the middle.

Really, it was nothing.

Neither of them were on their best behaviour though. On what
planet was this a good thing to say?

Louisa turned and held Angela's eye. *Richard is a good
man.*

I wasn't saying that. But she was saying precisely that, wasn't
she?

Louisa fitted the plunger into the mouth of the jug. *Melissa
is a good person, too.*

I know she is. Another lie.

There are two slices in the toaster if you want. Louisa picked up the cafetière and swept out.

Was it jealousy, perhaps, this childish desire to drive a little wedge between the two of them, the knowledge that they possessed something she and Dominic had let slip through their fingers?

A sudden memory of 92 Hensham Lane. Donny getting drunk one night and cutting the lawn with a pair of scissors for a bet. That German girl putting a padlock on her room. Angela remembered the day she and Dominic moved into their own flat. There were earwigs in the bread bin and someone was playing 'London Calling' at stadium volume upstairs, but it was theirs, and she could feel the relief even now, nearly thirty years later.

Dominic ate a spoonful of Shreddies. *'We believe this to be a tragic case of mistaken identity. We are calling on everyone in the local community to come forward with any information.'* Crack and genocide, then you turned the page and it was cloned sheep and solar power, everything going to hell in a handcart, and heaven just around the corner. It all levelled out in the end. People stopped smoking and got fat. Polio was cured and AIDS killed millions in Africa. When was the Golden Age, anyway? Child prostitution, gin epidemics, the Crusades . . . Alex sat down beside him with a bowl of Sugar Puffs and a mug of tea. *How was the run?*

Good. Yeh, it was good.

Don't you ever just want to lie in bed?

Of course. But you can't, can you?

He hadn't crashed the car or got a girl pregnant, for which they should be thankful, but there was a distance. He thought at first it was genetic, the same self-containment he saw in Richard. But maybe it was just part of being a teenager. *Your job is to be completely and utterly in the wrong.* They didn't need you in the end, generations like leaves, the young taking over a world you no longer really cared for.

All those photographs of Andrew in Amy's house. Hospitalised seven times with asthma and chest infections. He was moved, at first, by the care with which Amy looked after him, and it was only gradually that he came to resent the way that this young man whom he'd never met intruded upon their most private moments and began to suspect that Andrew's continual fallings-out with bosses, flatmates and girlfriends were not a symptom of his medical condition but scenes in a long drama of interdependence besides which Dominic was only a sideshow.

Incidentally, said Alex, *I think I saw Melissa hitting the road.*

Richard's father had died of testicular cancer at the age of forty. Richard was eight, Angela nine. 1972. Hewlett-Packard were making the first pocket calculator and Eugene Cernan was making the last moonwalk. His father was working for the police firearms unit at the time and Richard believed for some years that he had been killed during a shoot-out, though whether this was a lie his mother had concocted or one he had concocted himself and which his mother did not contradict, he never knew.

He still has his scrapbook of news clippings from that year, 1972 in silver foil on the front cover. Vietnam, Baader-Meinhof, Watergate. His father's death goes unrecorded. Not even a pause in the weekly entries, because it was not his father's death which divided his childhood in two, not directly.

His parents drank regularly, at home, in restaurants, at the squash club, so perhaps it didn't seem unusual at first, but by the time he was ten he knew that other children's mothers did not open a bottle of sherry in the afternoon and finish it before bedtime. He and Angela never discussed it. What they discussed was the cleaning and the washing-up and the household bills that fell increasingly to them to sort out. Within a couple of years he was signing his mother's name perfectly on cheques, and even now when he loses the car keys he finds himself looking in the places where he hid them from his mother thirty years ago, the washing machine, the sugar jar. He was nervous of inviting friends to his house and equally nervous at their houses, wondering what might be happening at home, so that school rapidly became the refuge where the tasks were straightforward and the rewards immediate. Geometrical diagrams. The House of Hanover. He regularly cooked for his mother, put her to bed, bathed her sometimes, and the more intimate the task the more she resented the intrusion. At least when she lashed out she was drunk and uncoordinated and he was able to avoid the second blow.

Melissa's gone. It was Louisa, standing behind his shoulder.

What do you mean, gone?

She's taken her bag with all her stuff. Alex thinks he saw her walking down the road.

So, she hasn't been abducted.

I'm being serious.

So am I. Professional habit. Consider all possibilities. He stood up. *Let's go inside and gather some information.*

Alex came downstairs waving Louisa's mobile as they stepped through the front door. *You can get a couple of bars on Vodafone in our room when the wind's in the right direction.* He handed it back. *I left a message.*

Everyone had gathered in the dining room. The scene struck Richard as a little over-dramatic. *She vanishes once a week at home.*

But we're in the middle of nowhere, said Louisa.

Which is a lot safer than a city centre on a Friday night. Richard's voice was noticeably slower and softer than usual. *She'll be sitting in a café somewhere, enjoying the fact that we're panicking. If we ring the police they'll laugh and tell us to call back tomorrow.* Louisa seemed short of breath. He rubbed her arm. *She'll let us worry for a while, then she'll get in touch.*

Angela was thinking, *It's your fault*, and trying hard not to say so, but Dominic was impressed. How did Richard reassure everyone despite knowing nothing? Did all doctors do this?

If we haven't heard anything, said Richard, *we'll ring her from Raglan.*

OK, said Louisa, *OK.*

Except that she wasn't OK, thought Angela, she was simply obeying orders, like a dog with a stern owner.

Benjy stood on the flagstones of the utility space between the kitchen and the downstairs bathroom. It contained a chest freezer, a dishwasher and a deep china sink set into a long wooden draining board as thick as an old Bible. The chest freezer was made by Indesit. He picked up a battered octagonal tin from the window sill. On the lid it said *Dishwasher Tablets* in Dymo Tape and bore an orange sticker reading *If ingested seek medical attention*. The tin rattled as he turned it over. On the bottom the label said *Praline Cluster* and *Coffee Cream* and *Turkish Delight*.

Angela announced that she'd skip the castle and take the bus into Hay. *There's a bus?* Richard had said, incredulously. *Possibly pulled by cows*, she'd replied, a little too tartly and there was a sudden chill in the room. Daisy said softly, *I'll go with Mum*, because she wasn't any keener on Richard's company than Mum was, which meant that Dominic had to go to Raglan to accompany Benjy who never knowingly turned down a castle.

So Angela and Daisy found themselves walking down the hill to the little stone bridge, just the scuff of their boots and the rustle of their waterproofs. A dirty white horse observed them from behind a gate. Angela was angry with Daisy for hijacking her solitary expedition and simultaneously relieved that she wasn't going on her own. So much of one's self depended on the green vase and the rotary washing line that turned in the wind and she was slipping her moorings a little. Daisy liked silence but Angela was used to the clatter and echo of four hundred children in one building. Richard's Mercedes passed them en route to Raglan, Dominic, Alex and Benjy waving like passengers on a steam train.

Where do you think Melissa is? asked Daisy.

But Angela had forgotten about Melissa completely.

Melissa stood on the corner paralysed. Where the fuck was she going to go? Dad wasn't going to fork out for a plane ticket to France without an explanation. Donna in Stirling? She looked around. A shop selling windchimes. A shop selling green wellingtons and crappy silk scarves like the Queen wore when she took the corgis out for a shit. Scabby public toilets. People from London pretending to enjoy the countryside. She checked her wallet. £22.68 and a debit card that might very well get swallowed by the machine on the far side of the road. God, she was hungry.

Do you think Benjy's OK? asked Daisy.

I think Benjy's fine, said Angela.

He seems lonely.

He's good at being on his own, said Angela. The little bus growled up a steep and sudden incline. A tiny church with a garden shed for a tower. A woman hosing a Land Rover down in a muddy yard. *If you can't be alone you join a gang, you drink instead of going home, you marry the first person who comes along because you're scared of going back to an empty house.*

Daisy thought of her mother as stupid. What other reason could there be for the constant friction? Then she said something like this and Daisy remembered that she was a good teacher, and what Daisy felt wasn't admiration or guilt but fear, because if her mother was in the right then she was in the wrong.

The bus idled while a red Transit reversed into a driveway for them to squeeze past. Farmhouses with roses and swing-seats. Farmhouses with chained-up dogs and rusted cars. A hunchbacked woman at the front of the bus, so old and ragged she must surely have come from a gingerbread cottage up in the hills.

Are you and Dad all right? She meant to sound caring but she wanted her mother to admit some small compensatory failure.

We're . . . OK, said Angela gingerly.

And it came to Daisy out of the blue. Her mother was a human being. How rarely she saw it. She wanted to reach out and hold her and make everything good again but the intervening years seemed suddenly like a dream and she was five years old, going into town with Mum to do the shopping. So she turned and looked out of the window and watched the bus rise above the trees and hedges onto a kind of moorland, the grey ribbon of the road and plantations of pine across the valley like scissored green felt.

I'm sorry about Richard, said Angela.

Sunday

It's all right, said Daisy. *I can look after myself.* This dance she and Mum did. Reaching out and pulling back. Stroking and snapping.

He was being a bully.

I can't believe he's your brother.

I'm having a bit of trouble myself in that department.

People counted Dominic as their friend but no one counted him as their best friend. Angela thought of it as cowardice, though she tried not to think of it very often. A failure to engage properly with the world. The mortgage arrears, the car being towed to a scrapyard. Nothing *mattered* enough. (In the back seat, Benjy and Alex were playing Benjy's version of Rock, Paper, Scissors called Wee, Poo, Sick.) He thought of it as a blessing once, not being haunted by the terrible wanting that blighted so many lives, but he looked at Daisy's screwed-up religion, Alex being carted away in an ambulance after that race, Angela trying to save some white-trash kid who'd end up in prison anyway, and he realised that all of them had reasons to be alive in a way that he didn't.

Raglan Castle was built in the mid-1430s by Sir William ap Thomas, 'The Blue knight of Gwent', who fought alongside Henry V at the battle of Agincourt . . . (Richard is reading the free information pamphlet thoroughly) *. . . but the castle was undermined after a long siege during the Civil War and what remains is largely a picturesque ruin . . .* Consequently it takes a dedicated historical imagination to stand on the mossy cobbles of the Pitched Court and conjure up the falconers and the manchet bread and the clatter of billhooks, and what Louisa notices mostly is the absence of a café where she might sit in the warm with a cappuccino and a magazine and rid herself of the image of Melissa naked and broken in a ditch.

Alex walks the battlements of the Great Tower, *which sits at the centre of its own moat and is connected to the main fortifications by a drawbridge*. A little single-engined plane is flying overhead sounding like a lawn mower. He thinks about that flight last year in the Piper Cherokee with Josh's uncle, being frightened during take-off, then feeling smug about not being frightened any more, then enjoying it, then being rather bored because basically there wasn't much to do apart from sit in a cramped seat watching clouds. He glances down into the big stone box of the castle's main hall and sees Louisa pacing. Now that Melissa has gone he is beginning to realise how fit she is. She's nearly fifty, which makes it sound pervy if you say it out loud, but she's in really good nick and he keeps imagining her taking off that cream rollneck jumper. Big tits. All that hair.

But Dominic is listening to Joe Pass. 'Stella by Starlight' from the first *Virtuoso* album. BbMa7 ... Em7b5 ... A7 ... Those incredible runs, just ragged enough to make them feel human. Ever since they arrived at the castle he has been experiencing a disturbing sense of *déjà vu* for which he is unable to account, having never been to Wales before, until he remembers Robert Plant's swordfight in *The Song Remains the Same*. It was filmed here, wasn't it? He'd owned a Welsh farm during his dungeons and dragons phase. 'Bron-Y-Aur Stomp' and so forth. But there's no one here with whom he can share this satisfying pop trivia nugget.

Benjy can't really concentrate on the castle because a weird ginger boy is trying to befriend him. *We're from Devon . . . Have you seen Pirates of the Caribbean . . .? My dad's got a quad bike.* He has a dolphin T-shirt and no eyebrows to speak of. Benjy wants to be left alone because if you concentrate and no one disturbs you the knights stand up from their stone tombs and a cornfield of spears rises beyond the moat.

Do you like football?

He still hasn't quite got the politics of the playground, that low-grade scuffle over space and status. He expects more logic, better tactics. He's spent too much time with his older siblings. He knows quite a bit about homosexuality and communism and income tax, and with Pavel it's easy because they both like making potions and Lego massacre tableaux, but if Wayne Goodrich calls him a spaz . . .

That's my dad, says the ginger boy, turning briefly, *over there.* Benjy runs.

The problem with Jennifer . . . Richard paused. He had never talked seriously about her with anyone except Louisa. *She didn't really care about other human beings. I'm not talking about the way she treated me. You make your bed and you have to lie in it. But friends, patients.* The image of that girl in her wheelchair passed briefly through the headlights of his mind.

Dominic was transfixed by Richard wrestling with difficult ideas in real time. *Why did you get married?*

We were both ambitious, both somewhat unsentimental, neither of us wanted children. In the circumstances I think that was wise. She would have made a dreadful mother. I'm not sure I would have made the perfect father, but in my darker moments I feel a good deal of regret.

Dominic wondered if he could tell Richard about Amy, but he didn't know whether clinical detachment would win out over fraternal loyalty.

Plus, Richard laughed, *she was a very determined woman who was used to getting what she wanted.*

Dominic had met Jennifer only twice, she had no small talk and she watched the children the way a snake might watch a cat. Yet if she had given him her undivided attention? If she had wanted him . . .? Benjy appeared out of nowhere and tugged at his sleeve. *Can we go now?*

Do you remember that scary German woman? said Daisy. *Or maybe she was Dutch. The one who used to throw her son into the water and shout, 'Schwim! Schwim!'*

You and Alex had a race.

And I won.

And he never swam again. Men. Honestly. Angela laughed. What was it? The carnival release of holiday? Being out of habit's gravity? Why could they not do this at home?

They had this amazing toaster. At the hotel.

I'm not sure I remember the actual buffet details.

Benjy was totally in love with it. You put the bread on this conveyor belt and it came out the other side toasted. He called it the Wallace and Gromit toaster. He must have had, like, ten slices every morning.

She glanced over Daisy's shoulder . . . *Bandits at nine o'clock.* Daisy turned round. Melissa, in the window seat of the café on the far side of the road, something hunched and beaten about her.

Daisy said, *I'm going to talk to her.*

What? Now? Had Daisy not noticed? Their two lives were changing course right now.

Perhaps you should give Louisa a ring, said Daisy, setting off across the road because her mother had become simply her mother again, the person you came back to after the adventure.

Please? said Benjy, holding up a short wooden sword with a handguard of plaited rope.

Benjy. Dominic rubbed his eyes. *You've already got six of them.*

I've got five and they're different. He had two broadswords, a katana, a cutlass and a dagger, whereas this was a gladius for stabbing in close combat with a groove down the centre of the blade to let air into the wound so you could easily pull it out without a sucky vacuum holding it in.

It's the acquisition, isn't it? Richard was holding a hardback book about the castle. *Don't you remember?* He had slipped into a more casual register as if the Jennifer conversation had made them friends. *The football cards which came with chewing gum? A part of you knew it was going to be another Peter Shilton, but that didn't matter.*

You promised, said Benjy. *You said I'd get £10 holiday money.*

I know, but . . . Ten pounds was a lot of money. *Why don't you wait for a few days and then decide what you want to spend it on?*

On the far side of the window Louisa was examining the ground in front of her feet and hugging her coat tight around her.

But we won't come back here again. Ever. Benjy was desperate now.

He wanted to say that no means no, but you couldn't say that these days. You had to be friends with your children. He squatted. *You know what always happens. You'll go into another gift shop tomorrow or the day after* . . .

I'll get it for you, said Richard. *My holiday present.*

Dominic's phone went off. The first ten bars of 'Flight of the Bumble Bee'. He fished it out of his pocket. Richard was handing the sword to the woman behind the till. *Hello?*

Panic over. It was Angela. *We found Melissa in a café.*

He felt a vague disappointment. If she'd been murdered they could all go home. *I'll pass on the good news.* Though when he did this Richard simply said *Excellent*, showing neither surprise nor relief so that Dominic wondered for a moment if you could shape the future by predicting things with sufficient confidence.

Thank you, Uncle Richard, said Benjy.

You're welcome.

And he was off, through the glass door and out into the sunlight of the car park, thrusting and parrying. *Oof . . .! Yah . . .!*

Melissa was listening to Cally's phone ring at the far end when she saw Daisy come in. She was annoyed and relieved at the same time. She hung up.

Daisy sauntered over. *I'm going to get a coffee. Do you want anything to eat or a drink?* Super casual, like they were still back at the house. She should have left more theatrically, shouldn't she? *A flapjack would be good.* She'd babysat a mug of cold tea for the last hour. *And a black coffee.*

She watched Daisy walk over to the counter. The steely thing made her uneasy. She had absolutely no idea what Daisy was thinking or feeling or planning. There were Christians at school but they kept their heads down, whereas Daisy . . . She wasn't a moose either, she hadn't got a big arse or a weird face. She knew it, too, something about the way she carried herself, deliberately choosing to make herself look shit, a provocation, almost.

Daisy returned to the table with two black coffees and two flapjacks. *They always put the napkin under the food. Which misses the point, don't you think?* Like she was thirty-five. *How are you doing?*

I'm dandy. Just dandy.

And how's Ian McEwan?

Melissa thought Daisy was talking about a real person

until she remembered the closed novel lying under her hand. *It's OK.* They were playing a game, but it was against the rules to say so. *We're doing it at school.*

I'm reading about vampires.

Melissa took a swig of coffee and relaxed a little. *Twilight?*

Daisy took *Dracula* out of her bag. *Jonathan Harker travels to Transylvania to do some work for a mysterious count and it all kind of goes downhill from then on.*

OK, said Melissa, carefully.

Except that Daisy wasn't playing a game. This was serious. Usually she became tongue-tied and foolish when she wanted someone to like her, but with Melissa . . . Was this a kind of acting, too? Putting on your best self and coming thrillingly alive? Was this the Holy Spirit? *God be in my mouth, and in my speaking. Sorry about Alex.*

Sorry in what way?

The slobbering.

Oh, I think I can handle Alex. Melissa wondered if she could make Daisy a sidekick for a few days. That would throw Mum and Richard. Her phone vibrated. *CALLY*. They watched it tango across the table. She looked at Daisy. What was her weak point? It wasn't the religion, was it. But that first night, the way Angela reached across to stop her saying grace . . . *Your mum thinks you're stupid, doesn't she?*

We don't exactly see eye to eye.

Your dad seems OK, but your mum . . . Is she, like, really unhappy or something?

That's exactly it. Because Melissa was right, and no one

else said it, did they? *She doesn't enjoy things, she doesn't get excited.* She bit off a piece of flapjack. *Your mum seems pretty happy.*

I'll give it two years.

Yeh?

Tell me one thing they've got in common.

Daisy laughed. No one said this either. *So . . . are you still running away, or are you coming back?*

Melissa looked at her. *Crazy hazy Daisy.*

Daisy felt as if she was in a film. Something hypnotic about that gaze. The snake in *The Jungle Book.*

What do you think I should do? asked Melissa.

I think you should come back.

Then I shall come back.

Angela finished her second Twix and put the scrunched wrapper into her pocket. Little canvases of dancing naked women, sheep made of welded nails. She wanted to buy the big bowl with ducks on because that's what you did on holiday, bought stuff you didn't need. Lovespoons and wall plates. Except they couldn't afford it now. They'd stopped talking about money. He was sane again. Don't look a gift horse. Five years of mortgage left, assuming they caught up with the payments. Then she could buy sheep made of welded nails. She tilted her head, as if taste were simply a matter of angle, but all she could think was, *I like the ducks.*

The china tramp. The Pineapple. She'd got it completely wrong. It wasn't her house, was it? Like stepping out of a plane. It was Juliette's house. She walked to the little wall and sat down beside an elderly couple eating cornets. She felt light-headed and shaky. It was Juliette's dad who played Oscar Peterson. She tried to remember what music her father played, tried to remember her own bedroom. She realised for the first time that her parents had died taking secrets with them. Where was Juliette now? New Zealand? Dead? The pennies, the train to Sheffield, that was home, yes. But the doorway from which her father was always vanishing, what was in there? If only she could get closer and see into the dark.

She needed to tell someone, she needed to tell Daisy, and in her untethered state of mind it seemed entirely natural that the thought itself should conjure her daughter into being fifty yards further up the high street, but she was shoulder to shoulder with Melissa and they were laughing and Angela felt as if she had been slapped.

Benjy loves being in the countryside, not so much the actual contents thereof, horses, windmills, big sticks, panoramas, more the absence of those things which press upon him so insistently at home. He occupies, still, a little circle of attention, no more than eight metres in diameter at most. If stuff happens beyond this perimeter he simply doesn't notice unless it involves explosions or his name being yelled angrily. At home, in school, on the streets between and around the two, the world is constantly catching him by surprise, teachers, older boys, drunk people on the street all suddenly appearing in front of him so that his most-used facial expression is one of puzzled shock. But in the countryside things are less important and happen more slowly and you know pretty much exactly who might or might not appear in front of you. And his hunger for this calm is so strong that he keeps a little row of postcards along his shelf at home. Buttermere, Loch Ness, Dartmoor. Not so much windows on to places he would rather be but on to ways he would like to feel.

Those first five years with Dominic were the first sustained happiness she had ever experienced. She worked in a travel agency, he played in two jazz groups and taught piano to private pupils. She can recall very little of what they did together, no romantic weeks in Seville, no snowed-in Christmases, finds it hard now to picture them doing anything together that isn't recorded in a photo album somewhere, but that was the point, the ease of it, finally not needing to notice everything. Twenty-four years old and she was off duty at long bloody last. And nowadays when she thinks about her marriage, this is what depresses her, that she is back on duty again. Has Dominic changed? Or is his blankness precisely what she once found so consoling? She doesn't mind the lack of love, doesn't mind the lack of physical affection, doesn't even mind the arguments. She wants simply to let go for once, wants not to have to think and plan and remember and organise. Cows like toy cows on the far hill. When she imagines the future, when she imagines the children leaving home, the truth is that she's on her own. That dusty pink house sitting up there squeezed into the edge of the wood, for example, a little dilapidated. She can imagine living there, she can imagine it so vividly that it is like a taste in her mouth. Butterscotch. Marmalade. Job at a village school somewhere nearby. Tidy house, little garden, one day blissfully identical to the next and only herself to please.

Daisy and Melissa are sitting in the back seat of the bus talking about *Juno* and Pete Doherty and Justin Bieber and the kid on crutches at Daisy's school. Angela sits five rows forward feeling abandoned and petty for feeling abandoned, trying to read an article about the possibility of a coalition but being led astray by an interview with Gemma Arterton (*they made a Lego figure of me*).

The walk from the bus stop is twenty-five minutes and the girls chat the whole way, or seem content in one another's silent company while Angela trails behind. She catches herself thinking Melissa is Karen. She wonders what Karen is like now, what Karen might be like now. Another Daisy but with Melissa's confidence, perhaps, her physical ease. She remembers that line from the Year 12 poetry project. *When I look ahead up the white road there is always another who walks beside you.* Or something like that. Phantoms and guardian angels, like those people in the Twin Towers, trapped in a smoke-filled stairwell. Someone takes their hand and says, *Don't be afraid*, and they walk through the flames and find themselves alone and safe.

She forgets completely about Melissa's disappearance until they walk into the dining room and Alex and Louisa and

Richard look up and Melissa and Daisy are visibly *together* which catches everyone by surprise and Melissa is clearly not planning to apologise or explain if she can possibly help it, and Angela realises the whole thing is one long performance. Melissa says, *I'm going to freshen up* and sweeps stairwards, bag over her shoulder and Angela can see Richard biting his tongue very hard.

Dominic and Benjy go outside and sit together on the rusted roller beside the woodshed and Benjy uses Dominic's Leatherman to whittle a stick. The knife is unwieldy and Benjy is ham-fisted but it's a good stick because Benjy is an expert in these matters (Dominic will let him have his own penknife next birthday), neither too green so that the shaft is whippy nor too rotten so the wood crumbles. Dominic lets him do it without offering to take over, because he's not a bad father. Indeed he's able to enter Benjy's world in a way that no one else in the family can, perhaps because the adult world holds him in a weaker grip, perhaps because there is a part of him which has never really grown up. And now Benjy has finished making the sword, stripping the bark and sharpening the point. *There you are.* Dominic takes it. The naked wood is the colour of margarine and waxy under his fingers. It makes him think of woodlice and Play-Doh and paper planes. *En garde.* Benjy dies four times, Dominic five. Afterwards they lie on the damp grass looking at the featureless grey sky because this is how Benjy likes to talk sometimes. *I've been thinking about Granny.*

In what way have you been thinking about Granny?

Because you said it was a good thing she died.

She wasn't really Granny any more, was she?

She called him *the little boy,* but he liked Mum explaining who he was each time. He also liked the photo of the cocker spaniel and the cogs of the carriage clock moving silently in their glass box and the biscuits the nurses brought round on a trolley at four o'clock. *I see her at night sometimes.*

You dream about her?

Yes, it was a dream, Benjy supposed. *But she's standing in my room.*

Are you worried that she might not be dead?

Is that possible?

No, it's not possible.

He thought about Mum and Dad dying and being looked after by strangers and it was like someone standing on his chest. He rubbed the cuff of Dad's shirt but it wasn't the special shirt. Then they heard Melissa shouting, *Fuck off,* which was the second rudest thing you could say, so it made him laugh and Dad got up and said, *Hang on, Captain.*

Melissa patted the bench beside her.

Daisy sat, obediently. *You were telling me about Michelle.*

She's a drama queen is what actually happened.

Daisy had accepted a glass of wine so as not to seem like a prude and the world was a little fuzzed already. *But still.*

We were at this party. It was a relief telling someone who would vanish in five days. *Michelle disappears upstairs with this skanky guy none of us have seen before.*

That kind of party had always scared Daisy, the smell on your clothes the next day and something else that couldn't be washed off.

We go into the bedroom and she's sucking this guy off. She paused to gauge Daisy's reaction, but it was hard to read. *He looks at us and smiles. You know, come in, why not, like he's making a sandwich. I take a picture and Michelle doesn't even notice because she's, like, way too busy down there.*

Daisy was thinking about the giant cockroach at Benjy's animal party, how the hard little segments of its body glowed like burnished antique wood.

There's some stupid argument a couple of days later and Cally grabs my phone and waves the picture in Michelle's face. Michelle goes apeshit, punching Cally, pulling her hair. So it's knives out and Cally sends the picture to Uncle Tom Cobley and all.

I'm not surprised she tried to kill herself. Daisy felt soiled just hearing the story.

Had Melissa heard right?

That was a really horrible thing to do.

Whoa there. Was this what she got in return for her friendship? She stood up. *Well, you can fuck off, then, Miss Goody Two-Shoes.* She flounced grandly towards the house.

Everything in the garden became suddenly vivid as if some general membrane had been peeled away. The bootscraper, the ivy. Then Dad rose from behind the wall. *Trouble at mill?*

Daisy felt as if she were broadcasting the story wordlessly. Like he's making a sandwich.

He sat down and put his arm around her. *Hey.*

She's a nasty person.

Read all about it, said Dad. *Do we need to take retaliatory action?*

No. She was returning slowly to herself. *I think being Melissa is punishment enough.*

Benjy, you crouch down at the front, said Alex, *like you're holding the football.*

Perhaps you should take the apron off, said Louisa, but Richard liked the idea of being a modern man. The all-round provider. *Where's Melissa?*

Don't worry, said Dominic. *Alex can Photoshop her in later. Little square in the top right hand corner. Like the reserve goalkeeper.*

Which was good, thought Alex, because then he would have to take a picture of her on her own and you couldn't wank over a photo that contained your parents. *Hold still.*

People assumed Melissa was vegetarian out of cussedness, or maybe as an outlet for the empathy she didn't expend on human beings, but it was sloppy thinking she hated. She cared little for the suffering of cattle or sheep but why eat them and not dogs? It wasn't so much a belief as the obvious thing to do. She hated injustice without feeling much sympathy for those who had been treated unjustly. She thought that all drugs should be legal and that giving money to charity was pointless. And she liked the fact that these opinions made her distinctive and intelligent. In many respects she was like her father. Not the dirt under his nails, not the prickly pride in his under-education but the way his sense of self depended so much on other people being in the wrong.

Ian's been offered four hundred thousand for the business, said Louisa.

So he'd be an idiot not to take it.

But what's he going to do? She put the milk back in the fridge. *He's fifty-one. Too young to retire, too old to start all over again.*

Richard quartered an onion and laid it between a parsnip and a sweet potato. *They'd keep him on as manager, surely. Or would that be beneath his dignity?*

Angela came in with a glass of wine and sat herself on the window seat. *Am I interrupting?*

Not at all, said Louisa. She hoisted a stack of white plates from the shelf. *I'll set the table.*

Angela gathered herself. *Look. About Juliette.* She realised how rarely she apologised, for anything, to anyone. *You were right, I did spend a lot of time at her house.* She explained, about The Pineapple, about Oscar Peterson.

It doesn't matter now. It's water under the bridge.

She felt herself bridle. *But it does matter.* He wasn't giving enough weight to this. *I'm saying sorry.*

He stood to attention, clicked his heels and dipped his

head like a tin soldier. *Then I forgive you.* He leant his weight on to the flat of a knife blade and crushed three cloves of garlic. *Besides, I couldn't wait to get out of there myself. But this is good, though*, said Richard, *us talking about it, laying ghosts to rest and so forth.*

Except she had never got out of there, had she, not the way he had got out. The ease with which he sailed through his A levels, the confidence with which he strode off into the world. Was it childish to resent someone for being blessed with such good fortune? At sixteen she'd felt so much more skilled at the task of being human than her gauche and solitary brother. Then suddenly . . .

He arranged the crushed garlic. *I should have visited Mum more. I realise that.* How long was it since he'd used that word? *Jennifer never liked me having a family. I don't think that's a revelation, is it? I didn't really understand what family meant till I met Louisa. Even Melissa. Because that's part of the package, isn't it? You have to work at these things.*

But she wasn't really listening, because underneath it all ran the fear that it had nothing to do with good fortune, that he had earned this, and she resented him because she could have done it, too, if she'd applied herself properly, become a lawyer, moved to Canada, run a business, and what she saw when she looked at Richard was not his success but her own failure.

Benjy is playing with his GoGos at the far end of the dining table, arranging them in colour-coded ranks. Gold, silver, red, orange, yellow. They have official names like Pop and Kimy and Kichi which you can look up on the website but Benjy and Pavel have given them names like Spotty Lizard and Pooper and Custard-Dog. They play a flicking game with them, like marbles, but when he's on his own Benjy likes to arrange them in battle array.

Angela, Dominic and Daisy like them because they're rather beautiful en masse and, refreshingly, not weapons, but when Louisa steps into the dining room laden with plates she feels only mild annoyance. She hasn't really talked to Benjy yet this holiday and the guilty truth is that she doesn't like him much. Clothes that don't hang quite right, stained more often than not, flopping constantly as if he is operated by remote control by a person some considerable distance away. *Benjy . . .?*

Louisa works for Mann Digital in Leith. They do flatbed scanning, big photographic prints, light boxes, Giclée editions, some editing and restoration. She loves the cleanness and the precision of it, the ozone in the air, the buzz and shunt of the big Epsons, the guillotine, the hot roller, the papers, Folex, Somerset, Hahnemühle. Mann is Ian Mann who hung on to her during what they called her *difficult period* because she'd manned the bridge during his considerably more difficult period the previous year. She started on reception, learnt how to do the accounts and now did most of the Photoshopping because the boys were just techies, really. Years back she'd started an art degree at Manchester but she hadn't slept with another woman or been permanently stoned or proud enough of the working-class roots which she was trying to escape, frankly, and while her draughtsmanship was near-perfect the bottom was falling out of the painting and drawing market so she left halfway through the second year. Plus she had to earn some real money because living in a shared house with a dirty fridge and peeling wallpaper held no romance and in truth she had felt uneasy with the idea of being an artist in the first place. Her father said going to university was *getting above yourself* and she hated him for it, not least because he was throwing her own suspicions back at her. And if Angela and Dominic assumed she didn't have a job and spent her days, what? shopping? at the gym? then it was an impression she was happy to give because it might not be art, as such, but it was creative and it was hers and it was precious and she didn't want it picked over by other people.

When Melissa came into the dining room Mum was laying the table while the little boy loaded half a million plastic creatures into a rucksack.

You and Daisy seem to be getting along pretty well.

Melissa was going to duck the question and head into the kitchen but Angela was sitting on the window seat looking kind of intense so she did a comedy pirouette and leant against the radiator warming her hands. She felt like an idiot. *Yeh, she's OK.* If only they hadn't made such a Royal bloody Command Performance of marching into the dining room together.

She seems like a really genuine person.

Melissa examined the pattern of cracks in the flagstones because, much as it hurt to admit it, Daisy was right. They knew Michelle was crazy and perhaps she had meant to kill herself, and there was no one she could say this to. It was dawning on her, like the clouds parting and the angels singing and a great load of shit pouring down, that she didn't actually have any real friends. Cally was probably stitching her up right now, and she could see Alicia and Megan laughing like a pair of fucking witches. She pushed herself upright and marched into the kitchen through the cloud of serious adult vibe and opened the fridge door. *Medical necessity.*

Are you OK? Richard was wearing oven gloves like a big pair of woolly handcuffs.

Hook Norton. Organic Fucking Dandelion. *I'm right as rain, Richard.* She grabbed an Old Speckled Hen, stood up, shut the fridge door, twizzled, clinked Angela's wine glass with the beer bottle. *Cheers, my dear.* And exited.

There were two shelves of books to the right of the chimney breast in the living room, so dulled by time and sunlight that most eyes slid over them as smoothly as they slid over the floral curtains and the walnut side table. Some were doubtless holiday reading left behind by the owners and their paying guests (*A Sparrow Falls* by Wilbur Smith, *Secrets of the Night* by Una-Mary Parker), some appeared to be gifts which had been banished to the second home (*Debrett's Cookbook, Fifty of the Finest Drinking Games*), some must surely have been bought for amusement only (*Confessions of a Driving Instructor* by Timothy Lea, *How to Be Outrageously Successful with Women* by John Mack Carter and Lois Wyse), while other tattered paperbacks bore glorious noir covers that no one had seen for years (*Fatal Step* by Wade Miller, *Plot it Yourself* by Rex Stout). *Eminent Victorians* by Lytton Strachey and Wittgenstein's *On Certainty*, however, had clearly slipped through some breach in the fabric of the universe and now sat waiting patiently for rescue.

When you are speaking to an older person, said Alex, *show that you are very alert and are paying due attention to what is being said to you.*

What's this? Dominic opened the fizzy water.

Pictorial Knowledge.

Benjy, mate, this is you, said Alex. *To loll awkwardly, ask for sentences to be repeated, be inattentive and uninterested is sheer bad manners.*

Can you clear some space, please? Richard bore the chicken aloft.

That looks delicious. Dominic rubbed his hands.

Broadly speaking we should take a bath every day whenever that is possible.

Alex . . .

In the absence of a bath, a quick sponge down and then a brisk rub with a rough towel does a great deal of good.

Daisy, said Richard, *are you going to say grace?*

It's all right, I don't have to.

Go on, said Richard, *I'm getting rather fond of it.*

Melissa looked at the chicken with disdain.

Dominic said, *Worry not, it was smothered with a silk pillow after a long, fruitful and contented life.*

It's OK, said Benjy, *because chickens aren't very intelligent.*

Some people aren't very intelligent and we don't eat them, said Melissa.

Mentally Handicapped Person Pie, said Benjy.

That is not funny, said Angela.

It is a bit funny, said Alex.

Richard returned with the roasted vegetables, borne similarly aloft.

I think it's an amazing vocation, being a teacher, said Louisa.

Vocation, thought Angela. Maybe that was what she'd lost.

But Dominic and Richard were talking about Raglan. *And then I realised*, said Dominic. *It featured in* The Song Remains the Same.

He's improving my mind, said Louisa. *He takes me to galleries. Museums, operas.* She leant in close. Alex could smell her perfume and see her breasts inside her shirt. *I'm not so keen on the opera.*

Melissa stared at her plate but she had lost the power to influence the atmosphere in the room. Richard patted her forearm gently and she didn't protest.

I felt rather deserted when you ran off across the road.

I'm sorry, said Daisy. The desire to save Melissa. It seemed laughable now.

What's the most horrible way to die? asked Benjy.

Huntington's disease, said Richard. *You go insane and lose control of your body slowly over many years. You can't sleep, you can't swallow, you can't speak, you suffer from epileptic fits and there's no cure.*

But Benjy had meant it to be a funny question.

A young doctor had stood beside her bed and explained why the foetus was deformed. He seemed pleased with himself for knowing the biology behind such a rare syndrome. She got the impression that she was meant to feel pleased, too, for having won some kind of perverse jackpot. The following morning they took the lift to the ground floor and entered a world full of mothers and pregnant women. She felt angry with them for parading their prizes so brazenly, and relieved that she herself had not become the mother of that thing. She cried and Dominic comforted her but he never asked why she needed comfort, because it was obvious, surely. She combed her memory to discover what she'd done wrong. She'd smoked during that first month. She'd stumbled getting off a bus on Upper Street. If only she could find the fault then perhaps she could turn back time and do things differently and arrive at the present moment all over again but with a baby sleeping in the empty cot.

Dominic came back into the bedroom holding his toothpaste and brush. *What's the matter?*

I look at people and I think they're Karen.

He remembered his grandmother dying when he was eight, seeing her everywhere. All those old ladies with white hair.

I think she's still alive. Out there. Watching. Waiting.

He was tired and this was scaring him. *She's not out there, Angela. She's not watching.* Had she ever been alive?

Don't you think about her?

Sometimes. Though he rarely did.

I hear her voice.

How long have you been thinking like this?

Not so much before, but recently . . .

You've got a real daughter.

I know.

And you give her such a hard time.

Dom . . .

It's not about the religion, is it?

Please, not now.

You're angry with her. He felt the giddy excitement of climbing a great tower and seeing the shape of the maze through which he had stumbled for so long. *She's not a consolation prize. She's a human being.*

Louisa sat on the edge of the bath, the little yellow tub of face cream in her hand. Melissa's disappearance had rattled her, not so much the thought of what might have happened as what else she might do, what else she might or might not say. Hard to believe it now, the facts blurred by the alcohol she'd drunk to blunt the unexpected loneliness after Craig walked out. Fifteen men, or thereabouts. She wasn't greatly interested in counting. One in the back seat of his BMW, with his trousers round his knees, his hand over her mouth, calling her a *dirty bitch* so she wondered if it counted as rape, though rape meant saying *No*, not just thinking it, which meant having some actual self-respect. One of them was a scaffolder. Blind drunk every time.

Annie had taken her to Raoul's that first weekend and she could feel them circling now Craig's scent was fading. Annie said she was punishing herself, but some things were just accidents. You took the wrong path and night fell. She never drank at home but the places she went for company were places where you drank, and if you were scared of going home you kept on drinking. Melissa encouraged her rebellion at first, then came back from a friend's house one morning to find a man she didn't recognise sitting at the breakfast table and said, *Who the fuck is this?* and Louisa couldn't say anything because, in truth, she didn't know who it was, not really. Even now she can't bring a name to mind. Or a face.

She didn't fall for Richard so much as grab him as she was swept past, fighting to keep her head above the water. They didn't have sex for six weeks while she waited for the result of an AIDS test. He thought she was just being old-fashioned. She thought that if she let go of the past it would be carried away by that same flood, but it was dawning on her for the first time that she would have to tell him before Melissa did. *Forgive and forget.* She was beginning to under-stand what it meant. You couldn't do the forgetting until someone else had done the forgiving.

*   *   *

I was having a nightmare about the Smoke Men.

OK, said Alex. *We're on two mountain bikes.* Because this was something he often thought about when he was falling asleep himself. *We're riding through a forest. It's summer and I've got a picnic in a rucksack.*

With bacon sandwiches, said Benjy, *and a flask of tea and two KitKats.*

We're going faster and faster and suddenly we come out of the trees and we look down and see the tyres aren't touching the ground any more.

Are they magic bikes?

They're magic bikes and we're flying and we're getting higher and higher and we can see the fields and a river and a steam train and cars. There are birds flying underneath us and there's a hot-air balloon and the people in the basket wave at us and we wave back and I say to you, 'We can go anywhere in the world.' He stroked Benjy's hair. *Where do you want to go, little brother?*

I want to go home, said Benjy.

Monday

Richard slots the tiny Christmas tree of the interdental brush into its white handle and cleans out the gaps between his front teeth, top and bottom, incisors, canines. He likes the tightness, the push and tug, getting the cavity really clean, though only at the back between the molars and pre-molars do you get the satisfying smell of rot from all that sugar-fed bacteria. Judy Hecker at work. Awful breath. Ridiculous that it should be a greater offence to point it out. Arnica on the shelf above his shaver. Which fool did that belong to? Homeopathy on the NHS now. Prince Charles twisting some civil servant's arm no doubt. Ridiculous man. *Hello trees, how are you this morning?* Pop a couple of Nurofen into the river at Reading to cure everyone's headache in London. He rinses his mouth with Corsodyl.

The intolerable loneliness after Jennifer left. The noises a house made at night. Learning the reason for small talk at forty-two. *Going to the pub.* He'd always thought of it as wasting time.

He spits out the mouthwash, sluices his mouth with cold water and pats his face dry with the white towel from the hot rail.

He turns and sees himself in the mirrored door of the cabinet, face still puffy with the fluids that fatten the face in the night, waiting for gravity to restore him to himself. They say you're meant to see your father staring back at you, but he never does. He pulls the light cord and heads to the bedroom to get dressed.

Alex hoists himself up and stands on the trig point. He is the highest thing for, what? fifty miles? a hundred? He turns slowly as if he is spinning the earth around him like a wheel, the ridges of the Black Mountains receding to the south, Hay down there in the train-set valley to the north. The wind buffets him. He imagines fucking Louisa against the bathroom door. Her ankles locked behind him, saying, *Yes, harder, yes*, the door banging and banging and banging.

They've created the largest fiscal deficit in recent history.

Dominic regretted broaching a subject about which Richard seemed to know rather too much and Dominic too little, for whenever he ventured into the financial section of the newspaper a dullness stole over him as if the subject were protected by a dark charm woven to dispel intruders. *So we elect a man who won't admit to having any actual policies?* But he was bowling uphill in fading light.

Down the table Angela was reading the *Observer* travel

section. A message had slipped over the hill during the night. *Missing U. Love Amy XX*. If he never told her about Amy then he would always be the better parent, the better person, because he loved Daisy unreservedly. And there she was, coming in holding a bowl of cereal. *People are greedy and selfish*, she said, sitting down as far away from Melissa as possible, though it was only Dominic who noted the geometry. *They just vote for people who promise to give them exactly what they want. It's like children with sweets.*

But she wasn't talking about *people*. She was talking about Richard and she was talking about Melissa, wasn't she?

But things improve, said Richard carefully. *It's a messy process but things do get better.*

For who? said Daisy.

None of them were greatly interested in the election except as a national soap opera in which the closeness of the result was more exciting than the identity of the winner. Individually, they were passionate about GP fundholding, academy schools, asylum, but none of them trusted any party to keep a promise about any of these issues. Louisa struggled to believe that she could change herself, let alone the world, and saving lives seemed to absolve Richard of any wider duty. Angela and Dominic had once marched in support of the miners in Doncaster and the printers in Wapping, but their excitement at Blair's accession had changed rapidly to anger then disappointment then apathy about politics in general. Alex was planning to vote Tory because that was how you voted when you were the kind of person he wanted to be. Melissa affected a disdain which felt like sophistication and Daisy affected an ignorance which felt like humility. Benjy, on the other hand, was interested mostly in the fate of the tiger, the panda and the whale, and consequently more concerned about the future of the planet than any of them.

Daisy had never really talked to Lauren till they were swimming for the school, up at six for seventy lengths at the Wheelan Centre before lessons. She was five foot eleven at sixteen, as graceful in the water as she was clumsy out of it, hunching her shoulders and speaking in a tiny voice to compensate, not quite a girl but not a woman either. She wore baggy clothes to deflect attention but when she was in her green Speedo Daisy was mesmerised by the length and whiteness of her legs and neck, the way you couldn't stop looking at someone with a missing arm or a strawberry birthmark. She attached herself to Daisy with an eagerness that no one had shown since they were six or seven so that they inhabited a kind of treehouse world together. Something about Lauren's size that made Daisy feel tucked away like a precious thing. Boys called Lauren a freak and kept their distance, though it was clear to Daisy that when she was older and more confident and they were less concerned about the opinions of their peers they would see that she was beautiful. Lauren responded by pretending they didn't exist, even Jack who hated being ignored by someone who still read novels with wizards in, a scorn she returned in equal measure so that Daisy grew rapidly tired of being the prize in a pointless competition.

But Lauren was the only person who wasn't fazed when Daisy joined the church. She should have been grateful, but . . . what was it? Lauren's smugness about having won the competition by default? The unshakeable puppyish loyalty? So she pushed Lauren away and when Lauren clung on she pushed harder, for surely it was insulting if a friend refused to react to your feelings? She gave up swimming, stopped calling, stopped answering her phone. Lauren knocked on the door once and Daisy asked Mum to say that she was out, and she wasn't sure which felt worse, the way she was behaving or Mum's delight at her unchristian hypocrisy.

Lauren's height and divorcing parents and the fact that she too had stopped swimming meant that it took a long time for anyone to notice her anorexia. Daisy didn't believe it had anything to do with her, for that would have been self-centred. But neither did she get in touch to offer help or support. Lauren was in hospital briefly, but Daisy didn't visit, and when Lauren's mother moved to Gloucester, taking Lauren with her, Daisy felt a relief that was no relief at all.

Benjy poured three centimetres of vinegar into the big plastic tub.

Now, said Richard, *fill the egg cup with bicarbonate of soda.*

This is going to be brilliant. Benjy filled it clumsily. *Did you do this when you were little, Uncle Richard?*

I was far too well behaved. He tried not to think about the children he might have had. *I'll do this next bit myself.*

Do you think it will go over the roof?

Let's see. Gingerly, he lowered the egg cup into the vinegar. The rim of the egg cup sat just proud of the liquid. Perfect. He pressed the top back on to the tub.

Can I do it? asked Benjy.

One shake and then step back quickly.

Ten, nine, eight . . . Benjy crouched down . . . *two, one . . . Blast off.* He shook the tub and sat his teddy bear on top and forgot to stand back so Richard grabbed his shoulder and pulled him away. And nothing happened. *Perhaps we should do it again,* said Benjy, but Richard could see the plastic lid bulging under the bear. *Wait.* There was a creak like a ship trapped in ice and the *POP* was considerably louder than Richard had expected, there was foam all over his trousers and a flatulent smell in the air (sodium acetate?) and while the bear didn't quite go over the roof it did get stuck in the climbing rose just under the first-floor window. Benjy was whooping and Richard could see it all from his point of view and it really was the funniest thing he'd seen in a long time and Benjy was saying, *Again, again, again,* which was when Angela appeared from the front door. *I thought a bomb had gone off.*

I can add you in later, said Alex. *Like the reserve goalkeeper.* She had no idea what he was talking about, but she ran a quick mental check of her outfit. Ugg boots, patterned tights under denim shorts, lumberjack shirt . . . She didn't know whether to be flattered or disgusted but it seemed like the wrong time to piss off yet another person. *Smile.* Click. *Turn towards the house.* Click. She knew she looked good. Her only worry sometimes was that she didn't look different enough, that people mistook her for part of a crowd. She'd see a girl in patterned Docs or with a dyed red pixie cut and wish she had the balls. Click. *Now sit on the wall.* Like some sleazy old guy. Click. You should be a model, love. Give us some arse. *I think we're finished now.*

Cheers, said Alex. *That's great.*

Except he probably wouldn't wank over the photo because he was becoming aware of a nastiness in Melissa that clung to her even in his sexual fantasies, though it didn't matter now because he fancied Louisa instead, and he was proud of the fact that his taste was maturing.

It's not far. Richard leans over the Ordnance Survey as if he is planning an aerial assault on northern France. *A couple of miles at most.*

Louisa brushes toast crumbs from her sweater. *Those little brown lines are very close together.*

Daisy is sitting in the window seat reading *Dracula* (*We need have no secrets amongst us. Working together and with absolute trust, we can surely be stronger than if some of us were in the dark*).

Angela appears in the kitchen doorway. *Any more sandwich orders? I've got mozzarella and tomato, cheddar and pickle, jam, ham . . .*

Can you bring those pears and bananas?

Benjy enters, absent-mindedly singing 'Whip-Crack-Away!'.

Did you flush the toilet?

He turns sullenly and retraces his steps.

Angela hasn't walked more than a mile in the last ten years but she doesn't want to abandon ship for a second day running and she is determined to prove Dominic wrong, to be a real part of the family.

Alex is reading the *Observer* sports section (*Bowyer received a gift of a cross inside the six-yard box but headed it wide*).

Distantly, the toilet flushes.

Where's Melissa? Richard finds himself worrying about her in a way that he hasn't done before. These vague thoughts of fatherhood, perhaps. *She hasn't made a second bid for freedom, has she?*

She's upstairs, says Alex. *Beautifying herself.* It's something his father might say.

Louisa thinks about going into the kitchen to help out but she is still uneasy around Angela. She still can't picture her as a teacher. She had expected more warmth, more openness.

Daisy turns the page (*When the terrible story of Lucy's death, and all that followed, was done, I lay back in my chair powerless*).

Dominic looks at Benjy's feet. *You are not walking up that hill in sandals.*

Click. Everyone briefly gathered and posed and smiling at their future selves. Beaches and cathedrals, bumper cars and birthday parties, glasses raised around a dining table. Each picture a little pause between events. No tantrums, no illness, no bad news, all the big stuff happening before and after and in between. The true magic happening only when the lesser magic fails, the ghost daughter who moved during the exposure, her face unreadable but more alive than all her frozen family. Double exposures, as if a little strip of time had been folded back on itself. Scratches and sun flares. Photos torn post-divorce, faces scratched out or biroed over. The camera telling the truth only when something slips through its silver fingers.

If we could rest for a bit longer. Angela's lack of fitness scared her. Luminous protozoa swam in her eyes.

Richard clicked his phone off and shook his head wearily. *You'd think at twenty-five you could arrange for someone to cover for you when you were on holiday. Actual human lives in their hands. I despair sometimes.*

Can we have a snack? asked Benjy.

You can have a banana.

But that's only fruit.

Monkeys like them.

Monkeys eat fleas.

Cool grey air. Angela looked back down the hill towards the shrunken house. So much effort to get, what? a hundred feet up? two hundred? It made you realise that we lived on the surface of a planet, moving backwards and forwards and round in circles, but forever trapped between earth and sky.

She pictured the view as a papier mâché model in the school hall. Gold Book for Seacole Class. She thought of the kids who'd never actually seen the countryside. Kaylee, Milo. Mikela's dad found the whole countryside thing utterly perplexing. *'Let's go for a nice walk', it should be written on the Union Jack.* Though the only time she and Dominic had stayed in a National Trust cottage it had slave trade prints on the walls. Black men in chains being canoed out to a waiting ship.

Daisy sat herself down beside Melissa and offered her the second half of her coffee. *Sorry about yesterday.* She wanted to tell Melissa about Lauren, but it was too long a story and she didn't want to give her any leverage. Melissa was saying nothing. Daisy got to her feet. Forgiven or not, she felt lighter for having apologised.

Do you have lots of friends?

Daisy wondered if Melissa was being sarcastic.

You know, like, other Christians?

We are allowed to have friends who aren't Christians.

Sorry, that was stupid.

Though Dad was right, her old friends had indeed drifted away, and what had seemed at first a kind of cleansing left a hole more painful than she'd expected. She knew it had been there all the time, that her friends had been a bandage over a wound she was now able to heal, but still she couldn't bring herself to answer the question, so she flipped it round. *You must have loads of friends.*

Melissa just laughed. *I fucking hate all of them.* She took a deep breath and turned to Daisy. *Sorry about all the swearing.*

We're allowed to swear, too. Though Tim had told her off for saying *Shit*.

I get so fucking lonely. A brief pause in the turning of the world. *There I go again. Fuck-fuck-fuckity-fuck.* She squeezed her eyes shut but couldn't stop the tears.

OK, people, said Dominic, *let's saddle up and move out.*

Daisy gazed at the ground between her feet. A little archipelago of yellow moss on a speckled grey stone.

Are you coming or not? shouted Dominic.

Melissa's got a splinter. We'll catch you up. She watched her mother get to her feet and realised that she was in some pain.

Thanks, said Melissa quietly.

New Leaves split from the Vineyard church in 1999. Tim and Lesley Canning were feeling increasingly alienated by the direction the church was taking. Rock music, the Toronto Blessing, speaking in tongues. They held meetings in their kitchen, spreading out to other prayerhouses as the membership grew, then taking out a lease on a hall vacated by a judo club. They were near the university and provided a safe harbour for young people who were often a very long way from home. Singapore, Uganda, the Philippines. They had a stall at the Freshers' Fair and ran weekly Frisbee and Donut afternoons during the summer. Most church members went out onto Lever Street for a couple of hours every week as part of the Healing Project. Tim had always disliked banner-waving street evangelism, for surely the Lord saved souls not crowds, so they struck up conversations with people who seemed lonely or broken in some way, many of whom were desperate for help. They formed a circle and prayed and often you could feel the presence of Jesus wheeling around that ring of hands like electricity. One man's cancer went into remission. A man possessed by demons was exorcised and no longer heard voices in his head.

Daisy found it preposterous at first, but the preposterousness would later became part of the appeal, the sheer distance between the church and the world which had served her so poorly. She accepted the invitation to that first service as proof of her own broadmindedness and needed a great deal of it to get through the sixty minutes. Embarrassment, mostly, at the way these people spoke and sang like over-excited children, and mild disgust when everyone was invited to hug their neighbour and she found herself briefly in the arms of a man who, frankly, smelt. Which would have been her remaining impression had not her beeline for the door been intercepted by a tiny Indian woman with bangles and a surprisingly red dress and a smile which seemed to Daisy to be the only genuine thing she had experienced since her arrival. She held out her hand. *Anushka. You must be Daisy.*

I've done bad things. They were sitting apart from the others, far enough away to feel private but near enough to prevent Richard shouting or storming off. That bell-jar feeling, everything muffled and far off. She really did think she might vomit.

Are we talking about a criminal record of some kind? He laughed, not hearing the crack in her voice.

No, not that.

He heard it now, but didn't think of Louisa as someone who had done anything of great significance, either good or bad, rather as someone who had put herself at the service of others so that they could do things of significance. *Tell me.*

She closed her eyes. There was no way back. *After Craig and I split up I slept with a lot of men.*

How many? The doctor talking.

Ten. Ten men. A little white lie. Did it sound that bad? Only if you knew the dates, perhaps. *I was drinking a lot at the time.* It didn't seem so awful now that it was out there. She'd been lonely. She'd made mistakes. *Say something. Please.*

I'm thinking about it. He wanted to know the details and didn't want to know them.

If only he would reach out and hold her. *I took an AIDS test.* But it didn't sound reassuring when she said it out loud . . . Blood and semen. *I'm really sorry.* Why was she apologising to him? Why hadn't he saved her sooner?

He couldn't think of what to say. Was he being a prude? Of course he was, but how did one change?

Richard . . . ?

It disturbs me a little.

What? Her anger surprised her. He was disgusted. She tried to keep her voice down so that Dominic or Angela didn't hear.

I'm just trying to be honest.

I trusted you completely. The girl. The one who ended up in a wheelchair. I never for one moment doubted you when . . .

That's different.

Why is it different, Richard . . .?

Because it wasn't my fault.

You think I deliberately set out to be . . .?

He couldn't stop himself. *You don't sleep with ten men by accident.* He wasn't trying to be unkind, it seemed to him to be simply a fact.

Do you actually love me, Richard? Or do you just like having me around as long as I don't cause any problems?

Of course I love you. Something perfunctory about his answer. They both heard it but he couldn't change the tone retrospectively.

I'm not sure you know what love means. She had never spoken like this before, not to Richard. There was a sickly thrill in riding the wave.

I know what love means.

So tell me.

It means . . . but what could he say? It wasn't something you put into words.

She got to her feet. *You come and tell me when you've worked out the answer.*

★   ★   ★

The priory, *fixed amongst a barbarous people* in the Vale of Ewyas, is now a hotel with four bedrooms, each one leading off the spiral staircase of the tower. *We advise guests to arrive during bar opening times so as to avoid waiting outside.* Ruined arches striding away like the legs of a great stone spider. Transepts, triforium, clerestory. Eight hundred years of wind and rain and theft. Sir Richard Colt Hoare sees the great west window fall in 1803. Banks of mown green baize. Holly Hop and Brains Dark in the cool of the vaulted bar. Snickers and tubs of Ben & Jerry's with wooden spoons under the plastic lids. Traffic making its way up the valley to Gospel Pass against the flow of the ghost ice, stopping for lorries to reverse, idling behind cyclists. Four pony-trekkers. A steel, a bay roan, two chestnuts. A brief Jacob's ladder of sunlight, as if heaven were searching for raiders moving over the earth.

Benjy peels the sandwich apart and licks the jam from each slice in turn.

Smile, says Alex. Click.

Hey. Dominic sits down beside Angela. He loves her again. Not loves, maybe, but feels a comfort in her presence which he has not felt for years. He is the one who cares. This does not need to be said. He can spend his forgiveness at his leisure. He'd gone to the toilet in the hotel and texted Amy, *Thinking of you must keep this short love D xx*. He wonders if Angela is actually sick, psychiatrically. This, too, is a consolation. *What do you make of that?* He nods towards Daisy and Melissa who are sitting on a ruined buttress, talking.

Her calves ache and she has a blister on her left heel.

Perhaps Melissa's leading her astray. Yesterday, when she walked off, Angela had seen it all from her own point of view. Which was Dominic's point, wasn't it? *Maybe it will be good for her.*

Why does the religion thing upset you so much?

She didn't want to talk about this now. *Because she thinks she's right and everyone else is wrong.*

Doesn't that cover pretty much every teenager in the world?

Angela felt Karen's presence.

Actually, said Dominic, *I think she's scared that she's wrong and everyone else is right.* He could hear himself play-acting the wise man, but that didn't stop it being true.

And suddenly Louisa was walking past them towards the bar, staring straight ahead. Dominic thought she might have been crying, but Angela was throwing a wet wipe at Benjy, saying, *You have jam all over your face, young man.*

White skin and loads of black hair, said Melissa. *Like, on their back as well. That is definitely the grossest.*

Big muscles. Daisy laughed. *Or tattoos. I hate tattoos.*

I've got a bluebird on my arse. Melissa paused. They were on the edge of the enchanted forest, kings and their judgement far away. *I'll show you later if you promise not to tell.* And drop the liquor of it in her eyes.

Well, I guess I'll have to make an exception in your case. Daisy wondered if the church was a bluebird tattoo. Doubt, that canker in the heart.

Prince Albert had a ring through his penis so he could tie it to his leg. Must have been a monster. Melissa laughed and

156

everyone turned and wondered what they could be talking about.

OK. You win. That is definitely the grossest.

So . . . Melissa touched Daisy's arm, to show her she wasn't mocking her. *Tell me about the religion thing.* It wasn't envy. More a kind of zoological fascination. And that steeliness . . . Maybe there was a little envy there.

Daisy paused. She had imagined this moment many times over the past few days but now that it was here . . . How did she say this without dispersing the nameless thing that hung in the air between them? *Don't you sometimes wonder if everything is pointless or whether it has some bigger meaning?* The Alpha line. She wished she could have been more original.

Sometimes, I guess.

Shakespeare, the pyramids, human beings . . . She looked at Benjy playing his Nintendo and really did think it was astonishing. *It can't be an accident, can it? I mean . . .* How could she express all that wonder? *You look up into the sky at night and it's beautiful but it's terrifying, too. Don't you think that?*

Sort of. But did she? Her fears lurked nearby with their feet on the ground.

What if you couldn't stop thinking about it?

I guess I'd take some really strong antidepressants. Melissa laughed. It was precisely what she would do.

I feel invisible sometimes. I look at myself and there's nothing there.

Melissa felt a shiver of recognition. Alex's attention drifting away. But she wasn't ready to cross this river.

I used to act, said Daisy. *As in, you know, drama, plays . . . And when I was someone else, then I knew who I was.* She'd never said this before.

You should act now.

What?

It's an exercise we did at school. You pretend to be someone else for the whole day. Blind person, deaf person, someone with a limp, someone who can't speak English. In truth she had never really stopped playing the game.

So what would I be?

Melissa smiled. *I think you should be a real bitch.*

Was it possible to be someone else? The forest, that faerie magic. My mistress with a monster is in love.

She would never be unfaithful to him. Foolish, perhaps, misguided, but never unfaithful, never dishonest. How odd that her revelation should make Richard certain of this. She wanted people to be happy. Was that the problem, pleasing other men, doling out her favours so prodigally? He wondered if he was simply the first half-decent man who had come along. He was disturbed, too, by the thought that these men had been, what? more adventurous? rougher? more masculine? and that she accepted his shortcomings in return for his reliability, his respectability, his money.

Jennifer's affair had precipitated the end of their marriage, not because of the betrayal or her failure to hide it, but because he cared so little. He couldn't imagine her giving herself or being taken. He thought of her as passionate at first. He had never quite known what women wanted, and he was both aroused and relieved to find someone who was so explicit about her needs, but there was always something mechanical about their coupling and he came to realise that the passion was at root an anger whose source he never fathomed.

Did the drinking excuse Louisa's behaviour or compound it? Perhaps everyone possessed a darker self kept at bay by circumstance. Who knows what life his mother might have led if his father hadn't died so unexpectedly? Airport novels shelved according to their height. The green melamine bowls.

They had crossed the top of the dyke and were walking into a chill wind rising out of the valley. He zipped the front of his orange waterproof. Misty rain, wisps of cloud trailing up the valley like ragged white curtains.

They'd reached the gravel track above the house. *You OK?* Dominic was calling. *I'm fine.* Angela paused before heaving herself over the stile. She needed a hot bath and Savlon and the sheepskin slippers she hadn't packed. She looked up. English Oak. *Quercus robur.* She'd done a biology degree in a previous life. Pedunculate, not sessile, because of the stalks under the acorns. She parcelled the knowledge and gifted it to children who forgot it straight after their exams. Or before. Mitochondria and ribosomes, the carbon cycle, Banting and Best. Nature with a capital N. How strange that she disliked it en masse. Walks on the heath and the occasional safari park with Benjy. Penguins and fruit bats. That was her limit, really. She'd been passionate once, collecting moths with a torch and a muslin net. Blair's Shoulder-knot, Magpie, Goat, Codling. It all faded. Hard to feel passionate about anything now. She thought about her mother. It was physiological, of course. Myelin breakdown, neural tangles. But you couldn't help wonder. Being bored of life, wanting to let go.

Something moved in the distance. Was it . . .? She had to stop this. If she talked to someone, maybe. A ticking clock and a box of tissues on the pine coffee table. She'd never asked Richard about Jennifer, why they were together, why they weren't any more. Dominic was right. She thought of herself as someone who cared, but she spent all of that concern at school. She put her foot on the little wooden step and lifted her aching leg.

We push an introductory needle into the femoral artery.

Is that in the groin? asked Benjy.

It is indeed. Richard reached over and picked up the jigsaw piece with the picture of the man being hanged. *Bingo*. He handed it to Angela.

Louisa was watching from the window seat. He wasn't even thinking about it, was he? At least Craig blew up and cleared the air. Had she made a monumental mistake? The degrees, the books, the music.

This, said Melissa, staring at the jigsaw, *must surely be the most boring activity in the universe*. But the edge was gone.

I think I'll save jigsaws until I'm in an old people's home, said Daisy. The two girls. Their little freemasonry.

I'll be in there soon enough, said Angela. *Sherry at five and drama students coming in to do hits from the seventies.* Except there wouldn't be sherry, would there, given that Richard wouldn't be paying this time round. Some council place. Dettol and the TV at Guantánamo volume.

Melissa found the man playing the lute.

X-rays are pretty harmless, said Richard. *Pilot. That's the job to avoid. Lots of breast cancer among female cabin crew.*

Is this subject entirely appropriate? said Angela.

Alex came and sat beside Louisa. *There.* He handed her a glass of wine. He was flirting, wasn't he? She hotched a centimetre closer so that their shoulders were touching. Richard glanced over. She clinked Alex's glass. *Cheers.*

Dominic sliced the florets off the head of broccoli and placed them in the steamer then opened the oven briefly to check on the sweet potatoes. How odd that it was such a manly profession now. Marco Pierre White, Gordon Ramsay. *I wouldn't give that risotto to my fucking dog.* He folded back the waxed wrapper, sliced a little pyramid of butter from the corner of the block and dropped it into the pan. *Exile on Main Street* in the background. Best double album in the history of popular music. Unless *Blonde on Blonde* was a double. Maybe second best, then. Recorded in that chateau the Gestapo had used. 'Tumbling Dice'. Keith Richards falling asleep with a syringe still stuck in his arse. All corporate hospitality now and VW sponsorship deals. Bob Dylan doing adverts for ladies' underwear. He dropped the sliced onion into the fizzy butter. He'd been vegetarian himself when he was a student. Animal fats in everything before BSE. Biscuits, ice cream. Shopping down the kosher aisle in the Stamford Hill Safeway with the Hasidic housewives and their fifties wigs. He washed the spinach in the colander and pressed it onto the onion. How odd to feel this contentment at the expense of Angela's failings. He was going to end the Amy thing when he got home. Couldn't see the point now. It was all about self-worth, wasn't it, trying to make himself feel better. He didn't need it any longer. The spinach darkened and shrank. Karen, the daughter he never had, blessing him from beyond the grave. Pint of full-fat in the microwave. But this thing with Daisy and Melissa. *I kind of like her, actually.* Unquote. That clumsy teenage eyes-down embarrassment he hadn't seen for so long. He'd help Angela get back on track, make the family work again, be a real father. He poured a little cone of flour onto the buttery spinach and stirred it in. He could take some private pupils again. Earn a little extra money. That honeyed scent of the sweet potatoes roasting. Everything was going to be all right. *Physical Graffiti.* That was a double album, too, wasn't it? Maybe *Exile* was third best.

Look. Melissa paused and glanced both ways down the landing. She lifted her skirt and pulled down her knickers and there it was, a little bluebird on her buttock where the tan faded to moony white. *And with the juice of this I'll streak her eyes.* Daisy wanted to say something complimentary but it seemed indecent. *Did it hurt?* Melissa was letting her look for too long and Daisy was finding it hard to turn away. *He was cute so I didn't mind too much.* She pulled her knickers up. *If you tell anyone . . .* But why would she? It felt like her own transgression, not Melissa's.

Angela enjoyed anything with a Latin flavour, Orchestra Baobab, Buena Vista Social Club (she'd sat through so many assemblies that English lyrics were always accompanied in her mind by a little white dot bouncing along the words). Alex liked Razorlight, Kasabian, music you listened to on open roads with the window down, whereas Daisy loved the rich sweep of choral music so that the portable keyboard at church gave her a guilty longing to be in St Catherine's on Christmas Eve, candles and holly-crackle, a church organ and boys like angels. But it was Benjy who listened more intently than any of them, ever since that night when he'd been sick and stayed up watching *Guys and Dolls* with Mum. Singing, dancing, everything squeezed into one vast sticky sugary cake. *My Fair Lady. Calamity Jane.* Why couldn't you have an orchestra in real life? Sometimes he sang 'The Deadwood Stage' or 'The Surrey with the Fringe on Top' when no one was watching, and when he was walking down the street clicking his fingers, doing wobbly little pirouettes only four people in the world knew he was doing the dance from the opening scene of *West Side Story*.

But now there was Monteverdi in the background. The roasting tin, battered and discoloured like Elizabethan armour. Wolf Blass Cabernet Sauvignon. Angela sees a tiny brown mouse run along the polished wainscot. Something storybook about it here, not like a mouse in the dining room at home. She decides not to mention it. *Let me guess*, said Richard. *The Vespers?* There was something under-powered about him tonight, thought Dominic. Perhaps he and Louisa really did have an argument at Llanthony. Now that he thought about it, yes, Louisa seemed a little flat, too. And when they sat down Dominic seemed to have inherited his seat at the head of the table, along with some kind of paterfamilias role. Indeed everyone's roles seemed to have been reassigned because Louisa was sitting next to Benjy, which wasn't the place she would have chosen, but she asked him what subjects he liked at school, he told her how much he hated maths and she showed him how to do long division on a napkin. Daisy and Melissa were huddling and Angela and Alex were remembering the disastrous holiday in Barmouth, the food poisoning, those people cut off by the tide and screaming for help. Dominic's pie was good. He'd sculpted a little dog from the spare puff pastry in the centre of the glazed crust which Benjy was allowed to eat. And afterwards, over coffee, while Daisy and Alex washed up, Angela found herself next to Richard and decided on the spur of the moment to tell him about Karen. An exorcism of a kind. Because she had never even told him she was pregnant, and afterwards it had seemed too fragile a fact to share with someone who was almost a stranger. But she swerved at the last minute and heard herself saying, *What do they do with dead bodies in hospital?*

They're refrigerated, said Richard, *then they're released to funeral directors after any autopsy is done. Why do you want to know?*

What about a stillborn baby? said Angela. The seconds rocked back and forth like water against a dock wall.

Depending on the length of gestation and the wishes of the parents it might be released to the funeral directors and given a funeral of some kind. He was holding a sugar cube so that it just touched the surface of his coffee, like Benjy did in cafés.

And if not?

It would be taken to a medical waste incinerator and burnt. He dropped the cube into the coffee. *But this is a rather grisly subject.*

If he'd asked the question she would have told him everything, but he didn't know what question to ask.

Hang on to your horses, yelled the shrunken head. *It's going to be a bumpy ride.* And the bus shot off into the night.

Benjy was insistent and all the other suggestions were too violent or too scary or contained romance which Benjy vetoed strenuously, so they bowed to his choice and, loath as some of them were to admit it, there was a pears-and-custard cosiness to it. Spells and potions, the Care of Magical Creatures. Because, ultimately, the place itself is immaterial, Combray, Meryton, St Petersburg, so long as it's over the hills and far away, the journey we once took with just a click of the fingers but which grows longer and steeper with the years.

Hey, Tiger, said Dominic. Benjy had curled up with his head on his father's lap. He was watching the film at an angle of ninety degrees, but he knew it so well he hardly needed to watch at all. *You should go to bed.*

If only he could sleep here, like he did when he was little, the dance and crackle of the fire, familiar voices, the beasts at bay.

Melissa turned the page and pressed it flat.

The bullet entered Tapp's chest, lifting him upwards and backwards. So many intense impressions were compressed into those two or three seconds that they felt like minutes. Tapp looked as if he were performing some kind of modern ballet. I remember with exquisite clarity, looking down and seeing a great tongue of red liquid arcing over the white tablecloth, thinking at first that it was Tapp's blood, then realising that it was the raspberry sorbet which had been knocked out of Jocelyn's hands.

The effort has, however, done him good. He was never so resolute, never so strong, never so full of volcanic energy . . . But Daisy couldn't read, didn't want to read, didn't want to be anywhere but here. She hadn't felt this eagerness for life in a long time. She'd meant to bring Melissa into the fold. *I get so fucking lonely.* The harvest of souls. But she didn't want to break the spell. Was it so wrong to have found a friend?

★   ★   ★

Louisa washed her face and patted it dry with the blue towel. She opened the mirrored cabinet and when she closed it again he was standing in the doorway behind her.

I'm really sorry.

Sorry was cheap, as Mum used to say. Buyer's remorse, soiled goods and all that. *Well, I'm sorry, too.* Now both of them had said it and had not meant it.

Why didn't you tell me before?

She took her toothpaste out of the cupboard. *And given you the chance to back out?*

I wouldn't have backed out. Was this a lie?

She brushed her teeth. Briefly he was another man looking at her. Other men. He felt dizzy. He closed his eyes. *I feel like a little boy sometimes.*

But she didn't want to be married to a little boy.

Marja, Helmand. The sniper far back enough from the window to stop sun flaring on the rifle sight. Crack and kickback. A marine stumbles under the weight of his red buttonhole. Dawn light on wild horses in the Khentii Mountains. Huddersfield, brown sugar bubbling in a tarnished spoon. Turtles drown in oil. The purr of binary, a trillion ones and zeros. The swill of bonds and futures. Reckitt Benckiser, Smith and Nephew. Rifts and magma chambers. Eyjafjallajökull smoking like a witch's cauldron. Sleep shuffling the day's events like a pack of cards. Cups and coins, the Juggler, the Traitor. Spearheads and farthingales smashed and scattered in the cities of the dead. The planet warming. Cadmium, arsenic, benzene. *Baby, please.* A ranch burns on the prairie. Brando and Hepburn pace their silver cages, over and over. Every mind at the centre of space and time. The fierce little star of *now*. Sparrows flying through the banqueting hall *where you sit in the winter months to dine with your thanes and counsellors*. A brief passage of warmth and light between darkness and darkness. The stepfather's hand over the child's mouth. *Mein Irisch Kind, wo weilest du?* A blue whale cruises the abyssal cold. Viperfish, fangtooth, gulper eel. A Burlington Northern pulls out of Fort Benton hauling hoppers of grain. Intercloud lightning over Budapest. The tide turning in the Thames. *Arklow Surf* to White Mountain, *Cymbeline* to Ford Jetty, vast Christmas trees of light above the black water. Vultures on a Tower of Silence. Creech Air Force Base, Nevada. A boy of twenty-three presses a button. Seven thousand miles away a Hellfire missile fizzes from the underside of a Predator drone. Three houses of stone and packed earth. A girl wakes and has no time to remember the dream about the birds.

Angela is standing in the kitchen. Moonblue dark. A shuddery jingle as the fridge motor cuts in. What woke her? Whose kitchen is this? The fear that has haunted her ever since her mother became ill, that she would go the same way. Names refusing to come. Lost objects. Keys, wallet. The mind's ordinary stumbles magnified perhaps. But sometimes . . . this utter blankness. Terrified of the simplest questions. *What year is this? What are your children's names?* She touches her own face but cannot remember what it looks like.

★   ★   ★

Then Nebuchadnezzar the king was astonished, and rose up in haste, and spake, and said unto his counsellors, Did not we cast three men bound into the midst of the fire? They answered and said unto the king, True, O king.

He answered and said, Lo, I see four men loose, walking in the midst of the fire, and they have no hurt; and the form of the fourth is like the Son of God.

Tuesday

Louisa had woken just after two. Halfway along the landing a sliver of light vanished from between the floorboards. Or was it her imagination? She waited, listening. Nothing. She knew she wouldn't be able to get back to sleep if she didn't check, and there was no way she was going to wake Richard, not now, so she made her way downstairs, the oak creaking under her feet. Walter Devereux, Earl of Essex, more alive then he ever was during the day, black table, black sideboard, the glowing grey circles of the plates on the dresser, as if a whispered conversation had been interrupted. The cry of a bird outside. She stepped into the kitchen and saw a silhouetted figure in the shadows at the far end. Jesus H. Christ. She flipped the light to find Angela standing beside the fridge, eating a bowl of Frosties, an open bag of caster sugar on the chopping board.

I didn't want to wake anyone.

Louisa could see now that the shabbiness was symptomatic of a bigger problem.

Comfort eating, said Angela.

You scared me rigid.

I was embarrassed. Angela put the bowl down delicately, as if she were stepping away from an angry dog. *So I turned the light out.*

Angela . . .? Was she sleepwalking?

I've been feeling a little unsettled. Something oddly formal about this. *I had another child. Before Daisy. Her name was Karen. She was stillborn.*

Louisa was sympathetic to friends who were depressed but this was something stranger and more worrying.

It's her birthday on Thursday, said Angela. *She'll be eighteen. Would have been eighteen.* She rolled and crimped the top of the sugar. *I'm going back to bed now.* She walked carefully round Louisa and out of the kitchen.

In other circumstances Louisa would have washed the abandoned bowl but she couldn't dismiss the idea that it was charmed in some dark way. She waited for the muffled clunk of a door overhead then followed Angela back upstairs, turning the lights on as she went so that there was no darkness at her back.

That's wonderful. Richard had approached so quietly and Melissa had been so absorbed in her drawing that she didn't hear him till he was standing behind her. *I didn't know you could draw so well.*

I am a woman of many mysteries, Richard. She turned and saw that he'd just returned from a run. *Are those new shoes?*

★　　★　　★

They meet you at the other end, said Alex, *and drive you back to your car.*

I'll come, said Benjy. *Canoeing is cool.*

Which meant that Dominic had to come, too, for Health and Safety reasons.

Count me in, said Louisa, because last night's anger had softened into a sense of superiority. Richard was normal, and she had been released from a childish respect she should never have felt in the first place.

Alex was running his hand slowly over the map, as if he could feel the texture of the land under his fingers. Contour, castle, cutting. *We can stop for lunch at the Boat Inn, Whitney.*

Angela?

You must be joking. She was ferrying a bouquet of dirty coffee mugs to the kitchen. *Drop me in Hay. I'll get some stuff for supper.* She caught Louisa's eye and looked away.

Louisa wondered if she should tell Dominic. Or Richard. Did Angela need help or was it a secret they should keep between themselves?

We'll stay here, said Daisy.

You go and do boy things, said Melissa.

You two sound as if you have a secret plan, said Dominic.

That's for us to know, said Melissa, *and for you to find out.*

Richard swilled the pan, flipped the brush over and used the wedged rear to scrape the cooked egg off the pitted aluminium base. They were experiencing a minor difficulty and he was making a hash of it, that was all. He rinsed the little tattered rags of cooked egg into the sink where they collected in the poker wheel over the plughole. He lifted it free and banged it clean on the edge of the bin. He'd run several hundred metres up the road that morning then been forced to walk, having underestimated the incline and over-estimated his fitness. Ashamed of returning to the house, he had walked up to Red Darren where he sat half appreciating the view and half pretending to appreciate it and being horribly aware of the stupidity of this combination. He squeezed a worm of lemon washing-up liquid onto the pan and waited for the water to run hot. He remembered the first time they had made love, the bulge of flesh above her waistband, plump and creaturely, the little fold where the curve of her bottom met the top of her thighs, the way she lay propped on her elbows afterwards like a teenager making a phone call. He moved the brush in swift circles and zigzags and figures of eight, each calligraphic figure swiftly over-written by the next. Those images. Two days ago they'd been a treasury of golden coins through which he could run his fingers, but now? *Of course I love you.* At this precise moment he felt only a dirty panicked entanglement.

Dominic appeared in the doorway. *Ready to rumble.*

He dried his hands. *Two minutes.*

The Mercedes pulls away and the sun is out. Angela climbs the steps to the ugly block that contains the tourist informa-tion office and the public toilets. A goth girl with Halloween hair and a pierced lip is pushing a young man in a wheelchair.

Cerebral palsy, perhaps? *I cried because I had no shoes until I met a man who had no feet.* One of her mother's gems. But in what kind of bizarre accident did you lose your feet? She'd never thought about that. Theo with Down's, the cheeriest kid in Year 8. So you couldn't assume anything. Though God knows how he'd cope when the hormones and the tribal stuff kicked in. Some ghastly special school, no doubt. She was trying hard not to think about the encounter in the kitchen. Handing Louisa so much ammunition in one go. The crazy lady with the imaginary daughter. She is going to buy some books. The *Yellow Sun* thing still unread at the bottom of her case. Hasn't read a book properly for months, come to think of it. She remembers being ten years old, jammed into that triangular recess behind the sofa with a tattered paperback. *The Log of the Ark. My Name Is David. Stig of the Dump.*

You have to wear this by law, young man. Mike handed Benjy a lifejacket of tatty orange rubber. Wiry and suntanned, workboots, ponytail. *And I strongly suggest that the rest of you wear these.* He took four more from the back of the Land Rover. *But as long as they're in the boat when you drown I'm in the clear, legally.* He put his hands on his hips. *No swimming from the boat. No extra passengers. No alcohol. Give me a call half an hour before you need picking up. If I hear nothing by three I put out an APB.* The mobile rang in his back pocket. *God bless you and all who sail in you.* He extracted the phone. *Brian. What can I do you for?*

Benjy put the lifejacket over his head. It smelt of mildew

and the air inside a balloon. Richard dragged the green Osprey into the shallows, Alex the Appalachian. *I'll take Benjy.* In truth he wanted to take Louisa, but he could still prove himself by paddling faster than the two men paddling together.

Dominic chucked the map into the boat. It was like a greasy-spoon menu. Water had seeped under a corner of the dog-eared laminate, blurring the ink. He turned to Louisa. *Willing to place your life in the hands of two rank amateurs?*

She stepped in. A disbelieving wobble then she was airborne. Waterborne. Holding her breath slightly. The faint tremor of magic. Like climbing into a loft, or vaulting the orchard wall.

Water loosening something in all of them. Jacques Cousteau. *The Man from Atlantis.* The twang and clatter of the diving board on its rusted roller.

Louisa is lying in the paddling pool at Mandy's house. Compared to the balcony Mandy's garden feels like a country park. She is seven years old and there is just enough water to lift her clear of the bottom. If she squints a little she can no longer see the pine tree or the roof of the chapel or the pink starfish on the pool's rim. Then she waits . . . and waits . . . and finally it happens. She floats free, neither her head nor her feet touching the plastic. The world has let her go and she is flying up into that burning edgeless blue.

It's so boring. Melissa blew a smoke ring. *So dreadfully boring.* Daisy stood demurely with her hands crossed in front of her. *Surely, madam . . .* But she couldn't think of what to say.

You have to say, 'My lady'. Melissa fixed her with an icy look.

My lady.

Melissa took another sip of Richard's brandy. *I was so very dreadfully bored yesterday that I ordered the stable boy to pleasure me in the rose garden.*

Daisy burst out laughing. *You've got this out of a book or something.*

The icy stare again. *You have to do this properly.* It was the exercise they'd done at school. Because there was no way she was going to be blind or deaf or limping. Carriage wheels on the gravel. *Pok . . . Pok . . .* The gamekeeper shooting rabbits.

Was it satisfactory, my lady? Because Daisy was good at this game, too.

I'm afraid not. She turned and held Daisy's eye. *He whacked my bottom and shouted, 'Tally-ho'.*

There was an ecstasy in not laughing, like stubbing your toe and closing your eyes and letting the pain rise and die away. But it was Melissa who choked first, dropping her cigarette and rolling sideways onto the bench. It was like being with Lauren, but different, Melissa's self-sufficiency, not quite knowing the rules, seduction almost, just a hint of danger.

Melissa sat up. *OK, now I really am dreadfully bored, darling.* She handed Daisy the last few dregs of the brandy. *Let's walk up that hill over there.*

Wow, said Daisy. *You're really getting into this whole countryside thing.*

I am a woman of many mysteries.

Angela had never really got on with modern poetry. Even stuff like Seamus Heaney, *Death of a Naturalist* and the other book. He seemed such a lovely man and she really did try, but it sounded like prose you had to read very slowly. Old stuff she understood. Rum-ti-tum. *Now sleeps the crimson petal, now the white . . . Dirty British coaster with a salt-caked smoke stack . . .* Something going all the way back. Memorable words, so you could hand it down the generations. But free verse made her think of *free knitting* or *free juggling.* This, for example. She extracted a book at random. *Spiders* by Stanimir Stoilov, translated by Luke Kennard. She flipped through the pages . . . *the hatcheries of the moon . . . the earth in my father's mouth . . .*

They were on a ferry. Richard was eight or so. He has no memory of the location, only that it was a chain-link ferry and this seemed extraordinary, the idea of being guided by underwater machinery. Rusted metal, sheer bulk and sea spray. He can't see his father but he knows he is there because of that radiation that throws all his needles to the right.

He has three photographs in a tattered brown envelope in the bottom drawer of his desk. He should have brought them along to show Angela. His father leaning against the bonnet of the Hillman Avenger, his father pushing a wheelbarrow in which both he and Angela are sitting, his father on a beach with a concrete pillbox in the dunes behind his right shoulder as if he is posing during a lull in the D-Day landings. Sideburns, burly arms in rolled-up sleeves, a cigarette always. Richard remembers the camera's soft brown leather case, the rough suede of the inner surface, the saddle smell.

In spite of everything he had been rather proud of having a father who died prematurely, because all the best adventures happened to orphans, though he can think of no incidents from his childhood which might count as adventures per se. He told other boys at school that his father had been a soldier, that he was a spy, that he had a false passport, that he had killed a man in Russia. He remembers a conversation with the headmaster. *If this becomes a habit you will find yourself in great difficulty later in life.* The only moment he had ever felt genuine shame. Aftershocks every time he remembers, even now. It never occurred to him to tell anyone what was happening to his mother. It would be different nowadays, of course. Taken into care, possibly, which was an astonishing thought.

There was a gull. Was this part of the same memory? It landed on his head and he screamed and his father was laughing in spite of his tears. The scratches bled and scabbed and for days he kept finding crumbly nuggets of dried blood in his hair.

Benjy is trailing his hand in the water, watching the glitter and flex of the light, the silky fold in front of his fingers. He wonders if there's anything down there that might bite his fingers, a pike perhaps, or a crayfish, but it is a small fear and he's learning to be brave.

When he was six he had an imaginary friend, Timmy, who had shaggy blond hair and a Yorkshire accent and the sandals Benjy coveted in Clarks with green lights that lit up when you stamped. He was over-sensitive, which annoyed Benjy sometimes, though at others Benjy liked having someone he could take care of. Because adults forgot how porous that border was, the ease with which you could summon monsters, and find treasure in any basement. Besides, adults talked to themselves. Was that any more rational? And on the glacier, when the ends of your fingers are black and your companions are gone into the howling dark? You open your eyes and see to your surprise that there is a person sitting calmly at the other end of the tent. They seem familiar, but this is such a long way from anywhere. You know your brain is starved of sugar and oxygen. You know your hold on reality is slipping. But that green duffel coat. You thought they'd gone away, but you realise now that they have been waiting patiently through all these years for the moment when you needed them again.

XIX

i went out for a walk
under the canopy of high trees
and waited upon the firemakers
restlessness
uncertainty
ice dissolves in the ponds
that warm wind rising

it begins
the savannah bubbles and overflows
60 million stars babbling in unknown tongues
gooseberry wild plum peppermint
every cell on fire
hoops and carols and coloured eggshells
the raven stiff-legged dancing
and the hatcheries of the moon
blown open

How sad they must be, those only children. Growing up in a house of adults, outnumbered, outgunned, none of that unbridled silliness, no jokes that can be repeated a hundred times, no one to sing with, no one to fight with, no one to be the prince, to be the slave. But siblings can be cruel, and companionship refused is worse than loneliness, and you could cast your eye over any playground and not tell who comes from a brood of seven or one. But later, when parents fall from grace and become ordinary messed-up human beings and turn slowly from carers into people who must be cared for in their turn, who then will share those growing frustrations and pore over the million petty details of that long-shared soap opera that means nothing to others? And when they are finally gone, who will turn to you and say, *Yes, I remember the red rocking horse . . . Yes, I remember the imaginary bed under the hawthorn tree.*

★   ★   ★

A torrent after winter rains but quiet now, central shallows and the banks hidden under chestnut, hazel and sycamore. Pontfaen. The salmon catch a fraction of what it once was (a fifty-one-pounder at Bigsweir in '62 but less than a thousand every season now). Otters and pine martens. Pipistrelle and noctule bats sleeping in ancient beeches. Cabalva Stud (Cabalva Sorcerer, 1995, £3,000, honest, eager to please, big scopy jump). The ghosts of Bill Clinton and Queen Noor. Flat stones down the centre of the river so that if the level were just right you could skip across the water like Puck (Richard and Dominic run aground twice). The Black Mountains a smoky blue in the day's haze. Rhydspence. A moss-greened hull upended against a tiny shed. The five arches of the toll bridge at Whitney-on-Wye. White railings at the top, twice washed away and rebuilt. 10p for motorbikes, 50p for cars. Inexplicably, the sound of a flute from somewhere nearby. The Church of Saints Peter and Paul. The Boat Inn. Scampi, shepherd's pie . . .

Dominic looked at the map. There was a road half a mile away. It seemed impossible. The swill and chatter of water, those little birds darting in and out of the greenery overhanging the banks. How many more worlds were hiding round the corner and over the hill? He remembered the big ash on the wasteground behind the junior school, climbing up into that plump crook where the trunk split, sitting there for hours with a Wagon Wheel and a Fanta, the world going about its business below.

Up at the prow Richard had fallen into a steady rhythm that calmed him somewhat, bears in cages and so forth, though people lived entire lives with this level of anxiety, not even pathological, just part of the human condition. Alex was up ahead quite clearly revelling in his superior maritime skills. *Sweet Thames run softly till I end my song . . . With falling oars they kept the time . . .* Of course the one thing he missed since marrying Louisa was that solitary hour each day, a place of comfort and safety in which he returned to himself, Monteverdi or Bach in the background usually, turning over the day's events in his mind, or more often thinking absolutely nothing. He wished he had kept the flat or bought himself a smaller one nearer the hospital, though the former would have been wasteful and the latter an insult to Louisa. Nor would she have understood. She liked company, she liked noise, she liked knowing someone else was in the house. He turned and smiled at her and she returned something that was neither quite a smile nor a scowl.

Louisa turned to Dominic. *My go.*

The boat swayed precipitously as they swapped positions. She sat on the little bench in the bow. This was more like it. Bows and arrows and dens and scrumping, the childhood she once dreamt of having, like Richard's childhood, except not like Richard's because his childhood wasn't like that, was it, as she regularly had to remind herself. *Incidentally . . .*

What? said Dominic.

Last night. She wouldn't mention the cereal or the sleep-walking or the turning out of the kitchen light. *She said something about Karen. A baby called Karen. Your daughter.* Was *baby* the right word? Was *daughter* the right word?

She's having a rather difficult time, said Dominic.

But this was eighteen years ago.

I'm afraid so.

Something dismissive about his tone, and for the first time since they had arrived she felt a kind of sisterhood with Angela. Men are from Mars. All that stuff. She'd come on holiday expecting to be a spectator, to cook and help out and be good company while Richard got to know his family. But they were her family too, weren't they, in the same way that Melissa was his family. Somehow she had never seen it this way.

There's a dead fish, shouted Benjy excitedly. They waited and, sure enough, it floated past, huge and silvered, milky eye skyward.

Overhearing their conversation, Richard realised too late why Angela had asked him about stillborn children. He felt bad for not having pressed her further, and with this guilt came a longing for that armchair, the solitude, the empty mind.

What Angela finds is not *My Name Is David* or *The Log of the Ark* but *The Knights of King Arthur*, a book her mother had been given when she was a child and which she in turn gave to Angela when Angela was eight or nine. The memory is so strong that when she finds the words *To Kathleen from Pam, Christmas 1941* written in crabbed fountain pen on the endpaper she feels a sense of real grievance and trespass. 40p. She'll buy it and read it as a kind of penance.

Scampi, shepherd's pie, a stuffed pike in a glass case, polished copper bedwarmers.

You should try it sometime, said Alex. *Waking up under canvas.*

If you built a log fire and gave me a bottle of whisky, maybe, said Louisa. *And some very thick socks.*

So, said Dominic, *where would we end up if we just carried on paddling?*

Hospital, said Alex.

Richard could see that he was flirting with Louisa, but he had no idea how to stop it without causing grave offence, possibly to everyone around the table. He held up a spoonful of crumble. *This is surprisingly good.* His marriage to Jennifer had been a contract with explicit and renegotiable terms. He was belatedly realising how uncommon this was. There was an art to marriage, which depended not just on skills and rules but something more nebulous. That image of the gull and his father laughing. Why did it trouble him so much?

The path was not as clear on the ground as it was on the map, the mud was surprisingly deep in places and Melissa wasn't really getting into the countryside thing after all. *I am going to get an apartment in Chelsea and the only time I am ever going to look at a field is from the window of a fucking plane.*

They crossed the little stream and worked their way up the hill and were nearly at the road when Melissa slipped and spun and landed on her arse with such perfect comedy timing that Daisy laughed out loud. She offered Melissa her hand but Melissa grabbed it and yanked and Daisy yelped and found herself lying on her back next to Melissa staring into a canopy of horse chestnut leaves with damp seeping into her knickers. She imagined grabbing Melissa and rolling over, wrestling, like she might have done with Benjy.

Sod this for a game of soldiers. I'm heading back.

Ten more minutes. Daisy got to her feet. *We're nearly there.*

I need a hot shower.

Come on, said Daisy, *you can cope with a wet arse.* She began walking up to the fence and when she opened the gate onto the road she turned briefly and saw that Melissa was following and it gave her a pleasure she hadn't felt all week.

Queen Guinevere lay idly in bed dreaming beautiful dreams. The sunny morning hours were slipping away, but she was so happy in dreamland that she did not remember that her little maid had called her long ago.

But the queen's dreams came to an end at last, and all at once she remembered that this was the morning she had promised to go to the hunt with King Arthur.

He walked to the edge of the car park to listen to Amy's message. *Dom. It's me.* She was crying. *I'm really sorry. I know I said I wouldn't ring but Andrew's been taken into hospital with pneumonia and I'm frightened, Dom. If you get a chance, can you ring me, please?*

Episode 39 of the Mother and Son show. He deleted the message. The truth was that she disgusted him, something moist and wretched about her, a child at forty-two. He couldn't remember her once expressing real unadulterated joy, only that desperate hunger when they made love (*fill me up . . . push it right inside me . . .*) which was thrilling at first but which now sounded like a need to be crushed out or used up. If it wasn't him it would be someone else. Deep down she wanted things to go wrong. If she was happy she would have to face up to all those things she hadn't done, the law degree, the second child, New Zealand, those precious hypothetical ambitions stolen from her by a string of bad men. He loved his family. Why had he risked losing them for this?

He heard a rumbling clang and turned to see Mike's Transit coming into the pub car park, the trailer bouncing and yawing behind it. He turned the phone off and slipped it into his back pocket.

Angela assumed at first that her mother had started drinking again, the dirt and clutter, the mood swings, but there were no bottles and no alcohol on her breath. She might have realised earlier but their conversations had never been intimate and you didn't ask someone to name their grandchildren or do their five times table as her GP finally did that freakish Saturday morning, the cloud so low and thick it felt like an eclipse. She expected him to set in train some boilerplate process, health visitor, social worker, nursing assistant, leading gradually towards residential care, but they stepped out into a biblical downpour with nothing more than an invitation to return when things got worse, and in two hours her mother's terrified incomprehension had become a vicious anger at everyone who was trying to interfere in her life, Angela, the doctor, the neighbours.

She rang Richard who said there was nothing they could do. Something would happen, an accident, a stroke, something financial, something legal, and the decision would be taken out of their hands. She thought, *You selfish bastard*, but he was right. An icy pavement outside Sainsbury's. Lucy at school said she should sue and Angela laughed and said, *I should pay them*. Hospital threw her mother completely. *Who are all these people?* Her mind held together only by the scaffolding of a familiar house and a routine she had followed for ten years. Two weeks later she was in Meadowfields. *Beckett meets Bosch*, said Dominic, and it was true, there really was screaming every time they visited. A couple of months later she was transferred to Acorn House. Grassy quadrangle, actual menu, two lounges, one without television. The previous occupant of her room had left a framed photograph of a cocker spaniel on the bedside table. Mum was insistent that it had been their dog which had recently passed away, though they had never had a dog and she was never quite able to remember its name.

They crossed the little car park and began climbing the Cat's Back, a rising ridge of grass and gorse and mud. Sweaty now,

Melissa had tied her shirt and Puffa jacket around her waist and was walking in a blue vest, her freckled shoulders bare. Daisy was embarrassed to find herself in second place. *You do secret sport, don't you?*

Hockey. Melissa's enjoyment had caught her by surprise. Middle-aged people did this stuff, but she felt like a kid again. The mud, the effort, Daisy's uncomplicated company, except that she'd never been that kid, had she, because Mum needed counselling if you spilt coffee on the carpet. Hence Dad fucking off, possibly.

The spine of the hill flattened out, the grass and mud giving way to a rough path weaving its way around little rocky outcrops, the slopes on both sides falling away so steeply that you could glance up and think for a moment that you were flying.

OK, said Melissa. *This is as far as I'm going. End of argument.*

They turned round, breathing heavily. All that wheeling space. The cars were Dinky Toys. Miniature sheep and miniature cows. *There's the house*, said Daisy, pointing. She imagined opening the hinged front so you could rearrange the furniture and the model people.

You win, said Melissa. *This is pretty cool.*

Angela sat in Shepherd's eating a bowl of ice cream with chocolate sauce. She hadn't pictured herself alone at a table when she was at the counter and only when she sat down did she see herself from the point of view of customers at the other tables. Discomfort eating. She'd bought *Notes on a Scandal* but it refused to hold her attention. There was an exhibition of framed watercolours hung around the room which looked as if they'd been done by a talented child, a poppy field, a lighthouse. It was her, wasn't it, the person who couldn't be alone, who married the first man who came along because they were scared of going back to an empty house. At home she moaned constantly about the chores she had to do because everyone else did them badly or not at all. *For once I'd just like to put my feet up.* But she was doing that right now and hated it. She looked up at the clock. Twelve minutes past two and sixteen seconds, and seventeen seconds, and eighteen seconds. She was in Maths with Mr Alnwick again, each minute a rock to be broken.

She picked up the bag of books she'd bought for Benjy, to replace that terrifying *Two Worlds* thing, and opened the *Tintin*.

Blue blistering barnacles . . .
What is it, Captain?

We should be getting back. Melissa puts her hands on her knees, preparatory to standing.

Wait, says Daisy. She wants this moment to continue for ever. She turns and looks at Melissa. Those freckled shoulders, sweat cooling in the wind. She can see it all so clearly now and she is both surprised and relieved. Her whole life has been leading towards this moment. She has turned a final corner and seen her destination at long last. Is time slowing down or speeding up? She puts her hand on Melissa's forearm. *And with the juice of this I'll streak her eyes.* Like being on a rollercoaster, no way of getting off now. She puts her other hand around the back of Melissa's neck and pulls her close. The barn roars in the night. Daisy kisses her, pushing her tongue into her mouth, but something is wrong because Melissa is shoving her away and shouting, *What the fuck . . .?* She's on her feet now. *Get off me, you fucking dyke.*

No, says Daisy. *I didn't mean . . .*

What the fuck do you think you're doing?

I only . . . Crashing back into the bright light and the hard edges of the day.

Just . . . Melissa takes four steps down the hill, backwards, keeping her eyes on Daisy, as if she is holding a gun. *Just . . . stay the fuck away from me, OK?* She rips the shirt from round her waist and fumbles it on, covering her flesh as quickly as she can, then the Puffa jacket. *You're weird and your clothes are shit and the only reason I was even spending time with you was because it is so fucking boring here.* She turns and strides away till she is swallowed by the curve of the hill.

Daisy sits rigid. For two, three, seconds everything is very clear and quiet, as if she has dropped a china plate on a tiled floor. If she stands very still and concentrates hard she will be able to find the matching fragments and put them all together again. She got carried away. For the briefest moment she lost any sense of where she stopped and Melissa began. When Melissa has calmed down she will be able to explain everything.

Then she realises that Melissa will tell Louisa and Richard, Louisa and Richard will tell Mum and Dad, Alex will find out, everyone at school will find out and they won't understand that it was a mistake. Because it isn't a china plate, it's her life and there are too many fragments and they're too tiny and they don't match. A woman is standing in front of her wearing a blue cagoule. *Are you all right?* Daisy stands and turns and runs, further up the ridge, away from the woman, away from Melissa, away from the car park, away from the house, hoping that if she runs far and fast enough she will find the edge of the world and the beginning of some other place where no one knows her and she can start all over again.

Economics, History and Business Studies, says Alex.

Why History? asks Richard.

Because I like it, said Alex. *And because I'm good at it.*

Richard finds it reassuring, the swagger. It makes Alex seem like a boy again. Of course he's flirting with Louisa. It's only natural. Richard feels jealous, almost. Because he never had it, did he, the swagger. That sudden spurt of growth just after he arrived at university. Rugby, judo, 400 metres. Turning suddenly into a person that was never quite him, waking in the night sometimes, convinced that he was trapped in someone else's life, heart pounding and throat tight till he turned on the lights and found the family photographs he kept in the back of the wardrobe like passports, for the route out, the route back.

Dominic is sitting up front with Mike. *So, what's it like living out here?* Because he is still enchanted by the idea of the cottage and the garden and the job in the bookshop. Mike bridles slightly at the metropolitan presumption of *out here* so Dominic tries to be more conciliatory and asks how easy it is to make a living. Mike sucks his teeth and says he does a bit of tree surgery in the winter, *and some other stuff*, in a tone which suggests that the other stuff might not be legal.

So do you live up in them thar hills?

And freeze my bollocks off? They go over a bump and the trailer clanks and shakes. *Got a flat in Abergavenny.*

Dominic realises that he has misread the ponytail and the workboots. He isn't Davy Crockett after all, just a chancer who props up a saloon bar and sells pills to bored kids on a Friday night.

Louisa is sitting next to Benjy. *Did you enjoy that?*

Enjoy what?

Did you enjoy the canoeing?

Yeh.

What did enjoy about it?

Just, you know . . . He shrugged. *Being in a canoe.*

You're not very chatty today, are you?

No, not very.

Sorry, that was a mean thing to say.

It's all right.

How hard it was to talk to children. They made no effort to ease your discomfort. But it was hard to talk to Melissa sometimes and at least Benjy wasn't going to swear at her. *What do you want to be when you grow up?*

Don't know.

Boys always wanted to be train drivers when I was little. What did girls always want? She can't remember now. Married to one of the Bay City Rollers, possibly.

Some boys in my class want to be footballers, but I'm not very good at football.

What are you good at?

He shrugs. Perhaps he wants to be left alone. *It's because I don't know you very well.*

What is?

Not being chatty. Even though I know you're meant to be my aunt.

The word moves her in a way that catches her by surprise.

Is it OK to be quiet?

Yes, she says, *it's OK to be quiet.*

Melissa wanted to walk back via the road but she had absolutely no idea where the road went so she had to retrace the path back through all the fucking mud. Christ. She wanted to ring someone at home. Tell them about Dyke Girl. Except they'd laugh, because if she told them about the kiss they'd be, like, *How did you let it happen?* And if she didn't tell them about the kiss, then what was she being so horrified about? Just some girl fancying her. Which sounded like showing off. Because the truth was that it wasn't the kiss that made her angry, it was the way she'd reacted. She was cool with people being gay, even getting married and having kids, and she rather liked the idea of another girl fancying her as long as the girl wasn't ugly. So she kept rerunning the moment in her head except this time she gently pushed Daisy away and said, *Hey, slow down, I'm not into that kind of thing.* But she'd said all that other stuff, and now they were going to have to spend the next three days in the same house. Jesus, this fucking mud.

Daisy couldn't run any further. She came to a halt and fell to her knees, lungs heaving. She had sinned. She had wanted everything Melissa had. Now she was being punished with exquisite accuracy, that envy pushed to its poisonous extremity. *For I know my transgressions and my sin is always before me.* People would be disgusted. She would be mocked and reviled. She looked around. Bare and bleak, no fields visible now, just high empty moorland, the further hills black under the massive off-white sky. Where was her coat? You could imagine hell being like this. Not the fire, nor the press of devils, but a freezing unpeopled nowhere, the heart desperate for warmth and companionship, and the mind saying, *Do not be fooled, this is not a place.*

You're weird and your clothes are shit. Melissa, of all people. So vain, so nasty. But the fault was hers alone, Melissa merely an instrument. She had never pretended to be anything but what she was. It was Daisy who had deceived herself.

The image of Melissa telling Alex. She rolled over onto the wet grass, curling up, as if she had been punched in the abdomen. *Oh please, God, help me.* She was crying now, but God wasn't listening, He had never been listening, because He knew, didn't He? It was why the Holy Spirit hadn't come.

He had peered into her soul from the very first and seen the pretence and the false humility.

She was lying in muddy water. *Cursed is the ground.* Thorns and thistles and coats of skins. She rocked back and forth. She imagined stepping off a tall building or standing in front of an oncoming train, head bowed, eyes closed, and it was the sweet pull of these images which revealed her cowardice. She had to remember. The hurt was her only way out of this place, the long walk through the flames.

The taste of Melissa's mouth, the freckles. Diamonds and pearls. How cruel time was. The future turning into the past, the things you've done becoming your testimony for ever. *I think being yourself is punishment enough.* Where had she heard those words before?

Angela carries the shopping into the kitchen and starts to put everything away, sausages, cheese straws, pears. The house is silent. Melissa and Daisy must be out somewhere. £26 for the taxi, tiny round man, Punjabi Sikh. She didn't catch his name. Talked about his sister being married to a drug addict, how he and his brothers were forced to *take him in hand.* She didn't press him for details. Plastic Taj Mahal swinging on the mirror, Bon Jovi on the radio.

Half an hour later and the explorers return. Benjy runs for the living room, shouting, *Can I watch a video?* and vanishes before anyone can countermand him. *So,* says Angela, *did you reach the source of the Nile?* Richard laughs. *Not at the speed we were going.* The blare of the *Robots* theme tune. *Benjy, can you shut that door, please?* Alex picks up the paper. Audrey Williamson has died. Silver in the 200 yards at the London Olympics, 1948. Melissa sweeps into the room, cleansed and fragrant. *Where's Daisy?* asks Dominic. *Oh*, says Melissa breezily. *I think she went out for a walk.*

One person looks around and sees a universe created by a god who watches over its long unfurling, marking the fall of sparrows and listening to the prayers of his finest creation. Another person believes that life, in all its baroque complexity, is a chemical aberration that will briefly decorate the surface of a ball of rock spinning somewhere among a billion galaxies. And the two of them could talk for hours and find no great difference between one another, for neither set of beliefs make us kinder or wiser.

William the Bastard forcing Harold to swear over the bones of St Jerome, the Church of Rome rent asunder by the King's Great Matter, the Twin Towers folding into smoke. Religion fuelling the turns and reverses of human history, or so it seems, but twist them all to catch a different light and those same passionate beliefs seem no more than banners thrown up to hide the usual engines of greed and fear. And in our single lives? Those smaller turns and reverses? Is it religion which trammels and frees, which gives or withholds hope? Or are these, too, those old base motives dressed up for a Sunday morning? Are they reasons or excuses?

★   ★   ★

Benjy waited for his eyes to grow accustomed to the dark then approached slowly and quietly, because rats could run up your trouser leg, which was why thatchers tied string round their ankles. Except that it was not a rat, nor a mouse, but something halfway between the two, with a rounder body and a long pointed nose. Some kind of shrew perhaps. It was clearly sick and not going to run anywhere fast, so he crouched down and was about to reach out and touch it when he saw that several flies were sitting on its fur. It moved again, just a twitch really. There was blood coming out of its mouth and out of its bottom. It was going to die if he didn't do something, but if he went away some other animal might find it and kill it. A fox maybe, or a crow. He had to be quick. *Mum . . .? Dad . . .?*

Richard appeared in the hallway. *What's the matter, young man?*

I . . . The words got jumbled in his mouth.

OK. Slow down and tell me. I'm sure we can sort the problem out.

He didn't like being upset in front of someone who wasn't proper family but Richard made him feel safe, like a good teacher. *There's an animal. An animal in the shed.*

What kind of animal? Richard assumed it would be an errant cow or somesuch.

I don't know, said Benjy, calmer now that an adult was sharing the responsibility. *It's like a mouse.*

And you're scared of it? He nearly laughed but there was something desperate about Benjamin's reaction that warned him off.

It's really ill.

Come on, then. He patted his nephew's shoulder and they headed outside, and his sorrow at never having been a father was briefly equal to Benjy's sorrow for the shrew. They had reached the woodshed. *You show me.*

Benjy was afraid of getting close this time. The fact that Richard was a doctor made him think of rabies. Richard squatted by the little body. It was still moving. Richard took a piece of kindling from the woodpile and poked the creature. Benjy wanted to say, *Don't hurt it, please,* but you weren't allowed to tell a doctor what to do.

Rat poison, said Richard, standing. *Internal bleeding. I'm afraid there's nothing we can do for the little chap now.*

Benjy felt dizzy. He couldn't see where it had come from but there was suddenly a spade in Richard's hands. Benjy tried to shout *No!* but it was like being in space or under-water. Richard held the spade above the animal, aiming carefully. Benjy shut his eyes and Richard brought it down as hard as he could. There was a smacking crunch as the spade dug into the gravelly earth of the shed floor. Benjy opened his eyes, he couldn't stop himself. The animal was in two bloody halves and its insides were leaking out. Blood and tiny broken purple bags.

Richard scooped everything up on the spade and said, *Let's give this little man a proper burial.*

But there were tears streaming down Benjamin's face and he was running away, weeping.

Benjamin . . .?

★   ★   ★

A car was pulling up outside the house. Dominic had started to worry about Daisy and for the few seconds it took to get to the window he wondered if it was the police with bad news, but it was a green Renault and Daisy was getting out of the passenger door. He stepped outside to see the car turning and driving away.

Daisy? Her trousers were crusty with dry mud.

She looked at him. Had Melissa said anything?

Are you all right?

He didn't know, did he. She was safe for the moment. *I got lost.* A white lie and therefore not a real lie. *This man and woman gave me a lift. They were really kind.*

You look freezing.

I lost my coat. I'm sorry. Because they'd have to pay for another.

Let's get you inside.

The truth was that they had given her more than a lift, though precisely what she didn't know, something between helping her to her feet and saving her life. There was a blankness, like having a general anaesthetic, coming round with no sense of time having passed. She thought for a second or two that she was holding an elderly man's hand to stop him falling, then she realised that it was the other way round.

They paused in the hallway. Where was Melissa? *I need to be on my own for a bit.*

Can I bring you anything?

I'll be fine.

Daisy?

She paused and turned and almost broke.

I'm glad you're safe, said Dominic. *Don't worry about the coat.*

Thanks. She turned and carried on up to the landing.

But he knew somehow that she was neither back nor safe. He wondered whether to tell Angela but didn't quite trust her. He'd keep it a secret, just Daisy and him. He'd go up later and check how she was.

Angela poured boiling water over the dried mushrooms. A smell like unwashed bodies she always thought, but it was the simplest vegetarian recipe she knew. Made her want to roast a pig's head for Melissa, all glossy crackling and an apple in the mouth. Make Benjy sad, though. Earlier she had told Dominic that she wanted to go home, and thought for a moment that he might actually agree but he had slipped into the grating paternal role he'd been adopting more and more over the last few days. *You'll regret it . . . insult to Richard . . . hang on in there . . .* Him being right made it worse, of course. Sherry, tomato purée. Risotto Londis.

Louisa came into the kitchen, placed a glass of red wine in front of her and retreated to the window seat. Some change in her aura that Angela couldn't pinpoint. *Sorry about last night.*

Last night? Angela had suppressed the memory so well that it took a few seconds to unearth. *I think it's me who should apologise.*

Or how about neither of us apologises?

A sense that Louisa had, what? jumped ship? changed sides? A little warmer than before. Angela poured the rice into the pan and stirred it.

Dominic said you were having a difficult time.

Are you having one, too? asked Angela, because she didn't want to talk about herself, or Karen.

Is it obvious?

You had some kind of argument at the priory.

I am a woman with a past. She wanted a cigarette. Eleven months without, and her hands still felt empty sometimes. *Richard would prefer that I was a blushing bride.*

Ah. Angela felt a burst of queasiness. Richard and sex. Then it all seemed very funny. *Poor Richard.* She added the liquid to the rice.

In what way?

He's getting it from all sides. Me giving him a hard time for not looking after Mum . . . She drank some of her wine.

Louisa wasn't laughing. *He's facing an inquiry at work.*

Dominic mentioned something.

This girl ended up in a wheelchair after an operation went wrong. Richard X-rayed her. The CEO sent her a less-than-fulsome letter of apology, the family have taken it to a solicitor and now the surgeon's passing the buck and trying to dump him in the shit.

What might happen to him if he's found guilty?

He's hoping it never comes to court, said Louisa. *But in the last couple of days . . . People make mistakes, every day, even honest people.*

Angela found herself wanting to defend Richard despite

knowing none of the details, blood trumping everything. She thought carefully about where to position her sympathy. *I hope it works out OK. For both of you.* Her hands were slippery so she handed the sun-dried tomatoes to Louisa who twisted the jar open with a satisfying pop. They were silent for several minutes. *She had a genetic deformity. Karen. She wouldn't . . . The foetus wasn't viable. I have this photo album in my head. The life she never had. I can see the pictures so clearly.*

That chilly subterranean hum. *And tomorrow . . . ?*

I'm frightened. She turned the heat down.

What of?

That I might turn a corner and see her standing there. Melissa's voice a couple of rooms away, briefly audible above the Handel. *Or the opposite. That she'll disappear completely. You know. Eighteen. Leaving home and so on. And I don't know which is worse.* A longer silence.

Well, that's cheered us both up.

It has actually, said Angela. The gentlest bubbling now. She put the lid on the pot, leaving a gap so that it didn't boil over. *I don't talk about it much. Which is not good, perhaps.* But *cheered up* wasn't the right phrase. She felt . . . *engaged*. Talking to Louisa, finally something to grip in this great sliding nothing of this forced leisure.

Louisa got up and walked over and laid her hand on Angela's shoulder and left it there for three or four seconds. A low-rent laying on of hands. *I'll go and warn the troops. Twenty minutes, right?*

★   ★   ★

Alex had no real interest in the arts. He liked some music, a few paintings and the occasional poem, but it all came down to taste, and taste seemed like a pretty pointless thing to teach at school. Languages were important, but you could move to Italy or Poland and be halfway fluent in a couple of months. As for maths and science, he always imagined that if he needed these skills later in life he would hire someone who had them. But history . . . It had been sheer pleasure at first, plastic knights and horses giving way to Airfix models of Avro Lancasters giving way to TV documentaries about Galileo and Hadrian's Wall. Something murder mystery about it, answers you could dig out if you knew where to look, lost in attics, buried in fields, Roman roads across a map, obscene carvings under pews. He had a *Penguin Atlas of Early European History* that he loved. The ebb and flow of Celts and Saxons and Vikings. Something solid with something fluid moving over it, which seemed like a good model for pretty much everything, stuff you could rely on interacting with stuff you couldn't. Facts and opinions. Feelings and thoughts. Because he still didn't really understand that this was only one way of looking at the world, and that there were people who looked around and saw no fixed landscape whatsoever, only an ebb and flow over which they had no control.

Dominic put the bowl of risotto on the chair and sat on the edge of Daisy's bed. She was still wearing her jeans. Pink mud on the blanket. Her eyes were damp and sore. *I told everyone you were ill.*

Thanks.

But you're not ill, are you?

Dad . . .

What's wrong?

Daisy closed her eyes.

If there's anything I can do . . .

There's nothing you can do.

I'm worried about you.

She mustn't lie. That was how she'd got into trouble in the first place. *I did something bad.*

I can't imagine you doing something bad. It was true. *Are we talking bad in the eyes of the church?*

Please . . .

Has this got something to do with Melissa?

Something about the way she curled up tighter, trying to move further away from him. *It has, hasn't it?*

Real fear now. *Don't say anything to her. You have to promise me.* She could ask this favour, couldn't she, because it wasn't being selfish. It was protecting others.

If Melissa has hurt you in any way . . .

It's not her fault. Please, Dad, you have to promise me.

He wanted to lift her up and hug her like he did when she was tiny. He put his hand under her face and she rested the weight of her head on his palm. *I would never do anything to hurt you. You understand that, don't you?* Because he couldn't make the promise, because if Melissa had hurt Daisy he wouldn't let her leave this house unpunished. *Have some food, OK?*

I'll try. The thought of eating made her feel sick.

I'll bring you a cup of tea later on.

Richard raised his glass at one end of the table and caught the attention of Angela sitting at the other end. *A superlative risotto.*

You're welcome. She turned to Dominic. *I should go up and see Daisy.*

She's all right. She just wants to be on her own.

I thought you said she was ill.

This was a ridiculous game. *She asked me to say she was ill. She's feeling really upset about something.*

About what?

I honestly don't know.

I'll go up and see her after supper, said Angela.

Angela . . .

So, we're going to leave her up there on her own?

No.

She's my daughter.

Melissa glanced over at Mum and Richard. They looked as if they were in different rooms. Richard had found out, hadn't he? She just knew. Still that child's shameless radar for the weak point. Blood in the water. She wondered how it would pan out.

Do you believe in reincarnation? asked Benjy.

Course not, said Alex. *I mean, can you remember who you were last time round?*

It was the wrong answer. He needed Alex to say, *Yes, yes,*

of course I believe in reincarnation. Because Benjy wanted to come back as a panda or a gorilla, but he would agree to come back as anything if he could only be assured that he was coming back. He didn't want to think about what had happened to the shrew, what had happened for Granny, so he stopped listening to what Alex was saying and wrote his name using risotto to stop himself crying.

Melissa brought in the two plates on which the treacle pudding bowls sat upturned. She placed them in the middle of the table and removed the bowls like a conjurer revealing rabbits.

Skinny jeans, for example, Louisa said to Alex. *I just don't get it. There, you see? That's the middle-aged frump talking.*

But I think you look really sexy, said Alex.

She looked at him, assessing whether this was just politeness.

Was Louisa doing it to spite him? Richard wondered. He forced himself to turn to Angela so that he did not have to watch the spectacle. *I have an apology to make.*

For what? said Angela.

Last night. You asked me a medical question. Should he explain how he knew? *You never told me that you'd had a miscarriage.*

Why should I have? Did that sound harsh?

Objection sustained. He took a spoonful of the treacle pudding. It was oddly dry. He rather wished he could mash it up with the vanilla ice cream like Benjy was doing. *But it's still a problem for you.*

I talked to Louisa earlier. I'm not sure I can talk about it twice in one day.

I understand.

He and Louisa weren't talking, were they? Angela could sense his sadness at being cut out of the loop.

He changed the subject. *I'm assuming you don't have any photographs of Dad.*

I don't have photographs of anything. Mum threw them all away. Or maybe they got carted off with everything else. I'm afraid I didn't make a huge effort to hang on to stuff.

I have three.

Three what?

Photographs of Dad, said Richard. *I'm no longer entirely sure how they came into my possession. I thought you might be interested. I should have brought them with me.*

A little explosion of, what? excitement? pleasure? fear? She is trying to imagine what the pictures might be like but panicking because she is unable to do this. Stems and slime, that empty doorway.

Remind me and I'll post them to you next week. To be honest, I'm not terribly fond of them, but I've always been chary of throwing them away. This fear that he would be angry with me. Absurd, isn't it?

Throwing them away? Without telling her? She gets to her feet. *I've got to go and check on Daisy. See how she's doing.*

Dirty orange street lights in the not-yet-dawn as she walks across the wet black tarmac of the Wheelan Centre car park.

Wet air and the clang of lockers, the flash of a blue verruca sock, pound in the slot, slam shut, keyband twisted out. She walks through the footbath into the hard white light of the pool, pushing her hair up into the rubber swimhat and snapping it down over her ears. The shriek and whistle of that ringing echo. She spits into her goggles and licks the rubber seal before flipping the elastic over the back of her head and sitting the lenses just right over her eyes. She stands and stretches beside the stack of red polystyrene floats, arms over her head, fingers laced, palms towards the ceiling. The black second hand ticks on the big white clock.

Getting in is like sliding feet first through a ring of cold. She dips down into the blue silence, looking up the pool to where the deep end vanishes in the chlorine blur, the air a ceiling of mercury studded with the red balls of the lane ropes. Someone kicks off beside her, trailing bubbles like silver coins. She stands and re-emerges into the noisy air. Sanderson is on the side wearing the world's worst shell suit, mauve and blueberry, bright yellow whistle. *People, people.* He claps and the building claps back. *Eight lengths warm-up. Let's wake those legs and arms.*

She pushes off, that first glide like slow flight, four butterfly leg kicks, then she breaks the surface, right arm arcing over, breathing behind that little bow wave the head makes. One, two, left. One, two, right. She tumbles at the end, flipping the world like a pancake. And Lauren is swimming beside her, that long stroke, the dolphin ease of it. They tumble together and swim in perfect unison. She is a bird of prey now, swimming up into the blue distance of the valley. The green of Lauren's Speedo. That tiny tractor. Tumble, push, glide. Four lengths, five. Still the muffled secrecy of underwater but they're no longer swimming, or are they? The air is warm and she can hear traffic. Or surf, maybe? The smell of cocoa butter suncream. They're on an island. Kings and their judgement far away. Lauren leans back and snaps her swimhat off, shaking her long red hair free. Freckles on her shoulder and blue veins so clear under the skin that you could trace them with your finger.

Hey. Lauren turns and holds her eye. *Crazy hazy Daisy*.

Alex is alone in the kitchen standing over the kettle, waiting for it to boil, when Richard comes in and walks over. Richard is never easy to read but Alex knows instantly from his expression what he wants to talk about and how he feels about it. He halts and pauses briefly, like a conductor, baton suspended before the downstroke. *Stop flirting with my wife*.

I'm not flirting.

Don't lie to me. Richard had expected Alex to crumble. He is surprised by his own anger.

I didn't mean . . . He had been concentrating on Louisa. I think you're really sexy. It never occurred to him that Richard might have been listening.

I don't give a damn what you meant or didn't mean. This in a forced whisper so that no one hears it in the dining room. Richard is frightening himself but there is a relief too which is blissful. *You're flirting with my wife and you're doing it in front of everyone and you're making me look like an idiot.*

Richard's hand is raised and for a second or two neither of them is sure whether this will become physical. Then Richard lowers his hand, takes a step backwards and breathes deeply several times. He looks like someone watching a horror film and perhaps this is precisely what he is seeing in his mind's eye. He turns and leaves the room.

Alex is shaking. The memory of Callum's leg being broken rears up. *Show some fucking respect.* The fear that Richard is going to come back into the kitchen carrying that length of scaffolding. Richard the doctor, his uncle, the admirable man. Fixed landscape turning into ebb and flow. Fear turning to anger. He marches out of the kitchen. If he bumps into Richard he really will punch him in the face and fuck the consequences, but only Mum and Dad are sitting in the dining room and Dad says, *Alex . . .?* and the ordinariness of this is enough to restore a kind of sanity. *Yeh. Sorry. I'm fine.* He goes out of the front door, closes it behind him and punches the stone wall hard so that all the knuckles on his right hand bleed.

When Angela got upstairs Daisy was already asleep, still clothed, white socks with grubby brown soles, holding a teddy bear Angela hadn't seen for a long time. *The Art of Daily Prayer* and Neutrogena hand cream on the bedside table. *Let's get you into bed or you'll wake up freezing in the middle of the night.* She eased the duvet from beneath Daisy's hips then turned her onto her back so she could unbutton her dirty jeans and slide them off, like she was five again. Flu, chickenpox. Daisy half woke and said something Angela couldn't quite make out. *Almost done.* She flipped the duvet back over Daisy and straightened it. *There.* Daisy turned to face the wall. Angela sat on the chair opposite. She was ill, that was all. Dominic was being over-dramatic, playing the old game, concocting a story that threw a little charmed circle around the two of them. That bear. Harry? Henry? She had to sew a leg back on after it was torn off in a fight, by Alex, presumably.

Was she warming to Louisa? Or did she just like taking sides? Was that little confession about Karen simply the price she had to pay to show her loyalty? It was a fault of hers, she knew, comfort in conflict, black and white, us and them, knowing where one stood, none of that muddy moral ambiguity. The relief at work when Helen finally slapped that boy in her class after years of just being a crap teacher.

Laughter downstairs and the chime of crockery. A brief Christmas feeling then a memory of sitting in her bedroom listening to Mum shouting in the lounge. Except it was Dad shouting, wasn't it, his voice suddenly so clear after all these years. Why didn't he come upstairs and say hello? Why was he so angry? She wanted to run downstairs and have him turn and see her and break into that big smile and sweep her off her feet.

Then she was back in the present again, Daisy's hands moving as if she were fending someone off in a dream. Angela got to her feet and stood beside the bed. She touched the side of Daisy's head and waited till she was calm again, then retucked the duvet and left the room, closing the door quietly behind her.

He was sitting on the edge of the bed. She was standing leaning against the chest of drawers with her arms folded. *This is not about you, Richard.* She closed her eyes to regather her thoughts. *I don't know who I am, sometimes. I'm not sure I've ever known. I've tried so hard to please other people, my parents, Craig, Melissa, you. I listen to your music, I go to your plays, I watch your films. And it's not your fault. I chose to be the person who fits in with your life.*

Are you saying you don't want to be married to me?

I'm saying . . . What was she saying? She was saying, *Let me think.* She was saying, *Give me space.* Just for once she wasn't rushing to reassure him. Perhaps he was right, perhaps she didn't want to be married to him. She wanted to turn this extraordinary idea over in her hand, like a shell she'd found on the beach, run her fingers over it, knowing that she might very well simply put it down again. *I'm saying I need to get some sleep. I'm saying we both need to get some sleep.*

Wednesday

Daisy put the milk back into the fridge, closed the door quietly and picked up the mug. When she turned to leave the kitchen, however, Melissa was standing in the doorway. Coffee slopped out of the mug onto the stone floor. *Please. I just . . .*

Melissa refused to move, she pushed her hands deep into the pockets of her hoody and rocked forward onto the balls of her feet as if this had to be squeezed out. *I'm sorry about yesterday.*

The apology was so unexpected that Daisy didn't know how to reply.

I just blurted, OK? I didn't think.

It doesn't matter. Really. I just need to go back to my room.

Wait. Melissa was angry. This had cost her and she wanted that cost acknowledged. *It's fine being gay. I'm not prejudiced.*

I'm not gay. Daisy realised too late how loud her voice was. She paused, listening carefully, terrified that someone else might be in the dining room. Her hands were shaking.

She put the mug down. *Please. I don't want to talk about this.*

Yeh, well maybe you should.

A sudden stab of utter loneliness. Melissa was the only one who knew, there was no one else she could tell. Daisy reached out towards her. *I need you to be my friend.* She wanted to be held but she couldn't say the words.

Cool it, lady, said Melissa.

Daisy saw herself standing in the kitchen, arms outstretched like a cartoon zombie. She'd made an idiot of herself for a second time. She threw herself through the doorway, pushing Melissa aside. She heard Melissa say, *You are so spectacularly fucked up*, then she was in the hallway and running up the stairs.

Abergavenny. Originally Gorbannia. Alex turned the page. *A Brythonic word meaning 'river of the blacksmiths'.*

Brythonic?

Of, or appertaining to the Britons.

What happened to your hand?

Alex glanced casually at his knuckles. *Mucking about with that roller in the shed.* He'd practised the explanation in advance. *Lucky my fingers are still attached.*

Dominic had taken over the guidebook. *It sits between two mountains, Sugar Loaf and Blorenge.*

Blorenge?

Richard appeared in the doorway. Alex hid his damaged hand under the table. Richard walked past and patted his shoulder and Alex thought, *Fuck you.*

Baron de Hamelin, said Dominic. *Tree of Jesse. Blah-blah. Goat's hair periwigs. Rudolf Hess.*

Are you making this up?

Scout's honour.

Benjy came in with his bowl of Deliciously Nutty Crunch and sat next to Dominic, squishing in close because he still felt bruised by his fears of last night which had not been banished entirely by the daylight.

Hey, kiddo.

Incidentally, has anyone seen Daisy this morning?

Nope.

Melissa?

What?

Have you seen Daisy this morning?

She came down to get some coffee. She seemed in kind of a weird mood.

I'll pop up and see how she is.

Hey. The town hosted the British National Cycling Championships. 2007 and 2009.

Paris of the West.

Now, don't be bitchy.

I'll be back in an hour, said Richard, chugging a glass of water. *I'll grab a quick shower and we can all be off.*

Enjoy.

Don't get lost, said Alex.

He was determined not to return home having spent so much money without running properly, plus he needed to

be alone for a while. It wasn't just Louisa. If he'd hit Alex
. . . Would there have been a better way of alienating every
single person in the house? He needed to step back and get
some distance.

Squatting on the slate path that led from the front door
to the iron gate he yanked the tongues of the trainers and
double-knotted the laces. The air was damp but somehow
clearer and more transparent this morning. The deep greens
of the foliage. You didn't get this in a city, the way the light
changed constantly. He walked over to the wall and put each
foot up in turn, leaning forward to stretch his hamstrings.
The house looked like an extension of the landscape, the
stone quarried from Welsh hills, the rafters from a forest you
might very well be able to see from the top of the dyke, the
moss, the rust, the burst blisters of weathered paint a record
of its passage through time and weather, like the scars and
barnacles on a tanker's hull.

He would jog up the road, walk the steepest part of the
hill and start running again when he was past the Red Darren
car park, conserve his energy this time instead of wasting it
in a private show of failed machismo. He checked his watch.
9:17. Looking around he was both disappointed and relieved
that no one was watching as he set off.

Dominic walked past the door of the living room and saw
Melissa sitting on the sofa. He went in and stood beside her.
She was drawing the little side table. Whenever you saw
Melissa drawing a picture you were meant to say how good

it was and she was meant to brush the compliment off. She refused to acknowledge his presence. *What happened to Daisy yesterday?*

I have no idea what you're talking about.

Of course you have.

I thought she was ill. She was relishing the confrontation.

You're lying.

That's a pretty serious accusation. I hope you've got evidence to back it up.

Who is more likely to be telling the truth, you or Daisy? In his own way he was enjoying this, too.

She laughed. *That is quite funny. In the circumstances.*

Don't bugger about. Something happened yesterday and it hurt Daisy a great deal and Daisy means more to me than anyone in the world.

Melissa put her pen down and turned to look up at him. *You don't want to know, trust me.*

Trust you?

Seriously, you do not want to know.

Try me.

She leant back and exhaled. *She's a lesbian.* She said the word as three distinct syllables.

What?

She tried to get her tongue down my throat. Which is not my bag, I'm afraid.

He felt punched. It was true, wasn't it?

I think she's having trouble coming to terms with it. A little show of theatrically fake concern.

You . . . He had to leave before he lost control of himself. *You shut your nasty little mouth.*

He walked into the dining room. Everyone was gathered at the table. Alex raised a hand to beckon him. He turned and walked upstairs, two at a time. He went into the bathroom, locked the door and sat on the toilet. An old memory of hiding in the bathroom when he was a child, the comfort of the only lockable room in the house, the bar fire high up, two orange rods in their little silver cage, the green rubber suckers that bit the corners of wet flannels. It seemed so obvious, thinking about it. He should go and talk to Daisy. Would she be horrified or comforted that he knew? Perhaps it was better to say nothing, because underneath the confusion he felt a distaste he would never have expected, the unnaturalness of it, the same distaste he felt about the church, strangers coming to claim his daughter and take her away.

The crumpled tissues, the fly crawling on the sill. Daisy had never thought of killing herself, even before she came to know it as a mortal sin. Now she could understand the seductive promise of oblivion. But what if one woke up in hell? A bowl of cold gluey risotto on the carpet by the bed. She'd left her coffee downstairs, hadn't she? Why had no one come up to see her? She couldn't be gay because being gay was a sin. She knew it seemed unkind but who was she to decide? *The decrees of the Lord are firm, and all of them are righteous.* You didn't discover God's love then argue about the small print. You submitted, you had to say, *I am ignorant,*

I understand so little, I am only human. Surely she would have noticed before now, it wasn't like an allergy to bee stings, something of which you were unaware until it put your life in danger. She should call her friends at church. She could go up to Alex and Benjy's room and get a signal. Meg, Anushka. Lesley, maybe. They would understand in a way that no one here would understand. So why couldn't she bring herself to do it?

She missed Lauren. She missed Jack. She needed someone who would simply be interested, someone who would say, *Tell me more,* not, *This is what you have to do.* But Lauren was somewhere in Gloucester and she lost the number when her old mobile was stolen. Just thinking about this caused a pain that made her grip the edge of the table till it passed. Jack. She took the mobile from her bag. Flat B, 47 Cumberland Street. She could ring directory enquiries. It was like a thin column of sunlight in the dark of the cell.

She knocked on Alex and Benjy's door. No answer. So she went in and stood on the magic chair in the far corner of the room. *Do you want the number texted directly to your phone?* Her hands were shaking, as if the seconds mattered. Eight, seven, seven, zero . . .

The owner of this Orange mobile number is unavailable. If you'd like to leave a message . . .

She saw Jack getting up from the table in The Blue Sea. *You fucking traitor.* Everyone staring, squid rings and tomato ketchup, the bottle of spilt vinegar leaking. The hurt in his face, and something she couldn't quite see, a figure on the edge of her field of vision that slid away every time she turned her head. She couldn't do it, she clicked her phone off and sat down on the chair. It looked as if someone had burgled the room, one drawer had been removed and upended, Benjy's dirty jeans lay on the carpet inside out, wearing a pair of red underpants, a crushed yoghurt drink carton, felt-tip drawings of carnage.

He had judged it rather well, fifty paces running, fifty paces walking, alternating the whole way up. Thirty minutes, not bad going. He said he'd be out for an hour but he was loath to turn around now that he was able to stretch his legs. Twenty minutes more or less would make no difference and he'd be a good deal faster on the way back. His legs were going to hurt like hell tomorrow but he felt better than he'd done all week. A tracery of gritty paths along the spine of the hill, blusters of wind. They'd walked up here only two days ago but how different it felt now, a sense of having earned this altitude, the way one lost any sense of scale when one was no longer able to see a human object.

Shit and damn. His left foot was suddenly gone from under him and he was tumbling sideways, breaking his fall with his open left hand on a hard little stone. *Damn and shit.* He rolled over onto his back and waited for a powder of stars to finish passing across his retina. He looked at his hand, a ragged pebbly graze across the centre of his palm, already starting to bleed. It reminded him of school, skidding bikes and falling off climbing frames. He sat up slowly. He had twisted his ankle, hard to tell how badly yet. He waited for a minute then rotated himself onto all fours and stood up carefully using only his right leg. He put a little weight on his left foot and flinched: not good. He tried to walk and realised he could accomplish only a kind of lurching hop. An hour and a half back? two hours? He would not be popular.

The drop in pressure. Bruised purple sky, wind like a train, the landscape suddenly alive, trees bent and struggling, swathes of alternating colour racing through the long grass, the sky being hauled over the valley like a blanket. An empty white fertiliser sack dances along the side of the hill. Windows hammer in their sashes, the boiler vent clatters and slaps. A tile is levered from the roof, cartwheels over the garden wall and sticks into the earth like a little shark fin. The bins chatter and snap in the woodshed, fighting the bungees that hold them down.

Then it comes, like a great grey curtain being dragged down from the hills, the fields smudged and darkened. A noise like wet gravel smashed against the glass. The guttering fills and bubbles and water gushes from the feet of downpipes. Drops fantail on the bench top and the stone steps and the polished roof of the Mercedes. Water pools and runs in the ruts of the drive, drips down the chimney and pings and fizzes on the hot metal of the stove; it squeezes through the old putty that holds the leaded windows fast to puddle on sills. The rain near-horizontal now, a living graph of the wind's force. All external points of reference gone, no horizon, no fixed lines. The house is airborne, riding the storm, borne on something that is neither wholly air, nor wholly water, Kansas vanished long ago, borders crossed and broken, the ground a thousand fathoms below.

Benjy stands at the dining-room window, spellbound by the sheer thereness of it, the world outside his head for once louder and more insistent than the world inside. Drops scuttle down the gridded panes, marbling the world, everything green and silver, the clatter against the glass now softer, now louder, as the great bead curtain of falling liquid swings back and forth.

Noah's Ark. *And God said I will destroy the world because human beings are sinful.* The animals went in two by two, marmosets and black widow spiders, Japhet and Daphet and Baphet. And everyone else was killed, like in the tsunami, cars and walls and trees pouring down the street, people ripped apart in a great wet grinding machine. And when the dove flew over the land there would have been bodies everywhere all bloated and black like in New Orleans. A sudden shadow and the smack of something thrown against the glass only inches from his face. He turns and runs, crying, *Mum . . . Mum . . . Mum . . .*

Dominic stands in the hallway, water creeping in under the front door, a sound like the chaos between radio stations. He should go and talk to Daisy, tell her it's all right, tell her they love her, that they will always love her. Why is he so scared of doing this? He has never thought about her as a sexual person. The idea disturbs him in a way he can't quite identify. All those little waystations. Daisy, Alex, Benjy, the first time they read to themselves, the first time they walked to school on their own. He remembers holding Daisy as a baby, those tiny perfect fingers gripping his thumb, the eczema, the blonde quiff. He imagines someone else holding her now, the two of them naked, and the clash of these two kinds of tenderness is like chariot wheels touching. Out of nowhere he thinks of Andrew, lying in a hospital bed, Amy sitting beside him, head bowed, holding his hand. He feels ashamed for having ignored the message. He has never really solved a problem in his life, he has simply averted his eyes and left other people to do the dirty work. The creak of wood. He turns and sees Daisy coming down the stairs. *How are you feeling?*

A bit better. She pauses, hand on the little metal dog of the newel post. *I'm just going to get something to eat.*

He wonders briefly if she is waiting to tell him about the encounter with Melissa but she doesn't and what he feels mostly is relief, that she seems happier, that he has over-reacted, perhaps, that Melissa was lying, that there is nothing for him to do.

A growing conviction that something was wrong, the hackles of the animal curled in the brainstem. Richard came to a halt so he could listen and watch more carefully. A sudden coldness, something about the quality of the light, a sense that other people were no longer simply absent but a very long way away. It was behind him, wasn't it? He spun round and saw horizontal rain coming out of a vast wall of lead-grey cloud. A sudden fear, then the rain hit him, a hard cold sideways shower, funny almost, once it had happened, thinking about the story he would be telling later on, about how he had been forced to hop through driving rain in the middle of nowhere wearing nothing more than a T-shirt and a pair of shorts. Ten minutes later and it was less funny because neither the wind nor the rain were slacking off, he was freezing, the pain in his ankle was, if anything, getting worse and it was going to be some considerable time before he got off the ridge. Childish scenarios began to play on repeat in his head: being rescued by the red helicopter they had seen two days ago, losing consciousness and lying down and night falling. He realised that he had not told anyone where he was intending to run.

Louisa makes a jug of coffee and puts it on the dining-room table, sugar, milk jug, a wonky tower of cups. Richard was meant to be back forty minutes ago and the storm is still raging outside. An air of mild emergency hangs over the house and however much people drift away there is a centre of gravity in the room which draws them back.

He'll turn up in five minutes, says Melissa, *showing off about how manly he is.*

I hope he fucking dies, thinks Alex. He wonders whether Richard told Louisa about the bollocking. Maybe he has bollocked her in the same way. Alex tries to catch her eye but she is too distracted by Richard's absence to notice anyone else.

Angela says, *Those paths will be a nightmare in this weather.* She means to be reassuring, explaining how he will have to take his time, but it comes out wrong. Louisa's nervousness is starting to infect her. Too many people lost, the membrane between here and the other place thinned almost to nothing by this unnatural weather, waiting for the foolish and the insufficiently loved to stumble through.

This is totally a record. Benjy has built a domino tower of nine storeys.

Alex wants to be asked to go and look for Richard, but he is not going to offer until he is asked. He wants it publicly acknowledged that he is the expert when it comes to running and walking in these hills. He wants it publicly acknowledged that Richard was pretending to be twenty years old and that he has made a fucking tit of himself in the process.

Daisy comes into the room and Melissa says, languorously, *Morning, Daisy*, but it is only Daisy who notices the barb.

Hello, love, says Angela. *How are you doing this morning?*

She is hoping Mum will offer to get her some breakfast so they can go into the kitchen and talk, but Angela seems distracted and there is no way that she is going to ask while Melissa is watching, so she heads to the kitchen where she puts the kettle on then leans on the draining board with her head in her hands.

And, *Oh!* says Benjy, and, *Oh!* says everyone else, as if they're watching a firework display but it's Benjy's tower

231

which collapsed next door, sending dominoes clattering all over the table and on to the stone floor.

An hour, says Louisa. A part of her wonders if he has done this to spite her.

Benjy is rebuilding his tower, placing the dominoes horizontally this time for greater stability.

He's Richard, says Angela. *He'll be fine.*

But Richard isn't always fine, he screws up, she knows this now.

You don't die by getting caught out in the rain, says Dominic.

That's not strictly true, says Alex. *People do die of exposure in the Brecon Beacons.* The room ices over.

Alex, says Dominic wearily, *that is not helpful.*

He's meant to say sorry but he's not in the mood for saying sorry. He stands and takes his coffee cup into the kitchen. Behind his back he hears Angela apologising for her son's foot in mouth disease.

Daisy is still leaning on the draining board, her boiled kettle cooling. She looks up. *Sister Daisy.* It's an old joke, so old he forgets it's a joke.

Not now, OK?

What's up?

Nothing.

Tell me. His own anger looms so large that he expects her to be angry with Richard for some as-yet-undisclosed reason, but he can hear a tone in her voice he hasn't heard for a long time.

She could tell him. He thinks she's a weirdo, anyway. Then

she laughs because it's what he's wanted to do since they arrived, isn't it, kissing Melissa, then she remembers. *Get off me, you fucking dyke.* That stab of panic, the way you can't rewind time.

What? says Alex. Is she laughing at him?

Now, before she changes her mind. *Look, I'm going to tell you something.*

Something what?

She stalls. What does she want him to say? That she is forgiven? That no one else is going to find out? That it never happened?

Alex? Mum is calling from the dining room. *Sorry.* He turns and walks away and she realises that telling someone will solve nothing.

Alex, says Mum. *Do you have any idea where Richard went running?*

Up onto the ridge, I guess. He has no real idea but he is assuming that Richard was indeed showing off, running up the steepest hill.

Will you go and look for him?

Suddenly he is paid back in full. *No problem.* He heads upstairs.

Benjy is twitchy and the dominoes are no longer holding his attention. The same fear as Louisa and his mother, but without her ability to hold it back and chop it down. The possibility of Richard dying out there in all that rain. *And God said I will destroy the world.* Sword-fighting isn't an indoors thing so he wanders around trying to lose himself in the details of the house, the smallness of things. He runs his fingers over the raised furry pattern of flowers on the wallpaper in the hallway. He looks inside the meter cupboard and imagines the whole house as a steampunk galleon, stovepipe hats and the chunter of pistons. He opens the leather cover of the visitors' book. The first entry is dated 1994. *Max (8) and Susannah (6). Canterbury. We woak up in the nite and saw some bagers.* Blue ink which has blobbed on the Y of Canterbury. *The Farmoors, Manchester. The Black Bull in Hay does a very nice Sunday roast.* Someone has covered a whole page with a superb pencil sketch of the house. *John, Joan, Carmen and Sophie Cain-Summerson, plus Grandma and Grandpa.* He sits on the stairs and works out which of the brass stair rods can be rotated and which are too stiff to turn. He goes into the toilet and looks inside the cistern. There is an orange plastic ballcock on the end of a rusty arm. When you push it down more water squirts out of the white spout. It looks like something you might find in a harbour, a tiny buoy among the lobster pots and fishing boats. Dad said the house belonged to a family and maybe they come here in the summer and at Christmas. Benjy doesn't know anyone who has two houses, though Michael's family have a mobile home by the sea in Devon. He can't see the appeal of having two homes because you would need your stuff in both houses, fluffy toys, PlayStation, animal posters. Then he finds a secret cupboard on the half-landing which he has never noticed before.

*   *   *

He is in serious trouble, that body shiver, guts and chest. He can't believe this is actually happening, he is two miles away from the house and he is getting hypothermia, not halfway up K2 or on the Ross Ice Shelf but in bloody Herefordshire. He is a doctor, and it is no longer wholly out of the question that he might die, not in a heroic way, but in a stupid way almost within actual sight of the house where there is a hot shower and a mug of coffee. He wonders if he should head straight down left off the hill to get out of the wind, but if he does that he stands even less chance of bumping into other runners or walkers, nor is he sure if he has the energy to clamber through hedges and over fences should he lose the path. The two options do a little back and forth dance in his head. Stay up, go down, stay up, go down. He realises that he is losing the ability to think clearly. Dying will sort out the Sharne case, if nothing else. He wonders if this is a kind of punishment, though that would be arrogant, thinking atmospheric pressure systems might be arranged in order to impact on his own life, and maybe the idiotic randomness is a more fitting punishment, but what is he being punished for? The rain has turned to hail. He can't remember precisely what he has done wrong. *Shit*. He snags his foot on a stone and the pain is both intense and suspiciously far away. He looks down and sees that his ankle is heavily swollen.

The owners? You didn't want to think about them too much. The idea that all this belonged to someone else. The suspicion that a wealthy family had over-reached itself and had been forced to rent the family silver. They came in the summer and at Christmas, then packed their more personal possessions into a locked cupboard on the half-landing, a stuffed owl under a glass dome, a box of tarnished spoons in purple plush. There was a clipframe of thirty-one collaged Polaroids, fading like photos of hairstyles in a barber's window, a student rowing eight hurling their cox into the Isis, a black retriever, Barbours and pearls, court shoes and ironed rugby shirts, faces rhyming from picture to picture, the plump girl with the laugh and the *Charlie's Angels* hair, the ginger man thickening over the years, playing tennis, posing in front of a Stalinist carbuncle in some Eastern European capital. But the London flat had been burgled during their last stay so they'd left in a hurry forgetting to lock the cupboard.

Alex jogs down the staircase wearing his running clothes and a woolly hat and his luminous yellow cycling jacket. Benjy closes the cupboard quickly, thinking he will be in trouble but Alex doesn't take any notice because he's going out for a run in the pouring rain. *See you later, Smalls.* Benjy waits until the front door bangs behind him and gently lifts the glass-domed owl out of the dusty dark. He is instantly in love with it. Serendipitously, he has already chosen a name for the owl he would have if he were a character in *Harry Potter*. Tolliver. This is Tolliver. He imagines writing, *Dear Pavel . . .*, rolling the paper tight as a cigarette, binding it with red ribbon and giving it to Tolliver who takes it in his sharp little beak and lifts his wide white wings and rises from the sill of the open window, the whole sky full of criss-crossing owls, knitting together a world of which Muggles remain utterly unaware.

How eloquently houses speak, of landscape and weather, of builders and families, of wealth, fears, children, servants. Hunkering in solitude or squeezed upwards by the pressure of their neighbours, proudly facing the main road or turning towards the hill to keep the wind and rain out of their faces. Roofs angled to shuck off, walls whitewashed to reflect the sun. Inner courtyards to save the women of the house from prying eyes. Those newfangled precious cars, Austin Morris, Ford Cortina, in little rooms of their own till they were bread and butter and banished to the kerb. The basement kitchen and the attic bedrooms where the servants worked and slept. Bare beams plastered and exposed again when they no longer said *poverty*. The front room that contains only the boxed tinsel Christmas tree and the so-called silver, where no one ever goes, and where you will lie for two days before your funeral. The new toilet replacing the privy in the garden that now holds only rusted tricycles and soft dirty footballs. Pipes and wires leading to reservoirs and power stations, to telephone exchanges and sewage farms. Water from Birmingham, power from Scotland. Voices from Brisbane and Calgary.

Time speeds up. A day becomes an hour, becomes a minute, becomes a second. Planes vanish first, cars are smeared into strings of coloured smoke then fade to nothing. People disappear, leaving only bodies that flicker on and off in beds in time with the steady toggle of the dark. Buildings inhabit the earth, growing like spores, sending out tubers, seeding new towns, new villages, new cities till drowned in sand or jungle. Girders and chimneys turning to mulch and rubble. Two thousand years, two hundred thousand years, two million years and a severe and stately house that once sat at the geometric centre of its square garden looking across the valley is now a ghost in the soil a mile below the surface of a snowball earth.

Daisy walks to the window seat at the other end of the kitchen and stares out into the rain. She tries to worry about Richard but can't do it. How grey the world is. So many words for red. Carmine, scarlet, ruby, burgundy, cherry, vermilion. But grey? She turns and glances into the living room and sees that Melissa has gone at last. The pressure in her chest builds. *Mum?*

What, love? Angela turns and touches her arm. *You look dreadful.*

Can we talk?

A momentary pause while Angela absorbs the oddity and intimacy of this. *Of course we can.*

Alex loves this weather, loves all bad weather, snow, rain, hail, mud, darkness, failing light, becoming a part of the landscape instead of simply observing it. Thoughts cycle as he runs. Song lyrics, conversations he's had or wished he'd had, sex he's had or wished he'd had. The encounter with Richard is on repeat as he runs up the road to Red Darren. *You're making me look like an idiot.* He thinks instead of Richard lying unconscious in the rain, a big wheeling pan from a film. He is not sure if he still fancies Louisa or not, the way she's so pathetically worried about Richard. The higher he gets the colder it becomes, the rain turns to hail and for the first time he starts to wonder what will happen if Richard is in actual deep shit and he realises that if he fails to find Richard then everyone will blame him even though he is the only one doing something to find him. Plus, of course, something might have happened which has nothing to do with the weather. Broken leg, heart attack, fallen down some bloody hole. But if he finds Richard and he's dead by the time he gets there Alex won't actually be blamed at all. He'll be *the person who found the body.*

He's up on the top now and, Jesus, it is fucking freezing running through this stuff, and it is entirely possible that Richard took another route and turned up at the front door five minutes after Alex left, which will really piss him off. He's having to pretty much close his eyes on account of the hail. Grey background and white dots coming straight at him like that old Windows screensaver. Was Richard wearing a waterproof? Should have grabbed a spare one from the hallway. Too late to worry about that now. Give Richard his own and earn bonus points. Who would win a fight between the two of them? Alex presumes it would be a smackdown. Richard had a few inches in height and reach but he also had that pudgy middle-aged look men got when they stopped looking after themselves. Fuck. And there he is, up ahead, limping like someone coming out of a war zone.

Richard wonders if this is really happening, and is sufficiently compos mentis to know that his unsureness is not a good sign. Not quite on the Glasgow Coma Scale yet. *Alex, is it?* In a luminous yellow jacket like a security guard. Shorts and a woolly hat. *Richard*, says Alex, in a casual golf-club manner. *Long time no see, a pint of the usual?* and so forth. Richard says, *I'm in a bit of a state*. So Alex removes his luminous yellow jacket. *Take this*. But Richard's hands are so numb that he can't grip it well enough to get his arms into the sleeves. His teeth are chattering. His teeth haven't chattered since school. Alex puts the woolly hat on his head. *Cader Idris* on the recorder. Frozen milk lifting the foil caps on the chunky bottles. Before Dad died. *Here, let me help*. He thinks of nurses helping elderly patients into cardigans. That girl in her wheelchair. Then the jacket is on and he realises he's going to see Louisa soon and he understands now quite how frightened he was and it is possible that he is crying about this, though hopefully the rain will disguise the fact. Alex lifts Richard's arm over his shoulder. *Come on, keep it up, or it's me who'll freeze to death*. Richard swings his good leg, hobbles, swings his good leg, hobbles. Alex is pushing him faster than he wants to go. It hurts a lot, but it's a good thing, going faster. He remembers the conversation of last night. He will apologise later. A hot bath, he can have a hot bath, but, God almighty, this ankle. *Thanks for this*.

Just keep walking.

*   *   *

Angela shuts the door and Daisy thinks of headmasters' offices and doctors' surgeries. They sit beside one another on the sofa looking into the empty stove. Daisy wishes it was lit but that's Richard's job. *What's the matter?*

You have to promise . . .

I have to promise what? asks Angela.

She's standing on the high board. One bounce and don't look down. *I tried to kiss Melissa.*

Angela is genuinely unsure if she has heard correctly but knows that she cannot ask Daisy to repeat it.

For God's sake, Mum, say something.

She shuffles through her memory of Melissa and Daisy in the dining room this morning. *And I'm guessing Melissa wasn't too keen on this.*

I'm not being funny, Mum.

Neither am I. It feels like a TV drama. *Are you saying you're gay?*

The words are thick in Daisy's mouth. She cries into Mum's shoulder. Angela can't remember the last time she held Daisy like this. Mostly Daisy is relieved that Melissa no longer has the same leverage.

Have you told anyone else? She remembers Daisy abandoning her in the street the other day and feels as if she has won a competition to regain her daughter's affection, beaten Melissa, beaten Dominic. She rubs her hand in a circle on Daisy's back. Ten years vanish. Those nightmares. *I don't mind if you're gay.* She squeezes Daisy a little harder.

Daisy pulls back. *I'm not gay, OK?* Panic in her voice.

241

OK. Angela is treading carefully because this is veering rapidly away from the script.

I'm not gay, OK?

So you kissed Melissa because . . .? It sounds accusatory but she's trying to understand. A click of the latch and Benjy is standing in the doorway. *Later, yeh?* He backs out. She turns to Daisy. *Did you join the church because of this?* Suddenly it all fits together.

That's not why I joined the church. The old anger in her voice. Why the hell is Mum doing this now?

Sorry, says Angela. She holds Daisy's hands. Again a flash of Karen, real and possible daughters, the Daisy that might have been if the church didn't have its claws in her. She should say, *I'll help. I'll stay out of the way. Just tell me what you want me to do.* But why is it any different from her being in love with a violent boyfriend? There are so many ways of crushing a human being. *Are you going to talk to someone at church?*

Why would I talk to someone at church?

What would they say?

What has this got to do with anything?

Listen to me, says Angela.

Daisy puts her face in her hands.

I love you. Maybe you're gay, maybe you're not. It doesn't make the slightest bit of difference to me. But you have surrounded yourself with people who . . .

Daisy takes her face out of her hands. *No. Stop this. You're not listening to me. This has got nothing to do with the church.*

This has got nothing to do with you and your prejudices. Where is this stuff coming from? She's opened a bottle of something poisonous but it has no label and she can't find a way of putting the top back on. *I made a mistake. I made a stupid mistake.* She stands up.

Daisy, wait, I'm sorry.

Just . . . fuck off, OK? And the door bangs behind her.

Angela sits for a whole minute. The lopsided tick of the grandfather clock. Then she kneels and opens the door of the stove, takes an old edition of the *Daily Telegraph* from the basket and starts making balls of paper to place in the bed of ash. She is standing on the far side of the room watching herself. She lays a little raft of kindling along the top of the crumpled paper and takes the matches from the mantelpiece. She's screwed up, hasn't she, yet again. *This has got nothing to do with you.* A door had opened and she'd slammed it shut. Christ. Alex and Richard. She checked her watch. What a mess of a day.

Everyone else had left the dining room so Dominic and Louisa were alone. Angela was having the conversation with Daisy that he should have had. What did he feel? Thankful that it was now Angela's problem? Aggrieved at his exclusion? Shame at his procrastination? Mostly a return of the torpor that had laid him low before Waterstone's, the sense of life going on elsewhere, too fast, too complex, too demanding to grasp as it swung occasionally through his purview.

But what Louisa felt mostly was anger, anger at Richard

who was meant to stop her feeling scared, anger at herself for being so self-centred, anger at the stupid timing, discovering how dependent she was precisely when she discovered how fallible he was. She thought about him not being there and she was terrified by what might happen to her.

The living-room door opened and banged shut. Louisa jumped, thinking it might be Richard, but it was Daisy and things had obviously not gone well. Louisa disappeared into herself again. Dominic got to his feet. *I'll be back*. He left the room and suddenly there was no one and the house was silent and she imagined running after him and looking in one room after another and finding them all empty and shouting and no one replying, just the sound of the wind and the rain hammering on the windows.

They were well down the road now, past the junction, only a few hundred metres to go. The rain was easing a little, but Richard was leaning on him heavily, his steps becoming less regular and more unsteady. They fell clumsily onto a verge and Alex had great difficulty getting him to his feet. The ends of his fingers were yellow. *Richard?* But Richard's words were slurred and Alex was ashamed of having imagined him being dead and because this was really starting to freak him out. *Come on. Bloody walk, OK? I can't do this on my own.*

Angela was kneeling in front of the open stove cupping a lit match. Richard had made the fire every day so far and it was disturbing to find herself stepping into his empty place.

The paper caught. She sat back and closed the squeaky metal door. *I've just been talking to Daisy.*

I guessed.

Where did she start? *She kissed Melissa.*

I know, said Dominic.

What do you mean, you know?

I talked to Melissa.

You discussed this with Melissa?

Talked, not discussed. Daisy wouldn't say what was wrong, so I asked Melissa.

When?

Today, this morning.

Dominic and Daisy and their charmed circle. *When were you going to tell me?*

I don't think she wanted anyone to know.

Of course she didn't want anyone to know, because those bloody people have convinced her she'll go to hell. Was this what they thought at the church? She wasn't entirely sure. *And you were just going to leave her feeling shit about herself?* Why were they doing this? Their daughter was suffering and they were using it as an excuse to rehash arguments that had been going nowhere for years.

What did you say to her? asked Dominic. *Just now?*

I said I loved her. I said what any halfway sane parents would say. She paused and rubbed her face and took a long deep breath. *Please, let's not do this.* Dominic was staring at his feet, hands in pockets. Shamefaced? Or just biting his tongue? *I mentioned the church, OK? Because I always do.* She held her

245

hands up in surrender. The clatter of a chair being knocked over in the dining room. *She says she's not gay. She says it was an accident.* The fire blazed in its dirty window. *Will you talk to her? Because she won't listen to me and if she thinks she's a bad person because of that place . . .*

I'll talk to her. But what if they were wrong? What if loving God was easier than loving other human beings? Was an easy life such a bad thing to want? *Later on, maybe. When things have calmed down a little.*

She looked into the flames. It was meant to be relaxing, warmth in the darkness, keeping the wolves away, but the heat-proof glass made her think of some infernal substance caged at the reactor's core, a little fiend on a treadmill. Those photographs, her hunger to see them is so strong. She is reading a magazine or watching a film sometimes, she sees someone and wonders for an instant if it's him. Big men, strong men, flawed but honourable, men you can rely on when the chips are down, this righteous anger they keep to hand, like a holstered weapon, ready to use as a last resort. The opposite of Dominic. All those presumptions you carry with you your whole life, about what a family should be. What a husband should be. What a father should be.

Louisa wrestled the door open and they spilt clumsily into the hallway dragging several coats to the floor and tearing one of the pegs from the wall. *Oh my God. Richard?*

I'm OK. He sounded drunk.

She threw her arms around him but Alex gently peeled

her away. *Downstairs bathroom. Take his other arm.* Mum and Dad were sitting in the living room doing absolutely bugger all. Jesus. *Richard. You've got to help us.*

I should call an ambulance.

He'll be OK. We just need to warm him up. Would he, though? Alex wasn't sure. But an ambulance wouldn't get here for, what? an hour on these roads? *Whoa.* Richard stumbled sideways again, Alex just managing to keep him upright this time. *Get the bath running.* Louisa ran ahead through the kitchen. Relief and panic, about what might have happened, about what might still happen. *Almost there.* He manoeuvred Richard through the kitchen. Up ahead he heard the twist and thunder of the hot tap. An image of Callum rocking back and forth on the pavement weeping, the broken end of the shin bone pushing up under the skin. Across the utility room, Richard unstable on the bumpy stone floor, like a child or an old man, the onion smell of his sweat. They negotiated the chicane of the bathroom door, into the steamy air, Louisa's hands literally flapping. How were they going do this? He lowered Richard onto the toilet seat, put a hand behind his neck and removed the hat and the yellow jacket. *Shoes.* Louisa yanked them off. No way he was going to be able to remove Richard's other clothes but it didn't matter. This would not be elegant. He heaved Richard on to his feet, sat him on the edge of the bath then stepped in behind him, muddy trainers turning the water brown. He pulled Richard backwards and let him slip arse-down into the water, legs flopping in after, spraying brown water up the wall and all over Louisa's shirt. Result. Alex stepped out and tentatively let go. Richard held himself upright. *Go and get a hot drink. I'll stay here.* Louisa stepped out of the bathroom. The hot water continued to rise.

Richard is frightened, endorphins spent way back, cold at the base of his spine, in his pelvis, under his ribs. His teeth are still chattering. Alex says something but Richard is not sure what. He has an abscess, he needs to tell someone this before they put him under. *Come away, fellow sailors, your anchors be weighing.* His father stands in the doorway, arms crossed, that surly expression, letting the tension mount. Richard wonders if he is going be picked up and slapped across the legs. The smell of cigarette smoke and Old Spice. God, this hot water stung.

The ping of the microwave and the clicky slam of the plastic door and Louisa reappeared with what looked like a mug of warm milk. Made Alex think of waking up in the night when he was a child. He can smell honey, Louisa doing her folded napkins and hospital corners even now. She kneels and offers it to Richard. He takes it in his hands, which is a good sign, though he clearly can't move his fingers independently. Christ, what a strange picture. Richard in his clothes in a bath of oxtail soup, Louisa leaning over in a flowery shirt, muddy footprints over the white fluffy mat, like some grubby dogskin carpet. He sees the bloody graze on Richard's hand and looks down at his own scabbing knuckles. Louisa takes the mug and puts it down on the corner of the bath and starts to remove Richard's running vest. The bath almost full now. It feels uncomfortably intimate, watching her do this, the hair on Richard's chest, pudgy man breasts, the sheer bulk of him, pathetic and threatening at the same time. Alex feels he should leave but he can't. He imagines Louisa on top of Richard, naked. Is it stupid not to ring an ambulance? He turns and sees Mum and Dad in the doorway. Louisa is oblivious but Angela says, quietly, *How is he?* Alex simply shrugs to punish them for being so fucking useless.

Can we do anything?

Food, says Alex. He remembers an episode of *Born Survivor*. *Have we got any chocolate? Something soft and sugary.* Though his intention mostly is to get them out of the bathroom, because he has earned his place here in the centre of the drama and they haven't.

I'm on it, says Dominic.

It never occurred to Melissa that Richard might be in any kind of danger, he being the person who sorted out other people in danger, but when she came downstairs to make herself a mug of coffee she found Dominic heating a tin of soup and Angela said, *He's in the bath*, and Melissa wondered who the hell she was talking about.

Alex brought him back, said Dominic.

He's going to be all right, said Angela.

We hope.

And then it dawned on her, but Alex had appeared in the doorway, sopping wet, still wearing his trainers. *We're out of the woods, I think.* He went to the bread bin and cut himself a two-inch doorstep. *I need a shower. Melissa, can you go and grab some warm clothes for Richard?*

She bridled but now was clearly not the time. *Sure.* Sweetness and light. She turned and headed back into the dining room.

Alex took a large bite of bread. *Give me a shout if you need help, yeh?*

Then he, too, was gone and Dominic felt proud of his son. The young taking over the world; maybe it wasn't so bad after all.

Daisy stepped on to the landing and saw Melissa disappearing like a hotel chambermaid bearing a folded pile of clothes. Then Alex appeared in his towel, with a chunk of bread in his mouth. *Bit of an adventure downstairs.*

Yeh?

Twisted his ankle. Touch of hypothermia. He's in a hot bath. He gently moved her aside. *Now I need a shower or I'm going to go the same way.*

Suddenly she couldn't bear the idea of being alone any longer. *Can I come into the bathroom with you?*

He raised his eyebrows. *If you really want, I guess.* Because, after all, it was the kind of day when the normal rules had been temporarily suspended, so they went in, she shut the door behind her and sat on the toilet. Vosene, Miracle Moist, Louisa's chequered pink washbag. He turned the shower on, took another bite of bread, placed the remaining crust on the rim of the sink then dropped the towel and stepped behind the big plastic panel, turning away from her to protect his modesty. Dints in the side of his bottom, the muscles in his back, unexpectedly at home without his clothes. She remembered how she felt about her body when she was swimming, not caring what it looked like, just enjoying the way it worked. They felt like *the children*, again.

So you're a bit of a hero, then?

I wouldn't go that far. But she could hear the pride in his voice. *God, this feels good.* His pleasure in the hot water oddly more intimate than the sight of his body.

She liked being in here together, hiding almost, comforting and secret. *But he's all right now?* His silhouette blurred and fogged behind the steamy plastic.

I think so. He bent down to clean the mud off his ankles. *He was pretty far gone when I got him back to the house.* Squirting shampoo onto his hair. *What a pillock.*

I saw he'd bought loads of new running kit.

Not looking very new now.

She sat quietly for a while. He turned the shower off and stepped out, turning away from her to pick up his towel and dry himself. Like a model, but like a little boy, too. He put the last piece of bread in his mouth and said, *Right. I need to pee at this point in time, which feels kind of weird so you might want to, like, stand over there and look the other way.*

I think I might be gay. As if someone else had spoken on

her behalf, as if someone had pushed her off that top board. Time stuck, rippled banners of light on the water's surface way below, the ring of cold and the blue silence.

You think? He really had knitted his brows, as if he were struggling with a crossword puzzle.

Does that sound totally insane?

A bit. Lesbian. Christ. He'd never met a lesbian, never really thought about them outside porn, except they weren't really lesbians. Too good-looking. Or was that being prejudiced? *Does this mean you're not a Christian any more?*

I'm scared, Alex. She was going to cry. *And now you have to say something. Please?*

He had to think about this and it was complicated. If she was male it would freak him out, trying not to picture the sex part. But this? He imagined her having a girlfriend which would be sort of like having two sisters. Unless the girlfriend was horrible, or ugly.

Please?

He tried to sit down on the toilet seat beside her but it was too small, plus he was half naked, so he knelt beside her and gave her an inelegant hug.

I kissed Melissa.

What?

I kissed Melissa.

Holy shit. Is she a lesbian, too?

It was kind of an accident. She ripped off four squares of toilet paper and blew her nose.

He moved to the edge of the bath. *I kissed her, too. She*

wasn't too keen on that, either. He expected Daisy to laugh but she didn't seem to have heard. *She is pretty fit, though.*

She called me a fucking dyke.

And suddenly he got it, why she was terrified. The shit she was going to get. Losing all her friends because of the church, those sanctimonious arseholes kicking her out, maybe. He wanted to slap Melissa's face. *Is this, like, a new thing?*

No. Yes. I feel like such an idiot.

They were silent for a few moments. This flatness. Surely the moment deserved more, mariachi trumpets, a thunderbolt striking her dead. *I told Mum.*

And . . . ?

She was crap. As usual.

Christ, said Alex. *This is one bizarre day.* Daisy looked offended. *Bizarre in a good way. You know, Richard not being dead after all, and you . . .* What? *You not being dead either?*

Alex? Dominic was calling from downstairs.

Alex stood up. *OK, now I really have to pee. Go and tell Dad I'll be down in a couple of minutes, yeh?*

She didn't move. He felt it, too, a sense that the event should be marked in some way. But how?

Dad shouted again. *Alex . . . ?*

He lay on the sofa, big jumper, mug of sweet tea, left leg up on Louisa's lap. She put the bag of frozen peas aside and began winding the elderly bandage around his ankle. First aid box under the sink from circa 1983. The door of the fire was open so that he could feel the heat on the side of his face. Franck

in the background, the violin and piano sonata, Martha
Argerich and Dora Schwarzberg. *There, that should do it.* He
felt a little queasy on account of the Mars Bars Alex had
forced him to eat in the bath, that jittery fatigue and joint
ache like when you had flu. Louisa fastened the bandage with
a safety pin. Little waves of anxiety rose and fell, the body's
alarm system saying, *This is not right*, though he knew, object-
ively, that he was recovering. Just clipped the edge of severe
hypothermia, if he remembered the textbooks correctly. Louisa
lifted his ankle and slipped a cushion under it to raise it a
little higher. Paradoxical undressing and terminal burrowing
in the final stages. Always unnerved him that image, the body
of the old man naked in the cupboard. Bit of a shock to find
that dying might be unpleasant after all. He'd always assumed
that the brain shrank to fit the little door you left by, Montaigne
being knocked off his horse and so on. Die in a hospital, that
was the lesson. Decent morphine driver. But it felt good, being
looked after like this. Louisa laid the frozen peas back over
his ankle and picked up her Stephen Fry. Ridiculous that it
should take such a big adventure to make them do this, simply
sit next to one another doing nothing. But that pillbox, the
one behind his father. They went inside, didn't they? He and
Angela. He can remember the smell of urine and a smashed
Coca-Cola bottle. Camping or caravan? Chips out of newspaper, trying to surf on a blue lilo.

Richard? She touched his shoulder.

He came round. *I'm just tired.* She was examining him
but he couldn't read her expression. Her words of last night.

Your plays. Your films. He was selfish, wasn't he? All those years with Jennifer, two single people sharing a house. *You're right. I do expect you to fit in with my life.*

I shouldn't have said those things.

But they're true. Up there on the hill, he had forgotten about her, hadn't he? He thought he might die and he didn't remember that he had a wife. *I worry that you might have married the wrong person.*

Hey. Come on. She rubbed his shoulder.

Trade Descriptions Act and all that. I wouldn't want you to think . . . It's not a binding contract.

You're exhausted. She put her arm around him. *Let's talk about this later, when you're warm again.*

How extraordinary that it should happen so quickly. Like flipping a coin. Inexplicable that she had not known before. Had it been standing behind her all along like a pantomime villain, visible to everyone apart from her? What strangers we were to ourselves, changed in the twinkling of an eye. Jack, too, of course, she understood now, that sense of betrayal, stone circles at midsummer, all those signs that meant nothing till the sun poured into the burial chamber. Katy Perry, *Maurice*, that article in the *Guardian* magazine, *Mulholland Drive*. She wanted to be held by someone who had been here before. Lesbian. The word like some creature lifted from a rock pool, all pincers and liquids and strangeness. Melissa of all people. What a fool she'd been. The church. There wasn't really an argument, was there? Meg, Anushka, Lesley,

Tim. *Fait accompli. And the walls came tumbling down.* So who was she now? She sank down so that she was squashed into the nook beside the wardrobe. The safety of a tight space. She hadn't done this since she was six, hiding from the monsters. She lifted Harry from the carpet and hugged him tight, rocking gently back and forth. Seedy passageways and sad hotels. Dogshit through the letter box.

Bizarre in a good way. No mariachi trumpets, no thunderbolt. But he just shrugged and accepted it. Mr Normal. What more did she want? *When you get the chance to be saved, you have to take it.* Silvered Bible flashing on the beach. How quickly she had found her faith. The twinkling of an eye. And now the footmen were turning back into mice and she was sitting in her sooty rags by the fire.

Dominic stopped halfway up the stairs. He imagined Alex in hospital, imagined Benjy in hospital. Like a lump of meat he couldn't swallow, finding it hard to breathe. His own fear of anything medical, just that blood pressure cuff at the doctor's, the tear of the Velcro and that squeezy black bulb. Maybe she *was* moist and wretched, but when was the last time he had felt real joy? She'd wanted to move to New Zealand, but he could feel the same pull, clean air, blank slate. And how far had he got? *Life is not a rehearsal.* The irksome truth of barroom platitudes. He had to call her.

Richard was falling asleep against her shoulder, twitching gently like a dog dreaming. What was it about this house?

Throwing everyone out of kilter, her and Richard, Angela in the kitchen at night, Daisy and Melissa being enemies then friends then enemies again, her own stupid confession. That chill, maybe it was our own ghosts. Maybe that was why she hated old houses, because we all had past lives that rose up. As if you could wipe out history with downlighting and scatter cushions. *You might have married the wrong person.* Perhaps he could see what she had spent so long trying not to see, that she was still the girl with the second-hand shoes, hanging over that woozy drop at the Hanwell flat, scooters and discos and Penny flashing her knickers so they could steal packs of John Player Special from the corner shop. Working in a petrol station now, that weird chance encounter last time back. The fire was going out, but if she moved she might wake him and she was scared that this might be the last time she was able to hold him like this.

They were having an improvised buffet lunch at the dining table when they heard footsteps on the stairs. Daisy paused in the doorway looking uneasy. It took Alex several seconds to remember because he'd helped dress a naked Richard five minutes ago, which had kind of taken up most of his short-term memory. He glanced across at Melissa. *Fucking dyke.* He decided to make this as obvious as he could. *Daisy . . .* He lifted his arm so that she walked over and stepped under it and let him squeeze her shoulders. He looked directly at Melissa and saw it in her eyes, she knew that he knew, Mum, too, a beaten look about her. And it was glorious and funny, seeing his parents and Melissa on the same team for once, at the other end of the pitch, several goals down. He turned to Daisy. *What can I serve you from this fine spread?*

But Daisy said, *What on earth is that?*

Tolliver, said Benjy, because the owl was sitting under its big dusty belljar in the centre of the table.

Cupboard under the stairs, said Dominic, trying to pull the family back together. *Belongs to the owners.*

The owners, said Daisy. She'd never thought about them, looking around as if she might be able to see them.

Alex did her a plate of cheese and oatcakes and assorted dips and they sat side by side eating, their radiant togetherness gradually driving everyone else out of the room apart from Benjy. Mum and Dad both touching Daisy on the shoulder as they exited, as if they were leaving a wake and she were the bereaved wife. Then they were gone and Benjy was building a model bridge out of hummus and carrots so Alex said, quietly, *Are you going to get a girlfriend, then?*

Alex. God. It's not like buying a toaster.

My bad.

Girlfriend. The lurch of the world. She remembered a freezing January morning. Coming out of the Wheelan Centre. Smoky breath and mauve sky and the street lights going off. She and Lauren had held hands for ten, fifteen seconds, no more, then someone was walking towards them along the pavement and they'd let go. Like cuddling up when you were half asleep and pretending it never happened. Lauren. *For now we see only as a reflection in a mirror; then we shall see face to face.* It wasn't simple, was it, or quick? The coin flipped, and flipped, and flipped.

Time speeding up now, Lauren answering a door in a street Daisy doesn't recognise. Husband, two kids, the telly on in the background, face tired and lined but beautiful. *We were at school together . . .? Are you sure . . .?* Turning and running down the street in tears. And now she was crying for real and Alex rubbed her back and said, *Come on, girl.* Benjy looked up. *Is Daisy OK?* And Alex was genuinely unsure if she was crying because she was happy or sad. It was all getting a bit beyond him. So Benjy got off his bench and came round and sat on the other side of Daisy and wrapped his arms around her and said, *Daisy sandwich,* because that's what they used to do with him when he was sad. They squeezed and let go.

Shit, said Daisy, wiping her eyes with an abandoned tea towel. *Shitting shit.*

They play cards, they eat toast, they watch *Monsters Inc.* and Richard says, *This is actually rather good,* like the queen getting a mobile phone for Christmas, and everyone laughs because he has suddenly become more teasable. The chequered rug, perhaps, the fogginess in his voice, the way Louisa is nursing his foot. Though it is extraordinary, isn't it? thinks Angela. She can remember the thrill of getting a colour television, she can remember when the *Thunderbirds* puppets were at the cutting edge of animation despite the fact that you could see the wires used to raise their eyebrows, whereas now . . .? *You can't tell the real dinosaurs from the animated ones*, as someone said somewhere.

Melissa tries to ring civilisation but they've swung out of the signal's orbit once again, so that when Angela challenges her to a game of Scrabble she is so spectacularly bored that she agrees and the two of them play as if it is a fight to the death. Orts. Beguine. Phalanx for ninety-five. Benjy and Alex concoct a fantasy in which the ginger man and the girl with *Charlie's Angels* hair are merely outer coverings for jelly-like aliens who feed on elderly people. Richard listens to *Idomeneo* (Colin Davis, Francisco Araiza, Barbara Hendricks . . .). Daisy looks at the pages of *Dracula* but the words just swim. Alex reads Andy McNab and Louisa reads Stephen Fry and Dominic goes away to start making supper and the rain stops and the world looks as if it has been serviced and mended and given back.

The owner of this Orange mobile number is unavailable . . .

Jack. Hey. It's Daisy. Remember? She looked around at the moraine of boy-crap. *I'm halfway up a small mountain on the Welsh border. We're on holiday. Listen . . .* She looked out of the window. Benjy was on the lawn getting sopping wet, doing Ninja moves with a stick, except it wasn't a Ninja weapon, was it, it was an umbrella and he was Gene Kelly. *I'm really sorry. I think I understand now. If that rings any kind of bell then give me a call, yeh? It would be really good to hear from you.*

*   *   *

Gingerly, Angela thinks about Karen, about the birthday, just grazing the subject, like touching an electric fence with the back of your hand to stop your fingers gripping the live wire. Nothing. It's the photographs of Dad, as if there's been an absence all along and she's been trying to fill it with the wrong person. A weight begins to lift. A little anxious, still, that Richard might not be able to find the pictures, that they might get lost in the post, that Dad might be turning away or obscured somehow, that he might not be looking at her.

Big pie, two enamelled baking tins, *Idomeneo* in the background, *Odo da lunge armonioso suono . . . In the distance I hear the sweet sound summoning me aboard . . .* Tomato sauce with onions and garlic, because they'd been planning to swing by whatever supermarket they could find in Abergavenny before the Richard debacle, so Dominic has offered to make what he has christened rather grandly Olchon Valley Pie which will include pretty much anything he can find in the fridge and cupboards, parsnips, carrots, spinach, butter beans, pasta shells, pine nuts, chopped apricots, the last two of which will turn out to be an unexpected hit. All topped off with mashed potato and that weird cheese with the lost wrapper no one can identify. And on the side, to prevent Richard getting anaemia, slices of Saucisson Sec Supérieur à l'ancienne. Oyster Bay Sauvignon Blanc, McGuigan Hallmark Cabernet Shiraz, Hooky Gold, Bath Ales Barnstormer, apple juice, mango juice, strawberry and banana smoothie. Fizzy water. Pistachios.

★   ★   ★

Are you going to say grace? asked Richard, which created an unexpected silence. He scanned the room. Melissa was grinning. *Have I put my foot in it somehow?*

Not at all, said Daisy. She lowered her head. *For what we are about to receive, may the Lord make us truly thankful. Amen.*

They sat down and Dominic pushed the big slotted spoon into the pie and Benjy said, *I want lots of cheesy topping.*

Louisa leant in close to Angela and whispered, *What was all that about?* and Angela said, *Oh, it's nothing.*

But Daisy could feel the coin flipping again, because it wasn't a *fait accompli.* You couldn't give your faith away like that. It wasn't a coat or a bicycle, it was a language in which you'd learnt to speak and think. *God be in my head and in my understanding.* Prayer, faith, redemption, consolation, how did you hold the world together without these things?

Richard shifted carefully in his chair, trying to find the least uncomfortable position, the Nurofen not quite taking the edge off. He looked across the table at Louisa. He had been humbled. Was that too dramatic a word? He had always seen his self-sufficiency as an admirable quality, a way of not imposing upon other people, but he could see now that it was an insult to those close to you. He had never been interested enough in Louisa's opinions, her thoughts, her tastes, her life. A stab of shame. *If this becomes a habit you will find yourself in great difficulty later in life.*

Daisy glanced sideways at Melissa, trying not to catch her eye. Had she misunderstood completely? Was this simply one more stage in her spiritual journey, a test she had failed and must retake? She tried to unpick her thoughts and feelings but there were too many. That smashed plate, so hard to see the broken pattern. The afternoon with Jack, Melissa pulling down her knickers to show her the bluebird tattoo. *She is pretty fit, though.* Lauren's hand in the cold dawnlight, images so vivid she was scared to bring them before her mind's eye for fear that they would spill out and be visible to everyone. *The Lord is the stronghold of my life.*

Dominic got a signal a couple of hundred yards up the road. He turned and leant against a fence and looked back down towards the house, golden windows swimming in the gathering dark. He could feel his heart beating. As always, the desire to carry on walking, to put this all behind him, over the hills and far away. He had to do it now, the longer it went on the more he would hurt her. Seven rings, eight. The hope that she wouldn't answer.

Dom.

Amy.

I'd almost given up on you.

We're in a valley. The reception is non-existent. Sinister, the pleasure one got from lying well. *How's Andrew?*

He's doing OK.

He felt cheated. *You said he had to go into hospital.*

He should be out tomorrow.

I thought he had pneumonia.

So did the doctors.

Had she been lying, too? It would make him feel better. *Listen.*

What?

Do it. *I've realised something. Over the last few days.*

Dom?

You and me.

What are you saying?

I'm saying . . .

I love you, Dom. Crying now.

But she didn't love him, did she, she needed him, that was all, needed someone. This was not his job.

Don't do this to me, Dom.

The way she said his name, like a child tugging at his sleeve, she suffocated him. How was it possible to explain that? A sudden anger at the way she used her weakness to manipulate him.

Dom?

I've made a mess of everything. It was meant to be a performance but he had unexpectedly stumbled on the truth. *I have to stop running away.* A balloon swelling and rising inside him. *From work, from responsibility, from Angela, from Daisy, from Alex, from Benjy.* Why had he not done this before?

I don't know what I would do without you. Is this real? Or is she crying wolf? *You're leaving me.*

He let this hang. He felt shitty and noble at the same time, but people did this every day, hurting people for the greater good. Collateral damage.

And you're doing it over the fucking phone.

The anger in her voice gave him more purchase. *You want me to lie now and say it to your face when we next meet?*

I want you not to treat me like dirt.

The Japanese paper lantern, her little breasts, the way her hip bones stuck out when she lay on her back. Suddenly he wanted her. What if he cashed in his advantage and re-established the relationship on more advantageous terms?

I'm not letting you do this to me, Dom.

The phone went dead and the great silence flooded in. The coloured screen hovered in the dark, then dimmed. She had outplayed him. He was angry that she managed to have the last word and frightened that it might not be the last. He had never thought before about what she might do to herself, or to him, or to his family. He put the phone back in his pocket and turned to look up the hill. A monumental wave of absolute dark that looked as if it was about to crash down upon him.

It seemed like a good time to mend fences after the marijuana thing and the Richard thing and the kiss thing so she offered to help Mum wash up after supper and while they were doing the glasses, she said, *I have some excellent gossip.*

I'm not sure I want to hear this.

Daisy's gay.

OK . . . said Louisa carefully. This was what scared her. How good Melissa was at keeping you on the back foot. The hoarder and user of secrets.

She tried to kiss me.

265

Melissa was too good a liar to risk inventing something as wild as this.

When we were out for a walk. She took the tea towel off the rail of the Aga and folded it neatly into a square one-eighth of its original size. *I said it wasn't really my thing.*

It was a peace offering, something freshly killed brought back to the cave. Louisa didn't want to be part of this, but it was too intriguing to drop. *I thought she was a Christian.*

I think she might be having a bit of trouble in that department.

Then Louisa put two and two together. The girls were friendly, then they weren't friendly. *Were you horrid to her about it?*

I'm just worried about her, that's all. Regaining her balance after being wrong-footed.

That wasn't what I asked you.

Like I said, I told her I wasn't into that kind of stuff.

Nor was that.

Why do you have to blame everything on me? Why is it always me who's done something wrong? She spun and swept out of the kitchen.

Louisa would find a way of talking to Daisy tomorrow, apologise for whatever her daughter had done this time.

So, tell me about the photos. Angela leant across the table and refilled Richard's glass, the Cabernet Shiraz finally doing what the Nurofen had failed to do.

They're Polaroids. Is that the word? The ones you had to shake.

Describe them to me. It sounds crazy. But this is her father.

OK. So . . . Richard rubs the corners of his mouth and looks over her head as if the pictures are hung, poster-sized, on the far wall. *One must have been taken on holiday. He's standing in front of a pillbox in the dunes. Normandy in 1968, I suspect, or possibly the Scilly Isles a couple of years later.*

She is taken aback yet again by the clarity of her brother's memory. *But him, what does he look like?*

He's wearing one of those check shirts, thin brown stripes on a cream background. He's enjoying this. You have thirty seconds to remember all the objects on the tray. *His sleeves are rolled up, he's smoking, he's smoking in all three photos, actually. God knows how long he would have survived if the testicular cancer hadn't got him.*

His casualness grates, but she knows that they are navigating through strong currents and she must keep the tiller straight.

Number two. He's leaning on the bonnet of the car, green Hillman Avenger, that long radiator grille with the square headlights at each end. Looks like he's just polished it. I think there's a shammy leather on the roof. He's wearing a short-sleeved white shirt.

Tell me about him. Not his clothes but him.

There is something disturbing about her intensity. *Do you really not remember?*

Just tell me.

Thick black hair, sideburns, big man, big biceps. He doesn't like this. It conjures his father a little too vividly. Rusted metal and sheer bulk and sea spray. Blood in his hair. He wonders whether it was not the gull, he wonders whether

it was his father who hit him, whether he has misremembered. *Why do you want to know so badly?*

He's my father. Wasn't it obvious? *If it was me who had the
photographs and if you'd never seen them, wouldn't you be curious?*

No. I really don't think I would.

Why not?

Because he was not a very nice man.

She shakes her head. Not disagreement, but disbelief.

Do you really not remember?

She is trying to work out a solution which will allow
them to disagree diplomatically. *We all look back and see things
differently.* She says this quietly, amused almost, as if it is he
who needs to be calmed down.

That's true. He sits back and takes a sip of wine. He wants
to let it go, send her the photographs, have done with it,
but this is more than simply seeing things differently. *Do you
not remember him hitting us?*

Everyone hit their kids back then. Though she is unsure
precisely what Richard means by *hitting*.

*I remember you being sick in the car. We were driving to
Hunstanton one summer. You kept asking to pull over but he
wouldn't, as per usual. So you were sick and then he swerved into
this gateway and took you out and put you over his knee and
slapped your legs. He was so angry, he just kept on hitting you.*
The memory upsets him more than he expects.

*Why are you doing this? Why are you trying to mess this up
for me?*

Because you are ill. The thought suddenly clear and sharp.

He veers away. *I think you were scared of him, too. And I think you've forgotten.*

Dad was not a monster.

I'm not saying he was a monster.

Then what the hell are you saying?

I'm saying he got angry. I'm saying he didn't care much about other people. I'm saying he didn't know how to deal with children. And he scared me and I don't particularly like looking at the photographs because it makes me remember what that felt like.

Is this what Mum told you? Is this her version?

I don't remember Mum saying a single thing about him after he died. The grieving process, 1970. He wonders if he should reach out and hold Angela's hand but he is not very good at judging these things.

You and Mum, she says. *You visited Dad in hospital, the day before he died. I wasn't allowed to go. I hated you for that. I had this recurring dream in which you'd both killed him.* She tries to make it sound like a joke but she can't, because she still has the dream sometimes.

You didn't want to go.

What?

Why on earth would you not be allowed to go?

Because that's what Mum was like, because she enjoyed manipulating people, because she never wanted other people to be happy.

After he died, after she started drinking, when she realised she was pouring her life away, then she was difficult, then she enjoyed manipulating people. He pauses and readjusts his focus. *I think it was the only power she had left.*

Why wouldn't I go to the hospital? He was my father.

He shrugs. He still can't quite grasp why this is so important to her. *I guess the extraordinary thing is that I wanted to go
myself.* He is looking for a way of saying this which isn't
accusatory. *Why would anyone want to see their father dying.
Me . . .? I don't know. Maybe there was a doctor waiting to get
out even then.* He wonders, on some deep level, if he did
indeed want his father to die, whether he went to make sure
it was happening, to say good riddance, to be certain he
wasn't coming back.

Stop. Wait. This is too much.

Sorry. He holds up his hands.

She wants him to be wrong, but he's not inventing it, is
he? He has no axe to grind, and she has no story of her
own to pit against his. She stands clumsily. *I need to be on my
own for a while.*

Going upstairs her legs feel weak. Is Dominic still out on
his walk? The room is empty. She sits on the edge of the
bed. The blankness again. *What year is this?* That woman on
the train, red string, liver-spotted hands. *I can't quite . . .* Dad
slapping her in the lay-by, a picture half forming on the wet
grey surface of the shaken photo. If she has the past wrong,
does she have the present wrong, too? Her father is vanishing
again. The empty doorway. Stems and slime. Another figure
materialising in the dark rectangle. Thickening in waves. A
high buzzing sound. Karen. She has betrayed her, forgotten
her, let her slip away. Rainbow-coloured windbreak, flicking
the hair out of her eyes. She's laughing and it is not a kind

laugh. Her birthday. It's tomorrow. In all the excitement over the photographs Angela had forgotten. She is going to be punished for this.

How are you doing?

Richard was sitting up in bed with Antony Beevor's *Stalingrad* closed on his lap. *Better. Significantly better.* He should have bought something trashy to read, though that was even harder work in his experience, like listening to someone play an instrument badly.

She sat on the bed and took her earrings out, leaning her head first to one side then the other.

I'm worried about Angela.

I never told you. She laid the earrings carefully in the lacquered Indian box with all the others. Elephants and jasmine flowers. *I found her in the kitchen the other night.*

Found in what sense?

She was standing in the dark, eating a bowl of cereal.

Why didn't you tell me?

Because I was angry with you and I wasn't sure that Angela wanted the fact broadcast.

He laid *Stalingrad* aside. *Are you still angry with me?*

When you said it wasn't a binding contract . . .

I don't appreciate you enough.

Is this a crappy roundabout way of saying you don't love me?

I think . . . He shifted up a little straighter in bed. *I think actually it's a crappy roundabout way of saying I'm not terribly keen on myself.*

Richard . . .

Wait. Downstairs the front door boomed shut. Dominic coming back from his late-night ramble. *When you asked me whether I loved you or not . . .*

Stop. Listen. Do you enjoy being with me?

I do.

Do you want me to be happy?

Very much so.

Do you find me attractive?

I think you know the answer to that.

What would you do if I left and you were on your own?

I'd think I'd very possibly fall to pieces, not immediately maybe, but . . .

Would you risk your life for me?

I'd risk my life for many people. A small child running into the road, a woman drowning in a river. *Correction. I think I would actually give my life for you. If it were me or you. Lifeboat, burning building.* He had never thought about this before.

Bloody hell, Richard. If that's not love . . . She sounded genuinely annoyed.

I've never really loved anyone, or been loved, come to think of it, as an adult, I mean. He looked at his hands as if the notes written on his palm no longer made sense. *Dear God, that was breathtakingly mawkish, wasn't it? The other men, by the way. Am I allowed to feel a little jealous?*

They were horrible and I was having a shitty time. She laid her head on his lap. *Incidentally, Daisy's a lesbian. Apparently.*

He looked at the ceiling. He felt suddenly exhausted. *You're going to have to tell me that again in the morning.*

Daisy wants happiness, of course, to belong, to be loved, but more than this she wants her life to have some kind of shape, not just this pinball zigzag from one accident to another. Even tragedy will do, so long as she can say, *I see now what it means. This is who I am.*

Has she discovered the truth or lost her way? What will happen at church, at school, at home? Jack hasn't rung back and she doesn't know what this means. She has no idea what Mum or Dad really feel, no idea, in truth, what she feels herself, except for a yearning so intense and nameless that she doesn't know if it is a longing for a girlfriend, or for God, or simply for those everyday discomforts which now seem in retrospect a blessing. She can't read, can't even lie down, so she paces, now staring out of the window into the dark, now squatting in the corner of the room, now sitting on the chair and rocking gently back and forwards. *Do not be fooled, this is not a place.*

Benjy lay for a while looking at the inverted cream pyramid of the lampshade. It reminded him of a film in which someone was wheeled into an operating theatre and the camera was looking up at the ceiling from their point of view. This, in turn, made him think of Carly's dad from school having his heart attack which made him think about Granny's funeral and he was scared that he might have one of those dreams that wasn't quite a dream. He looked at the clock. 11:30. Mum and Dad might still be awake. He went out on to the landing, walked to the top of the stairs, looked over the banisters and saw that the lights were on in the dining room. When he went down and stood in the hall, however, he could hear no one. *Mum . . .? Dad . . .?* He was afraid of stepping through the door for fear that someone was behind it holding their breath.

He was going to turn and walk silently back upstairs when he heard a beep and saw a light come on briefly in the pocket of a coat hanging by the door. It made him jump at first but it was a text message arriving on a mobile phone and this made the house seem more modern and humdrum. The phone was in Dad's coat. Mum allowed him to play the games on her phone, but he was never allowed to play on Dad's. So he invented a story in which Dad was receiving a vital message from someone who was in grave danger and who needed help. He would look at the message and take the phone up to Dad who would be cross at first then really grateful. He paused beside the coat, listening again to the silence. If it wasn't a message calling for help he could simply put the phone back and no one would know. He slipped his hand into the pocket and extracted it. He wanted a mobile of his own, not really for making calls, but for the way it felt so right in the palm of his hand, like a gun or a dagger. He pressed the main button and the face lit up. In the background was the photograph of him and Daisy and Alex on the big pebbly beach near Blakeney, and in the centre of the screen was a little blue square saying *Message*. He tapped it. Blakeney vanished and the message said, *call me I can't bear this any longer amy xxx* and he didn't know whether this was an emergency or a secret, only that he had done something very wrong.

Thursday

Louisa lies on her pillow, watching Richard sleep. Something first date about it, that shiver, not knowing whom you're inviting into your life.

Dominic shits in the half-light, blind down, opening the window afterwards to clear the smell.

Daisy almost wakes, senses something dangerous at the cave's mouth and turns back to the furs and embers and smoke.

Benjy thinks he has had a bad dream, except it's not a bad dream, is it, because it happened last night. He gets up, hoping to outrun the memory, makes himself a breakfast of Bran Flakes and red grape juice, plays *Super Mario* and reads *Mr Gum*, but when his mind's eye wanders he sees it watching him, like a hooded figure from an upstairs window.

Angela lies looking at the little rose-coloured lamp on the bedside table, knowing that something bad is going to happen, not knowing how to prepare for its arrival. Every day she finds out more and understands less. This lostness? Do other people feel this? Do other people live with this?

A tremor as Alex ran past the point where he'd found Richard. The narrowness of the escape. They'd come close on occasions, him, Jamie, Josh, slipping on Crib Goch, going over that weir with Aaron during one of the Watersides, but they were funny afterwards, whereas this upset him, the weird feeling that he had made it happen in some way. But it was fucking amazing up here, like a different place today, like being inside the sky. Sad to leave it behind. As if he owned it in some small way. He checked his watch. 10:15. Clocktower at 12:30, no problem. Last third pretty much downhill all the way. Almost disappointed by the good weather. Two thermals and a waterproof in the zip pocket of his bottle belt, cash, mobile, Twix. Quite liked the idea of running through another storm like yesterday, showing everyone how to do it. Plus the other disturbing thing was that he'd had a wank that morning thinking about Melissa kissing another girl, but the other girl kept turning into Daisy so he had to have one of those really quick wanks where you just went for it and didn't think about anything at all.

Daisy came down late hoping at least that she would be able to sit and eat alone, but when she was pouring herself a bowl of cereal Dad walked into the kitchen wearing his pyjamas and yawning. *Morning, you.* She was angry that he was intruding, that he knew, or didn't know, angry that he was going to say something stupid. He took a mug off the shelf, added a teabag and set it down next to hers. *Mum told me, about you and Melissa.*

It's not about me and Melissa.

I know, I know. He folded his arms and leant against the sink and looked at the floor, trying to take up as little space as possible. Like a dog cowering, she thought. *I just wanted to say that it's fine.*

Fine? As if she'd dyed her hair or got a Saturday job.

What I meant was, it doesn't change the way I think about you.

She put her hands on the worksurface and breathed deeply. One, two. The room was unsteady, because it wasn't fine, because it changed the way she thought about everything. So why was everyone else so fucking calm? Why was everyone else so fucking pleasant? At least Melissa *reacted*. Daisy wanted it to spin through their lives like a typhoon, ripping stuff apart.

He stood up. *I'll make my tea later.* He touched her shoulder lightly but the skin under his fingers felt like it was going to burn and blister.

They had decided to go to Hay again, like they were circling a black hole and no longer had the fuel to reach escape velocity. Richard was having trouble walking without the polished wooden cane they'd found in the umbrella stand and they knew what they were getting in Hay, whereas Abergavenny might turn out to be a disappointment, goat's hair periwigs and Rudolf Hess notwithstanding, and only Benjy was voting for the falconry centre. Plus, like Dominic said, this wasn't a *Michelin Guide* holiday, Palazzo Vecchio and the Boboli Gardens, this was the kind of holiday where you appreciated the things you really should have been appreciating at home, walks, conversation, communal meals, the passing of time itself. Also Louisa had seen that little jewellery shop as they were leaving last time and when Angela reminded Benjy about The Shop of Crap the falconry centre was dropped like a hot potato.

Richard was adamant that he could still drive, the Mercedes being automatic, and it seemed politic not to undermine his manhood any further. Louisa said she'd take a taxi and anyone else was free to join her, so that she could pay without it seeming like charity. Richard asked Angela to come with him because he wanted to continue the conversation of last night. He didn't say as much but Dominic, Daisy and Melissa all sensed the seriousness of something unsaid and opted for the taxi, whereas Benjy sensed nothing at all and said he'd go with them because the Mercedes was a really cool car and sometimes taxis smelt funny.

Is this OK? Handel Orchestral Works, Trevor Pinnock. Generic compilation stuff.

It's fine, said Angela.

The tyres slipped on the gravelly mud as he negotiated a tight little hairpin. His ankle hurt, but it was a good pain, like a bruise after a game of rugby. *I apologise for last night.*

It doesn't matter. Angela couldn't remember immediately what they had talked about last night. Then it came back, the imaginary father she never actually had.

But it does matter, said Richard. *I upset you.*

Really, said Angela. *It wasn't your fault.* She wanted to be left alone.

I'm not saying it was anyone's fault. What I'm saying is . . .

The way the road twisted and dipped and rose, thought Angela. It was like being in a film of your own life.

What I'm saying is that I'm worried about you.

Why? Not even a question, really, just knocking the ball back over the net.

Louisa said that today was . . . that today would have been her birthday. He glanced in the rear-view mirror to check that Benjy was immersed in a game on his little portable computer thing, then lowered his voice. *The baby you miscarried.*

Angela nodded. Strange that it didn't upset her, Richard not knowing her name. She felt numb, a heavy curtain between her and the world. *I'll be fine.*

He pulled into a gateway to let a muddy quad bike past, bale of hay tied to the back, young farmer at the wheel, wearing what looked like a comedy Christmas jumper, red, green and white, reindeer and zigzags. Maybe he should back off. But he'd been backing off for thirty years and he wanted to be a proper brother. But how did you help someone if they refused to ask for help? He reached over and touched her forearm. *You know you can talk to me if you want. I'll shut up and just listen this time.*

I know.

He wondered if he, too, had been damaged, by their father dying, by their mother drinking. He thought of himself as having put it all behind him, but his decision to marry someone who kept her distance, his failure to have children, his lack of interest in his own interior landscape . . . A sheep in the road. He slowed as it bounced and sprinted ahead. Such stupid animals, you'd think they'd learn to stand on the verge until a car had passed. It squirted through a hole in the fence. Wrong field, probably. Angela closed her eyes and leant back against the headrest, dozing or faking sleep. He readjusted the rear-view mirror. Benjy was still playing his game. Was he lonely or just self-absorbed? Both, maybe. Geometrical diagrams and the House of Hanover. 1972 in silver foil. Everyone in their little worlds.

They joined the main road and seven texts pinged onto Melissa's phone. *ring me we're so in the shit cal x . . . I'm really really really sorry. megan x . . . ring me megan has dumped us in it cally x . . .* She couldn't face reading the others.

Being the man, Dominic had been voted into the front seat to converse with the taxi driver who was telling him a story about how his brother lost his farm outside Llandovery during the foot and mouth epidemic. Green numbers on the meter flicking over, the little map on the satnav twisting, though this was probably the kind of place where it led you up cattle tracks and into ravines. He was having trouble concentrating on what the taxi driver was saying. Stupidly he'd left his mobile in his coat pocket overnight. He was relieved at first to find no message, then he checked the inbox and found one sitting there unflagged. Had someone read it? He wished he were sharing a car with Angela so that he could see her face and hear her voice and stop this churning anxiety. Amy's threat of last night. *I'm not letting you do this to me.* But what was his offence? They weren't going to spend the rest of their lives together, he was saving them both from a terrible mistake. It had always been an experiment. If she'd wanted more she should have said so. He had never lied to her. But where was the tribunal one could take these matters to? *LOVE* and *HATE* tattooed on the man's knuckles. Was that Hell's Angels or Skinheads? Dominic couldn't quite remember. The man seemed harmless now, pudgy, balding.

Louisa was sitting in the centre of the back seat being a buffer between the two girls, the place usually allotted to the smallest child. Daisy's proximity made her feel uncomfortable, the way their hips touched as they went round corners, a slight sexual discomfort, a sense of having been watched in a way she hadn't realised.

But Daisy was a thousand miles away, forehead against the window, a daydreaming child. Long stripes of fluffy cloud above the hill like something was in the process of being knitted. Dragonfly microlight. A cluster of semi-derelict buildings at the bottom of the valley which she hadn't seen last time, a mouldy green caravan. You could imagine some crazy guy with a gun, dirty children with little hairy tails snarling over a bucket of peelings. Big trees like lungs, roots underground like the same trees upside down in the dark, worms swimming through their branches. This inexplicable abundance, you could see why people dreamt up animating spirits. Naiads, zephyrs. But nowadays? Would the world look any different if there were no God? Could she believe that? It was an extraordinary thing to think, like tower blocks collapsing, like the touch of a feather.

Fine. It was the same anger, wasn't it, the anger she felt whenever Mum broached the subject of religion, the way she wanted Mum to say the wrong thing, the need to be offended, to be excluded. She liked it, didn't she, more at home with that anger than she had ever felt in the church. Maybe it wasn't equilibrium she was seeking. *Gemma's Choice.* The lime-green cardigan. Maybe it was release. Maybe it was the ability to say *Fuck you* to everyone.

Angela told Benjy that the way to stop feeling nauseous was to look out of the window but he was in the middle of some game and she wasn't in the mood for a fight. He held out till the car park at least, climbing out and vomiting copiously onto the tarmac, the tinny music of *Mario at the Winter Olympics* piping and chiming from the Nintendo at the end of his outstretched hand.

Richard hoisted himself upright using the cane and shut the car door behind him.

I told you. Angela fished in her handbag for wet wipes.

Benjy just stood there, head forward, letting a drooly trail lengthen.

Angela shook out the little damp square. *Come here.*

Richard turned away and gazed over the fields. Blood he could handle, but faeces, vomit, sweat . . . the smell of unwashed patients, stayed with you all day. The soothing green of the hills. He was upwind thankfully.

Drink some of that. Angela handed Benjy a plastic bottle from her handbag.

Benjy swilled the water round his mouth and spat it on to the sick to help wash it away a bit. He hadn't thrown up for seven months. Something reassuring about it once you'd got the taste out of your mouth, so long as it hadn't gone up into the back of your nose, like sugar and banana sandwiches, or rubbing an old blanket. That nice sharpness on the back of your teeth where acid had taken the plaque away.

They all regrouped at the top of the car park by the zebra crossing, waiting for Richard to negotiate the stone steps. Dominic and Benjy headed off to The Shop of Crap while Angela, Melissa and Daisy dispersed singly in various directions so that Richard and Louisa found themselves alone. *Coffee?* He liked the idea of sitting and talking.

Let's walk. Louisa took his arm in the old-fashioned way. *Keep mobile. Isn't that what the doctors say?*

And it was true, he did start to feel a little better for moving. Backfold Books. Nepal Bazaar. An old lady with five dachshunds, looking like a maypole. *Last night. You said Daisy was gay, or was that a particularly vivid dream?*

She tried to kiss Melissa.

287

Why would she do that? The surprise stopped him in his tracks. *That wasn't meant to sound quite so insulting.*

I have trouble understanding why anyone would want to kiss Melissa. Bit like sticking your head in the lion's mouth.

Do Angela and Dominic know?

I have no idea. They continued walking. *Melissa was horrible to Daisy about it. Predictably.*

He kept his own counsel and they walked past The Granary, turning left towards the river. In the centre of the bridge they stopped and leant against the balustrade so that he could rest and take the weight off his left foot completely. Daisy, Alex, Benjamin, he had managed to upset all of them. That shrew. He simply hadn't thought. But he liked them, he really did like them. Water purling between the shallow rocks, weed under the surface like green hair in the wind. Carl and Douglas, they hadn't come to the wedding. Too far, too expensive. *We should visit your brothers.*

Really. You'd have nothing in common.

We have you in common.

She used to picture it in bad dreams, Richard standing in that shabby room, ceiling tiles coming loose and that bloody dog yapping, TV left running at maximum volume since 1973. For the first time she could imagine him finding it simply funny, or interesting, or sad. Upstream a heron took off.

I'm going to go and talk to Ruth Sharne.

Ruth . . .?

The girl in the wheelchair. The operation that went wrong.

Is that advisable?

It's not advised, not by the lawyers. But 'inadvisable' . . .?

You're not going to say it was your fault, are you?

Nor Mohan's, just that we very much regret what happened. I don't think anyone's said that, except on paper.

Will it get you into trouble?

She comes into the OT unit. She must know that we're over there in the main building, a couple of hundred yards away. Can you imagine how that must feel?

Richard . . .

If it comes to court then I want to walk into that room feeling honourable, not scared.

Dominic picks up a cap gun, a proper old-fashioned cowboy pistol, dull sheen, sprung hammer, rotating chamber. Memories of childhood scooping him up and lifting him out of the troubled present. Yes. If you cracked it open at the hinge there was the housing where you placed the roll of caps and the ratchet which pushed the next cap into line. That smell, like nothing else. The little trail of smoke. Crawling through the long grass in the wasteground behind Fennell's. *The Good, the Bad and the Ugly.* Jumping out of trees onto cardboard boxes from the Co-op. Mr Hines stabbing their football with a breadknife. *Benjy, look at this.* He holds out the gun, expecting Benjy to take it, but he seems downcast. *What's the matter?*

It's nothing.

He squats so their faces are level. *Tell me.*

Really, it's nothing.

But you were so looking forward to coming here.
Really. It's OK.

Alex sat on the steps of the town clock eating two bananas from Spar, tired muscles buzzing, mind near empty. A blind man with a guide dog. Always golden retrievers, for some reason. Swallows overhead like little pairs of scissors. He closed his eyes and waited for the lime-green after-image of the street to fade to black.

How was that?

He opened his eyes to find himself looking up at Dad and Benjy. *Really good. Hour fifty-five.* But there was something wrong with Benjy. *What happened, kiddo?*

Nothing.

Sometimes Alex didn't notice Benjy because Benjy was eight. Then, sometimes, he remembered being eight himself and how hard it could be. *Why don't you come with me?*

OK, said Benjy. He smiled and Alex felt his heart lift a little.

She sits in Shepherd's stealing glances at other girls, other women. Panic, fascination, guilt. A tired young mum in a shapeless grey tracksuit, unwashed hair scraped back, baby in a high chair, two older ladies straight out of a sitcom, all cake and bosom and jollity. In the corner a girl of sixteen, seventeen, with her family but not really *with* them. Long brown hair, bangles, black T-shirt with a skull on that might be goth or ironic, it's hard to tell. That mix of sullenness and under-confidence, still not quite sure of who she is yet. She turns to look at Daisy, or something over Daisy's shoulder, or maybe nothing at all. Daisy glances away feeling both utterly invisible and completely exposed. The girl turns back to her family. Is Daisy attracted to her? She imagines talking to her, imagines touching her. The long ripple of her backbone as she takes that T-shirt off. A little jolt of what? desire? fear? disgust? But how did you know if someone returned your feelings? Was there a secret language? She feels unqualified, like she's failed to prepare for a vital interview. She stares at the table's plastic surface, tiny ticks and slashes, beige, brown, blue. Classic FM in the background, something orchestral and slushy. Because now that she thinks about it there's a feeling, isn't there, a feeling that's always been there, so constant she never really notices it. When she looks at women. Not even sexual, really, just a rightness, a comfort in their presence. Melissa, of all people. Magnetism and self-assurance. Was it so wrong to want these things? Was it so wrong to want someone who had these things? Maybe it wasn't God after all, maybe it was the heart which punished one with such exquisite accuracy.

Machine guns. Popguns. Potato guns. Cap guns. Bows and arrows. Axes. Tomahawks. Brooms. Dusters. J-Cloths. Nail brushes. Dog chews made of dried pigs' ears. Kendal Mint Cake. Butter dishes. Lovespoons. Skipping ropes. Golf balls. Tennis balls. Squishy cow keyrings that moo and light up when you squeeze them. Squishy duck keyrings that quack and light up when you squeeze them. Little forks for indoor gardening. Rubber knee mats for outdoor gardening.

Creosote. Weedkiller. Hanging baskets. Brillo pads. Orthopaedic pangrips and tin openers. Stanley 15-mm heavy-duty nails. Clout nails, galvanised, in ten sizes. Baby Bio. Itching powder. Whoopee cushions. Vampire teeth. Hoover bags. Alarm clocks with bells on top. Plastic farm animals. Videos of *Mall Cop*, *Hannah Montana*, *Transformers*. Fish food. Cafetières. Musical birthday cards. Peanuts in lard for overwintering birds. Wooden chocks to hold doors open. Ashtrays in the shape of tiny toilets. Sports whistles. Firedogs. Bootscrapers. Laces of assorted length. Postcards of hills. Postcards of sheep.

Cally picked up the phone at the far end. *Melissa.*

What the fuck is going on?

You are not going to believe this.

Just tell me, all right?

Megan the genius. She texted Michelle.

Saying what?

Oh, something along the lines of, 'You're a bitch and a liar.' Like, we're being accused of bullying her, so she bullies her. Sends actual proof to Michelle's phone. How fucking moronic is that?

Think, think. Over the road a fat man was stooping to pick up a piece of dogshit using a little pink plastic bag as a glove. Her brain wouldn't work. *I'll be back tomorrow, right? We'll have, like, a war cabinet.* It was starting to rain, dark spots on the tarmac. What if they blamed everything on Megan? Megan the loose cannon, Megan the bully. A blue umbrella popping open on the far pavement. She wanted to lie down and curl up and sleep, she wanted someone to come along and pick her up and look after her. She wanted someone to be kind to her for once.

Alex and Benjy were sitting on the bench at the side of the market square, just off the main drag so Mum and Dad didn't catch Benjy eating the ice cream Alex had bought him. *What's up, kid?*

Nothing.

This is a holiday and you're meant to be having a good time.

I don't want to say.

Was Dad horrible to you this morning?

No. But he had to tell someone and if he was going to tell anyone it was best to tell Alex. *I found a message.*

A message? It sounded like a rolled-up treasure map in a bottle on a beach.

It was on Dad's phone. He felt silly now for getting so panicked. *I went downstairs in the night, and there was a beep.*

What did it say?

It said, 'Call me'. And it said, 'I can't bear this'. He could still see it blocking out the picture of them at Blakeney.

And who was it from?

It was from someone called Amy.

Alex let it sink in. A kind of satisfaction almost, as if he'd been waiting all along for Dad to fuck up properly and justify his disdain.

Who's Amy? asked Benjy.

Amy . . . He had to take this slowly, he had to get this right. *Amy works at Waterstone's with Dad. She was stealing* books. Yes, that was it. *Dad caught her stealing books.*

Will she go to prison?

Poor Benjy. He looked so sad on this woman's behalf. *She wants Dad to keep it a secret.*

But he has to tell the truth.

Yeh, he has to tell the truth.

Benjy hated thinking of Dad being put in a difficult position like this, but he was flattered, too, by this brief view through the closed door of the adult world.

Spatters of rain out of a darkening sky. *You're wasting your ice cream, mate.*

Benjy changed hands and stuck all four creamy fingers into his mouth. Alex leant back against the wall. What an arsehole, what a fucking amateur. *It's a secret, by the way. So don't tell anyone, even Mum.*

It's OK. You can trust me.

Good man.

Can we go to the shop?

Which shop?

The Shop of Crap. I didn't want to buy anything before, but I do now.

What? Melissa guessed instantly but she was going to make Mum work for this.

That was your headmaster on the phone. Michelle tried to kill herself. After you, Cally and Megan bullied her.

We had an argument. Melissa tried to sound as if she were discussing a group of people in whom she had merely a passing interest. *Michelle can get a bit over-dramatic sometimes.*

Avison wants us to come in.

It'll be fine. Trust me.

Trust you? Are you serious, Melissa? You knew all about this and you didn't even think to tell me.

Because I didn't want to mess up your holiday.

Tell me about the photograph.

I think you're better off not knowing, frankly.

Stop patronising me.

OK, OK. Michelle was drunk. Possibly she'd taken a couple of her mum's diazepam, to which she is, like, a bit partial. She described the blow job with mild disgust. *So Megan grabs my phone and takes a picture.*

You're lying.

Hey. Chill out. We're, like, standing in the rain in the middle of a road here.

Don't treat me like a moron.

I'm bloody telling the truth.

I know you, Melissa. You're a little operator. If someone else took that photo you'd have covered your back by telling me a week ago.

I'll sort everything out when we get back.

You think you're charmed. You think you're a princess. You think it will just keep on coming, the money, the clothes, the friends, the easy life. My parents had nothing, your father's parents had nothing. It can vanish like that. She clicked her fingers. *No, be quiet. I'm having the last word for once. You are not going to blame anyone else. Give me your phone.*

★ ★ ★

The rain had stopped. Dominic stood on the raised pavement outside The Granary not knowing where to go or what to do. A need for something more central, cathedral, theatre, train station, but this was it, wasn't it, the Seven Stars and Jigsaw World. He would kill himself after a month here. Ageing hippies and inbred farmers and geography teachers with their bloody hiking sticks, eating their bloody scones. He took out his iPod, put the headphones in and scrolled. Steve Reich. *Variations for Wind, Strings and Keyboards*. He let music wash over him. That little green sports car, the fat woman with her arm in a sling. The way music turned the world into television.

Benjy decided to buy a catapult. £7.99. Alex was pretty sure Mum and Dad would have vetoed it on account of it being a Weapon of Mass Destruction but he couldn't give a fuck right now. Benjy could have it as a present from his big brother. They took it to the bottom of the car park and fired stones into the field.

Louisa held the earring against her cheek. Sunflowers, she supposed, alternating leaves of bronze and silver, hammered and cut. Different. But different *good*? She didn't want to make the same mistake she made with those ridiculous china puffins.

Richard was leafing through second-hand CDs, Bernstein, Perahia, some unpronounceable Czech playing Debussy on Naxos. Just showing willing, really, because he wouldn't actually purchase a second-hand CD. Also he was steering clear of books. *The Complete SAS Fitness Training Handbook* in a knotted bag at the bottom of the bin in the shed. Ah, but this . . . *Hommage à Kathleen Ferrier*. Looked rather good, 1950/51 recording, on Tahra, distributed by Harmonia Mundi, bit of Handel, bit of Purcell, Parry, Stanford, extracts from a *Matthew Passion* under Karajan.

Daisy was wandering around Hay-on-Wye Booksellers looking for something a little more addictive than *Dracula*, something to hold her attention completely. *The Girl with the Dragon Tattoo*? There was a gay and lesbian section. She'd seen the sign. Scared to look, scared she might be revolted, or entranced, scared she might be accosted by some terrifying gatekeeper. Big netball coach, some flinty girl with Hitler hair.

Melissa was looking at a remaindered volume of water-colours by John Singer Sargent. She loved the cool clean heft of big art books. But these pictures frightened her, how good they were, as if the paint had simply fallen into place. Sailing boats, women blowing glass in a darkened room in Venice, fountains in a park in Paris. She would never be able to do this, would she, because to be an artist you had to run the risk of failing, you had to close your eyes and step into the dark. The feeling of her empty pocket where her phone should be. Being treated like a ten-year-old. Fuck.

Sorry. Angela bumps into a second person. Little passages of blankness, like when you're driving a familiar route and come round to find yourself at the wheel. The health food shop. She is staring at a cold cabinet of cheese and salami and bean sprouts. Are Richard and Louisa cooking tonight? Karen's birthday. She keeps remembering then forgetting then remembering. She decides to go to The Globe early, fearing she might be carried off by the riptide unless she moors herself while she has the chance. Bohemian reclamation chic, an old chapel once, now a café-cum-gallery-cum-something else. She buys a cappuccino and a white chocolate muffin and sits down. There is a balcony made of scaffolding and some truly ghastly paintings. The pulpit still stands in the corner. Like being a student again. Foreign language films and patchouli and *Spare Rib*. She looks up and sees that Karen has walked in, that Daisy has walked in.

A second later and she would have turned tail but Mum has seen her now so she can't beat a retreat without making it seem like an insult. She walks over. Pews and hippy cushions and old blankets.

Hello, love. Mum is eating a muffin and huddling slightly, like she's cold, or hiding from someone.

Hiya. Daisy sits.

A long strange silence, as if Mum is a child and feels no pressing need to communicate with the adult world. It scares her. *Are you OK?*

Mum is using the tip of her index finger to move all the crumbs on her plate into a little central pile. *I'm having a difficult day.*

Mine's not exactly been a barrel of laughs. But Mum doesn't react. Another long strange silence. *I might be leaving the church.* She catches herself by surprise, saying this. Again Mum says nothing, just leans over and smiles and rubs Daisy's forearm. She seems sad. *Mum . . .?*

I just want you to be happy.

Something in her voice. An echo of Gran during that last year. The weirdest suspicion that she doesn't really know who Daisy is. *Mum . . .?*

It's Karen's birthday.

Who's Karen? She assumes it is some girl at school. Then she remembers. *Karen who . . .* She isn't sure of the word.

Not the day she died, but the day she would have been born.

But this was seventeen years ago.

Eighteen. It didn't used to bother me. Then all of a sudden . . . She sits up and gives a little shake, as if trying to throw off this passing strangeness.

That farawayness. As if Daisy is simply someone she has met on the bus with whom she is passing time. *Have you got some money for a coffee?* She needs to step aside for a few moments.

Maybe I'm just allergic to this kind of holiday, says Mum.

What kind of holiday?

Countryside, rain. She digs her wallet out of her bag and hands it over.

By the time the stripy mug of coffee is placed on the counter in front of her, Daisy turns and sees that Dominic and Richard and Louisa have arrived, thank God.

Phil the Fruit and Murder and Mayhem. The Great Outdoors (makers of fine leather goods). Teddy Bear Wonderland.

Crusty loaves and Bakewell tarts. *I had not thought death had undone so many*. Like a mist around the living, the crush of ghosts, the ones we can't let go. The outline in the bed, the empty place at the table. Siege Perilous. She crushes out the stub of her Silk Cut with the toe of her boot and fastens the top toggle of her green duffel coat. She stands on the bridge and watches the river flow to the sea. Silt and salmon, nitrates and mercury and human waste. Plynlimon to Monmouth, to the Severn Estuary, over the Welsh Grounds, down the Bristol Channel and out into the great downsweep of the North Atlantic Current.

Dominic assumed that Angela had found the message, her distance, her muted distress, but they drifted into a dog-legging conversation about a friend from college who lived in a squat in Finsbury Park, and the German student next door who was murdered, and the German club at school, and he realised that she hadn't found the message, had she? Something else was wrong, the way she was running on autopilot, radio silence and the cockpit windows frosting over. He was off the hook. His vow of, what? three days ago? Getting Angela back on track, making the family work, being a proper father and husband. He wasn't sure he had the energy now. He looked around the table. Richard and Louisa rebonded, Melissa absent in one way, Angela in another, some kind of sibling huddle at the far end, Benjy deep in his book. How rarely people were *together*. Gaps in the chain of Christmas lights. But Daisy and the kiss . . .

Perhaps they had already done the right thing by not making a song and dance about it, all part of life's rich pageant and so on. He tried and failed to catch her eye. A sudden stupid sadness, the worry that he had lost all of them, the urge to go and pick Benjy up and tell him how much he loved him. But you couldn't do that, could you, in the middle of a meal, just go and hug someone and tell them that you loved them.

Where's Melissa? asked Richard.

Louisa angled herself so that no one could hear and said quietly, *I got a call from school.*

About?

Melissa and her friends bullied a girl who then tried to commit suicide. Saying it to Richard made it sound worse, if that were possible.

The girl. Is she all right?

It seems so.

What did they do to her?

Louisa stalled. They never talked about Melissa and sex. That delicate boundary.

You can tell me.

She felt implicated by her own transgressions.

I'll keep my distance. I promise.

They took a photo of this girl, Michelle, at a party, having sex with some boy, then they sent it to everyone.

Charlie Lessiter. Those boys who force-fed him laxatives. *Swallow, Fatty, swallow!* Holding him in a headlock. *You're worried they'll expel her?*

I worry that this is not just a phase.

Children can be vicious. He wanted to talk to Michelle, find out how serious it was. Because killing yourself was easy if you meant it. He wanted to be the doctor, wanted to be the lawyer. He didn't like this blurry view from the outfield.

She thinks she can slip out of it like she always does. A bit of charm here, a few lies there.

Perhaps I shouldn't keep my distance.

Meaning?

Perhaps I should talk to her. The other man, the one who'd found her smoking in the woodshed forty-eight hours ago, he seemed like a stranger now. *I won't wear hobnailed boots this time.*

Two sweetcorn chowders, a slightly disappointing goat's cheese tart, two Stilton ploughmans . . . Alex and Daisy were sitting on either side of Benjy, conspicuously looking after him, showing their parents how to be parents. Benjy was reading *Guinness World Records. Look, this man lifted 21.9 kg using his nipples.*

Benjy, seriously, why would I possibly want to look?

Alex observes his father. It seems both impossible and completely obvious. They didn't love each other, did they, Mum and Dad, didn't like each other half the time. A little flash of sympathy for Dad, then he thinks of the dirtiness, the lying, the disrespect. He wants to tell someone, but who? Daisy has enough on her plate. He could tell Richard, perhaps, but there's something unmanly about handing over the responsibility. He has to confront Dad. If he doesn't then the knowledge is going to eat away at him, but every time he pictures this encounter his heart hammers and his palms sweat. Though it would resolve something, wouldn't it? Something that has haunted him since the night in Crouch End.

Guess the record for the most underpants worn at the same time.

Benjy, just eat that potato.

One hundred and thirty-seven.

Benjy . . .

I'm a bit full actually.

Of what?

Nothing.

We had some ice cream.

Daisy looks at Mum who seems a little better now, more awake, more focused, stringing actual sentences together with Dad. That echo of Gran. Made her blood run cold. Though when she thinks about it maybe Mum deserves a bit of suffering. All the shit she's given her over the past year. Schadenfreude. Is that a dreadful thing to think? Well, if she's leaving the church then thinking dreadful things without feeling guilty has to be one of the compensations.

Banana split, treacle pudding, cappuccino . . . Richard picks up the bill.

Daisy was waiting at the zebra crossing when she saw Melissa sitting on the stone wall across the road at the pre-arranged taxi rendezvous point. She bodyswerved rapidly towards The Shop of Crap and stood beside an aluminium dustbin full of brooms. No, wait. She was tired of feeling cowardly, feeling vulnerable. Fuck what Melissa thought, fuck what Mum and Dad thought. She turned and looked back across the road, Melissa still unaware of her presence. Spiteful and shallow. Like they always said about bullies. *Underneath they're fright-ened.* Because she had her own bluebird tattoo now, didn't she? And there were things she'd learnt in the church that remained true in spite of everything. Putting on the Armour of Christ, kneeling in the street, that drunk woman spraying them with a can of lager. If you believed with all your heart then none of it mattered. *What doesn't kill me only makes me stronger.*

Gay. What a wet fucking word it was.

She waited for a Post Office van to pull up then walked over the road. Melissa seeing her now and something extraor-dinary happening. The glossy thoroughbred look, the slow-motion hair, it counted for nothing. It was this confidence, wasn't it, the Armour of Christ. Melissa was shrinking just as she had shrunk in Melissa's presence four days ago. Daisy sat down beside her.

What? said Melissa nervously.

Daisy closed her eyes. She could let this moment run forever.

Once again, Dominic was deputed to sit up front and converse with the taxi driver. Young white guy in his twenties, poly-ester tracksuit top, tiny diamond earring, driving a little too fast, but not fast enough for Dominic to complain.

Five days and the landscape was fading already. The gash

of gold and the green distance. How pleased we are to have our eyes opened but how easily we close them again. The barn owl on the telegraph pole. It was picturesque, then it wasn't picturesque, then it was background.

Daisy stared through the window trying to discern a future that wasn't clear yet. These were not her people, this was not her family.

The mobile was sitting right there in Mum's bag. Melissa wanted to just grab it, have an all-out bitch fight, but Daisy would have loved that.

Louisa was remembering those family holidays in Tenby. Auntie May's boarding house, though she wasn't technically an aunt, of course. Deckchairs and slot machines, sharing a double bed with her brothers, the day Dougie smashed a crab with a rock and the time it took to die. There was an island out in the bay. She can't remember the name now. There was a monastery on it and there were boat trips, but they never took one. It came back to her in dreams sometimes. Of course Richard should meet Carl and Dougie. Why had she been so frightened of this?

Outside the damp green world sliding by. Ash and poplar. Cord moss and hart's tongue fern.

Angela had offered Alex the front seat on the way back so that she could sit quietly with Benjy in the back without being quizzed by Richard who was giving Alex a brief lecture on CT scanning. Iodine, barium, how The Beatles helped because EMI used their profits to make the prototype.

What's this? asked Benjy, dipping his hand into the green plastic bag that was squished between him and Mum.

Oh, said Angela, *it's something I bought.*

Alex looked round and saw that Benjy was holding a Victorian doll, stained lacy dress, blank china face, too broken to be an antique, too weird to be a toy.

Who's it for? said Benjy.

For me, said Angela. *For someone.*

Benjy slipped it carefully back into the bag, half believing that it might hiss and bite him if he treated it roughly. *Can you put it on your side?* He lifted the bag gingerly by the ends of his fingers. *I don't like it.*

What's that? Richard glancing into the rear-view mirror, now that they had exited the narrow chicane of high hedges. Alex caught his eye and gave the faintest shake of his head, meaning *Don't ask*, because he, too, knew now that something was wrong.

Louisa turned to him as he came into the bedroom. *What do you think?*

He scanned her top to toe. Hair? Clothes? *The earrings.* Metal sunflowers, bronze and silver. *They make you look younger.*

How much younger? Thirty is good. Sixteen is not.

Ten. Ten years younger. I like them. He swivelled and lay down with his head on the pillow. *Sorry about this.*

About what?

Family holiday. Not quite as restful as I had planned.

This is restful. She lay down next to him.

They stared at the ceiling, a king and queen on a tomb. The smell of cocoa butter. He liked Benjy, he liked Daisy, he liked Alex but he didn't like Dominic. Something weak about him, insubstantial. And his own sister . . .? They had the same parents, they had lived in the same house for sixteen years but he had no idea who she really was.

Hey.

What?

You're off duty. She checked her watch. *One hour.* She rolled onto her side and propped her head on her hand.

The spill of blonde hair, hips curved and creaturely. Desire coming back as strong as ever, that switchback of feelings. Wanting, not wanting. Anxiety, content. How fluid and unpredictable the mind was.

Wait. She put her finger to her lips, got to her feet and locked the door.

Are you sure this is a good idea?

I think it's an excellent idea. She lay down beside him again.

What if someone hears us?

You can apologise publicly over supper.

He lifted her blouse and put his hand on that little bulge of warm flesh above her waistband. *I'm afraid I can't be too gymnastic in my present state.*

Gymnastic? What were you planning?

What happened? Mum looked as if she had been standing in an inch of foamy water for the last thirty minutes. The same vacant expression she'd had all day.

I think there must be a leak somewhere.

Warm damp air, that flooded cellar smell. Alex splashed across the floor and turned the machine off. Wet clothing slumped and levelled in the glass porthole. At home she'd be shouting and swearing. *Go and get yourself a cup of tea and I'll sort this out, OK?*

Thank you, Alex. She walked off into the kitchen, the damp slap of her shoes receding.

Christ. He squatted and ran his hand round the front hatch. Dry. Something at the back, then, or underneath. He heaved on the big white box, rocking it gently from side to side so that it boomed and scraped out of its recess. He peered into the dark between the side panel and the plastered wall. Darkness, two disconnected pipe ends, a broken circlip lying in the suds.

My God. Dad was standing in the doorway, like a bloody lemon as usual, letting someone else get their hands dirty. *Washing machine broken?*

No. It's on fire. He wanted to go over and punch his father. But the china doll . . . Did Mum know? Was that why she was acting so strangely? She seemed so fragile. He shouldn't do anything to upset her. He reached into the recess and picked up the circlip. Tendrils of black slime, the little metal ridges sheared smooth where it had come free. He stood up. *You find a mop and clean this place up. I'm going out to the shed.*

The little fold where the curve of her bottom met the top of her thighs. He ran his hand down her back. The most adult activity, yet it made you feel like a child again, at home with your own nakedness, touching another person, skin to skin.

Something hovering that he could almost touch, some secret which had eluded him for a long time. But the warmth of her body under his hand, the quiet of this room, distant voices in the garden. He let it drift away.

In the corner of the shed, a crumbling wooden workbench, toy piano in sun-bleached red plastic, fishing net, spark plugs, filthy webs over everything. He picked up a coil of rusty garden wire thin enough to cut with the kitchen scissors. Red electrical tape. He wiped the roll clean on the leg of his jeans. Three-inch nail. Use it like a tourniquet. He sat down on the roller, light-headed suddenly. He hated being trapped inside other people's problems. He kept his life simple. Do your work, choose good friends and keep your promises. He didn't deserve this crap. He'd been dreaming about Coed-y-Brenin for weeks, nothing to do but cycle and eat and sleep. It scared him now, something happening to Mum while he was away. The idea that he might not have a home to come back to.

Are you making something? It was Benjy.

Washing machine's bust.

He's being a man, said Daisy.

He didn't want to be a man. He wanted to run away with them. But he couldn't say it. This gulf between them, a sudden flash of what Dad might be going through, of what he might have been going through for years. Fear and disgust, thinking how similar they might be after all.

See you later, yeh? Daisy laughed. *Send out the helicopter if we're not back in two hours.*

Little princess. She really did believe it on some level, the old dream, not that her real parents would come to claim her one day, purring Bentley, chauffeur, paint like a mirror. Nothing that naïve, simply that they were out there some-where. Because she looked at Mum's brothers and the word *uncle* made her skin crawl. Three years since she last saw them. Never again, hopefully. Fat and badly dressed, smelling of cigarette smoke and fried food. That awful dog with the patch of hair shaved off and the stitches crusty with dried blood, sleeping on the sofa. At least Dad wanted to be rich. You looked at Grannie and Gramps and you saw where it came from, polish on the table every day, antimacassars and family photos and the row of china figurines. But she was Mum's daughter, too. The fear that something genetic might rise up and claim her if she wasn't strong enough. That period when Mum was fucking everything in sight, echoes of that shitty estate, people with nothing to live for.

It takes twenty-five minutes to attach one stupid bit of plastic to another but there's no way Alex is going to ask Dad for help. The inane conversation behind him stops eventually, thank goodness. *It's great for a few days but I think I'd kill myself after a month in a place like this.* Fuckwit. The splash of the mop and the scrape of the bucket, the rhythm just slow enough to show that he wasn't putting any effort in. Will he make everything worse or better if he confronts Dad? He wants someone older and wiser to tell him what to do, but there is no one. He is out of the harbour mouth now and he can feel the long sway of the ocean proper. One more turn of the nail. He unrolls a length of electrical tape and bites it off with his teeth. Leaning into the recess he tapes the nail to the body of the pipe to keep his makeshift tourniquet tight. Round once, three, seven times. It's not pretty but it looks serviceable. He stands up. Soiled wet elbows, soiled wet knees.

Done? His father opens the back door and pours another bucket of dirty water into the stone gutter.

Alex twists the big dial to *Drain* and restarts the machine. The drum turns over a few times, then picks up speed, juddering. He looks into the recess. The makeshift junction holds without leaking. Result.

As he's leaving the room, Dominic touches his arm. *Alex.*

Alex fixes his attention on the light switch.

What's the matter?

Alex steps back very slowly to disengage from his father's touch. Like two spacecraft undocking. If he says anything now he will explode. He walks slowly towards the door.

Alex . . . ?

She didn't know who she was any more, that was the truth of it. The newel post, her fairy-tale father, 'My Funny

Valentine'. She had given up trying to remember her own bedroom. It was like moving to the edge of a cliff and gazing down through miles of empty air. You thought you were anchored by the tick of the clock, the sound of your children in the garden, these hands gripping the arms of this chair. Reality. It meant nothing. It was the story that mattered, the story that held you together, the satisfaction of turning those pages, going back to favourite scenes over and over, a book at bedtime, the reassurance of it. Saying, *This happened . . . Then that happened . . .* Saying, *This is me.* But what is her story? *Losing the plot.* The deep truths hidden in the throwaway phrase. She was coming, wasn't she? Karen was coming. Her vengeful little angel.

Kick, says Daisy. *Kick your legs right up.* And he manages it, just, despite gymnastics totally not being his forte. She holds his ankles and yanks them higher to straighten his knees.

And the world is suddenly upside down, his face fat with blood, a delicious wobble in his arms. He's like Atlas, carrying the planet on his upturned hands. And then he can't hold it any longer. His arms give way and he crumples onto the grass, shrieking and laughing and rolling down the hill. But he lands on a stiff little thorn branch. *Shit bugger bloody, shit bugger bloody.*

Benjy . . . ?

He gets to his feet and does a little anaesthetic dance. The pain is going down. But then he takes his hand away and sees the four red lines cut into the soft flesh of his underarm, tiny red drops blooming. He starts to cry and Daisy holds her arms open. *Hey, Action Man.* So he comes and slumps in between her legs and she hugs him.

Shit shit shit.

She rocks him gently. She remembers how this used to feel, how it still feels. Nothing you can do, just wait for the time to pass. The Armour of Christ. She's not angry now, nor as confident, just exhausted, mostly. Thinking and feeling too many things in too short a time.

But Benjy is crying not just about the wound on his arm, he is also crying about the woman who is being mean to Dad. He doesn't like to see adults suffering. He still believes that when he reaches the age of twenty-one he will no longer be sad, he will no longer be afraid, he will no longer be bullied. It is a hard clear star he can fix his quadrant on. But if that woman at work can bully Dad . . .

My turn, says Daisy.

Benjy dries his eyes and rolls away so that she can stand up. She finds a little pillow of grass. Forehead down, hands planted. A little push and her legs rise into the blue. Like diving into the earth. Absolutely vertical. The tiniest splash and little waves of earth spreading away from the spot where you vanished into the dark. Limestone, granite, basalt.

Mum bought a weird doll, says Benjy.

What kind of weird? She wonders how long you'd have to stay like this before it starts feeling normal, till it looks right.

She said it was for someone, then she said it was for her.

Daisy thinks about the baby who died, those scary thoughts

you got sometimes. What if I were someone else? What if I never reached the world? *It's something for school.* Just to reassure him. *A project.* Though God alone knows what Mum was up to.

That's all right, then.

Yeh, that's all right.

Can we go back now?

Of course. A few more precious seconds then she gives in to gravity.

Say it began with shadows, that it was shadows always. The sun above us, below us a dark figure that is ourselves and not ourselves. Look how it follows me, see how we dance in time. Narcissus, all of us, right from the beginning. Trace your hand on the rock wall of this cave, using flint, using charcoal. Now the ghost of you will live on after you have gone. Draw lines in the dirt. This is the wolf and that is the river. There are the hills and the men who live beyond them. This is how we can trap the wolf. This is how we can kill the men. Imagined futures breeding and branching. *We are, I know not why, double within ourselves.* So many different things to want and fear. Ghosts fighting for possession of a body.

Gather round the fire, says the old man. *Once upon a time . . .* And suddenly we are transported to a world that seems both strange and familiar. Angels and demons, wolves and shadows, the men who live beyond the hills.

★　★　★

The salmon wasn't going to fit into a single baking tray, was it? Louisa should have thought of that in the shop. She would have to rearrange it after baking, cut-and-shut, like a crashed car. She placed the jar of honey and the jar of olives on opposite corners of the cookbook to hold it open. Foil, peppercorns, mustard. Open the fridge. Sour cream, dill. Amazing you could get it here. She looked out of the window and saw Benjy and Daisy returning from a walk. It had happened this week, hadn't it, Daisy realising? Suddenly it was obvious, now that she thought about it. The way she held herself, some tension gone. Memories of that ghastly funeral, the way she sang the hymns, trying so hard to put her heart into something. She hadn't told her parents, had she? Or perhaps she'd told them and it had gone down badly. Angela's weird behaviour, perhaps it had nothing to do with the baby dying, or not that kind of baby dying.

She should have had two children. Or three. Or four. Melissa would have been a different person, surely. Sixteen years of ruling the roost, it couldn't be good for anyone. Forty-four. She wasn't old, was she? She could still have a child, with Richard. Was that an absurd thought?

Richard sat down on the bench and handed Melissa a mug of tea. That ridiculous cane. Like someone's grandad. She took the tea only because it would have seemed childish to refuse. He let the silence run for ten seconds. *You want to be successful, you want to be rich, you want to have a good job.*

And . . .? She didn't need any more of this stuff, not today.

You can offend some people. In fact, you have to offend some people if you're going to get things done. He should have talked to her like this a long time ago. He should have done many things a long time ago. *But you have to admit when you're wrong.*

I haven't done anything wrong. He refused to answer. *She told you, didn't she? Thanks, Mum.*

People are scared of you, Melissa. That's how you get them to do things. And you can do that at school but it doesn't work in the long run. You have to learn how to make people like you.

It caught her off guard. She was waiting for a lecture about knuckling down and toeing the line, but she was holding her shield in the wrong place and he had slipped a blade in under her ribs, because the shameful truth was that she wanted to be like him. The salary, the respect, the achievement.

A little column of midges rose and fell in the centre of the lawn as if contained in a big glass tube.

Richard rubbed his face. *You have to find something you really care about, then everything else falls into place. But I'm not sure you've found anything you really care about.*

I care about . . . But what did she care about? Out of nowhere she was crying. Sailing boats and women blowing glass. She would never be an artist, she would never love someone, she would never be loved.

Melissa . . .?

But she was standing up and running towards the house, her spilt tea dripping through the slats in the bench.

* * *

Daisy was passing through the kitchen when Louisa held out a glass of wine in a way that clearly meant, *You're staying*.

So Daisy clinked the glass against the chunky handle of the big knife Louisa was holding. *What happened in there, by the way?*

Washing machine. Louisa swept the carrot peelings into the bin. *Alex fixed it. Your dad mopped the floor.*

Sounds about right.

I'm sorry Melissa was horrible to you.

So, everybody knew.

I ought to come up with some sort of excuse, her being my daughter, but she can be an utter shit sometimes.

It was my fault, really.

Many boys have made the same mistake.

Daisy realised that they were talking about the kiss.

She should carry a government health warning, that girl. The kettle clicked off and Louisa poured the boiling water into the biggest pan.

Like it was the most ordinary thing in the world. And Louisa was on her side, Louisa of all people, Louisa who picked tiny pieces of fluff off Richard's jumper. The jar of honey and the jar of olives.

It happened this week, didn't it? Louisa slotted the kettle back on to its stand.

We went for a walk up Black Hill.

I didn't mean that. Louisa dried her hands on the tea towel and looked at her. *It's like there was a big knot inside you. And someone's untied it.*

God, she stumbled through life failing to understand everyone. Louisa. Melissa. Jack. Lauren. Herself most of all. *How did you know?*

You're a good daughter, said Louisa. *I don't think they're proud enough.* She halved the tea towel and hung it over the rail on the Aga. *Now. What do you think? Shall we pull out the stops for the last night?*

Good idea, said Daisy, because that was it, wasn't it? Nothing more to be said, nothing more that needed to be said.

There are no flowers so Daisy makes a collection of holly and grasses and a budding branch she can't identify and arranges them in the handpainted Spanish jug which she places in the centre of the table. Paper serviettes folded and rolled, a bishop's hat in every place. Two candles in wine bottles, flames multiplied in the wobbly glass of the leaded panes. Marks & Spencer's Chablis, the salmon cut and shut so deftly on a fresh sheet of silver foil that no one notices, flecks of grass green in the white of the sauce, asparagus, beans and carrots.

Why does it make your wee smell funny? asks Benjy.

Methanethiol, says Richard, *and some sulphides whose names temporarily escape me.*

Fresh bread, half the loaf sliced so the slices curled away like in an advert. The little bone-handled butter knife stuck into the pale yellow slab. *Whisper Not*, Dominic's choice. Keith Jarrett, Gary Peacock, Jack DeJohnette.

They're both solicitors, says Alex. *It probably counts as animal cruelty. The dogs are shut inside ten hours a day. I take them to the park and they go ballistic.*

Angela is drinking too much in the hope that it will calm her, though she can see, too, that it is loosening her grip on the real world.

Once more, Benjy is picturing the centre of the table as a city on an alien planet, the condiments, the wine bottles, the handpainted Spanish jug transformed to towers and gun ports. The two candles become refinery flares, an empty wicker mat the landing stage for which he aims as he weaves through the heavy laser flak in the scout vehicle.

How often is Angela like this? asks Richard quietly, because he had learnt over twenty-five years of being a doctor that normal was a very broad church and pathological too easy a diagnosis.

Just forming the word *never* in his mind makes Dominic realise how serious this is. His silence speaks for him.

I suspect she needs to see someone.

You're right, says Dominic, though he had lost the right to advise her on all but the most trivial matters after losing his job. As if one paid actual money for such rights. *I'll see what I can do.*

Louisa and Daisy are talking about swimming. *It was just a thing I was really good at.*

But . . .?

In the end it's just going up and down a pool. I think it's better doing something actually fun that you're not so good at.

Like?

How rarely she asked the question. *Acting. I liked acting.*

Louisa rests her knife and fork at half past six. *And your friends in the church?*

I'm not sure they'll be friends any more. What would she do? Walk away, like she'd walked away from Lauren?

It might be good for them. Louisa sips her wine. *There's a lot of troubled people out there.*

She was right, wasn't she? Meg, Anushka. Who could tell? So many ways of being saved. So many cold dark places.

Richard turns to Melissa. *I remember you saying you'd got a dodgy Oberon.*

He is being kind, and this, she knows now, is the thing that scares her most of all. Kindness, her inability either to give it or receive it. *I haven't really been thinking about the play.* It seems the least of her problems. *We'll work it out.* Down the other end of the table Mum and Daisy are gossiping, like she's been usurped and they want her to know it. She needs distracting, but Richard is talking to Dominic again so she turns to Alex. *Your dad said you were going to Wales.* Because she can do it, too, she can be kind, she can be interested. It's not hard. *Mountain-biking, right?*

He stares at her long and hard then laughs quietly. Utter disdain. *You'd hate it.*

And she thinks, fuck *nice*, fuck *kind*. Dust and tumbleweed. Her father's daughter, because no one treats me like that, no one.

Fourteen hours to go, says Dominic. *We seem to have made it without anyone killing anyone else.*

Thank you, said Angela. *For all this. For bringing us here.* As if she were a little girl remembering to be polite.

You're welcome.

A toast. To Richard.

And Louisa.

Cheers.

Something provisional about the two hours between supper and bedtime. Everyone kicking their heels slightly before tomorrow's departure. Daisy reads *Tintin* to Benjy. *Flight 714 to Sydney. Two hours and every trace of you and your friends wiped from the surface of the earth!*

Angela fills half a suitcase. Dominic means to say something, about her seeing someone, about her getting help, but he can't work out how to do it. He takes the cardigan from her hands and offers to finish the packing and this seems enough to absolve him of the greater duty for the time being at least.

Angela wanders downstairs and makes a cup of tea. Richard is putting the food they won't need for breakfast into a cardboard box. Flour, olive oil, two bags of cashews. He asks if she is all right. She summons enough self-possession to head him off at the pass because she is tired and a little drunk and not sure she could explain even if she wanted. He gives her a hug which feels clumsy because it catches her by surprise and she is not able to return it deftly enough. He holds her for a long time and she wonders if he is going to say something, about Mum, about Dad, about the two of them being brother and sister, perhaps, but he finally breaks the silence by saying simply, *Look after yourself.*

Half-eleven. Alex comes out of his and Benjy's room en route to the toilet. Something in the corner of his eye. Turning, he sees Melissa, standing at the end of the corridor watching him, leaning against the window sill, hair down, bare legs, man's shirt. He tries to turn away but leaves it just a moment too long. She pushes herself lazily upright and walks down the landing, face blank. He can't believe this is happening, all his previous opinions swept away by the fierceness of his wanting. She stands in front of him, arms hanging by her side, steps a little closer, angles her head and lets herself be kissed. He puts one hand round the back of her neck and pushes his tongue into her mouth. Pine fabric conditioner. Freakishly pliable. He lifts her shirt. White cotton knickers, the roundness of her arse under his hand. He pulls her towards him so that she can feel his erection, wanting to know what permissions he is being granted. She neither presses back nor pulls away but takes hold of his T-shirt, turns and begins leading him towards the bedroom. There is something about this that he doesn't understand, but there are many things he doesn't understand about Melissa. Perhaps this what she is like when she gets horny. He knows little and cares less.

Angela puts her mug of tea on the side table and opens the creaky door of the stove to make herself a fire, balls of paper, kindling pyramid, small log. She lights the paper, shuts the door and spins open the little vent, sits back and waits for it to roar and bloom and settle, then spins the vent almost shut.

Fatigue and wakefulness warring with one another. If she can make it through tonight perhaps everything will be better in the morning, but if she goes to bed now she will lie staring at the ceiling. She feels ill at ease being down here as the house grows empty and quiet, but if she is upstairs she will worry that these rooms are neither wholly empty nor wholly quiet.

From the wood basket she extracts the remaining pages of the *Observer*. Melvyn Bragg on Gödel and Leibniz. Honeybees in terminal decline. The awful truth: to get ahead you need a private education. God, the amount you read in a lifetime and how shockingly little stayed with you. Getting back to school will be good for her. Those burdens that seem heavy till you put them down to lift your own. Karim's impending statement. The creepy guy in the flat overlooking the Key Stage 1 playground. The Inclusion Unit closing and the Dillon twins coming back. Slipping away now. Rhubarb and Castrol. Behind everything there is always a house. You started the mower by pulling the plastic T on the end of the cord. She was never strong enough. The smell of greenhouse tomatoes, like nothing else. Almonds, bacon, nail varnish. Laughable, un-photographable. Sleep folds over her. Time passes. No real idea how much.

It is the cold that wakes her, the fire dying, the light off and only a dim glow from the landing upstairs seeping into the room. Karen is sitting in the armchair. A jolt of fear and relief. This will be over soon. But Karen is not Karen, not the Karen she had imagined. Bird bones and sunken cheeks, matted greasy hair. For a second Angela wonders if she is dead, then her glassy eyes open and turn. Such economy of movement, so little energy to spare. The unwashed stink of her, beyond animal, homeless all these years. Gypsy camps and the breakers' yards. A sore at the corner of her mouth, that tramp smell, urine and faeces, raw papery skin. Five thousand nights in the open air. She looks eighty, not eighteen. She does not speak, perhaps she has never learnt to speak. Angela is terrified, she wants desperately to move but her arms and legs will not answer her commands. She is trapped inside her body. Instead it is Karen who is moving, bony hands on the arms of the chair, straining to lift such a small weight. This is not about apology or explanation or penance, this is punishment, and Angela will have no say in it just as Karen once had no say. On her feet, unsteady but determined. She fixes Angela with her eyes and does not look away. Angela can see now how truly frail she is, the way her clothes hang, greasy brown rags, all colour gone. Things moving in her hair. Three steps and she is standing in front of Angela, the stink overpowering now, leaning down, her face changing shape as it closes in to kiss her. A ragged fin of grey flesh rising through the hair, eyes narrowing to gashes in the wet clay. Teeth and claws. Mouth on Angela's mouth, forcing it open, dry cracked lips. The dirty wet meat of her tongue.

Angela hears shrieking from high on the jagged rocks, the splintering of timber and the roar of water rushing in.

Bright light suddenly. Karen vanished and a girl kneeling in front of her. *Mum . . . ?*

Angela can't remember how to speak.

The girl stands and says, *Oh shit.*

Daisy. It's Daisy. This confusion. This is how her mother left the world. The nurses burning her hands. *When will Richard come to see me?*

But he's here now, her brother, the doctor. He leans on the arm of the chair. *Angela . . . ?* He clicks his fingers directly in front of her face, examines her eyes in turn. There's a woman in the room. Jennifer. No, the other one.

Richard takes her earlobe between his thumb and forefinger and squeezes it hard. *Ow.* She pulls her head away from his hand. She can move again.

Angela . . . ?

It feels like a very long time since she last talked. *I fell asleep.*

How are you feeling now?

It requires thought. Leafing through memories of the last few days. *What's the time?*

Half-two.

I heard something, says Daisy. *So I came down.*

Was it Karen she heard? She let the foolish question slide away.

We've been trying to wake you for some time, says Richard.

Louisa standing in the corner, watching. Angela wants to

hear her speak, the suspicion that she might not actually be there. She catches Louisa's eye. *You scared us*, says Louisa. So she's real.

Daisy touches her hand. *Seriously, how are you feeling?*

Suddenly she sees the situation from their point of view. That she has done this to them. *I'm really sorry.*

There's no need to apologise, says Richard.

She gets to her feet, a little unsteady at first. *I think we all need some sleep.*

Only as they are returning upstairs do they realise how deftly she has sidestepped the question they have been asking for the last ten minutes. What happened down there? But Angela is right and they all do need sleep and perhaps some questions are best left unanswered.

He doesn't get to take her shirt off, doesn't get to feel her tits, let alone see them. She rolls backwards onto the bed, he unbuckles his jeans and pulls down his boxers and leans over, left hand beside her head. He's not exactly an expert when it comes to this kind of thing and she seems really dry so it takes a while to get his cock in. Her face still blank, like she's looking through him. Fifteen, twenty seconds and he's about to come. Then everything changes, like she's woken up suddenly. She grabs his arm and shoves her free hand hard against his windpipe, a punch almost. He stumbles against the little dresser, regains his balance and slides onto the chair, trousers round his ankles, cock still hard, that weird tremor of being on the brink of coming, a big blunt pain in the small of his back. She slaps his face as hard as she can. *Now get the fuck out of here.*

Other people have hit him that hard, but no one has ever hit him with that venom. He raises one hand in a gesture of ceasefire and uses the other to pull up his jeans and boxers.

Really quiet this time. *Just fuck off.* Eyes narrowed.

Yeh. Don't worry. I'm going. He reaches down and retrieves his shirt. Trousers still undone and no time for checking the corridor before he steps out but that doesn't seem like top priority right now. Then he's gone and she holds it together long enough to hear his footsteps fade down the corridor, before rolling onto her side and holding the pillow against her face so that no one can hear her crying.

He doesn't even have time to grab any toilet paper. Just drops his shirt and lets go of his belt and steps into the shower and brings himself off all over the tiling in a couple of strokes. Holy shit. Did that actually happen? He fucked Melissa. He actually fucked Melissa.

Angela slipped into the bedroom. Little bedside light still on, Dominic stirring briefly then becoming still again. She sat on the chair and waited for the others to use the bathroom and return to bed. Silence at last. She leant over and then took hold of the green plastic bag that lay scrunched on the floor beside the chest of drawers, a tuft of hair protruding from the top. She stood up and went back out onto the landing, quietly closing the door behind her. She avoided the creakier steps then turned into the living room at the bottom of the stairs. The fire low but still burning. Bending down, she undid the little latch and eased the door open, slow as a second hand to prevent it squeaking. She took five pieces of kindling from the basket and laid them parallel in the single lazy flame. Little blonde sleepers. She took the doll from the bag. A brief hesitation, letting the doubts graze her before spinning away. She laid the doll along the kindling, the dress catching immediately, a poisonous blue flame leaping up. Slowly, she shut the metal door. The tiny muffled thud of the webbing seal. Latch closed. The toddler on the sheepskin rug, the rainbow-coloured windbreak, *OGDENS*. They were pictures of Daisy, weren't they? Flames licking round the doll now, as if she were falling through the air in a dress of sunset colours, violet, orange, green. A fierce little star. *And they cast her bound into the midst of the fire. And she had no hurt.*

Friday

$\mathbf{A}$lex wakes early for one final run, south to Hatterall Hill via the grouse butts and the little disused quarries, thinking how he will probably never come back here, looking around, storing it, another place to visit in his head. He has returned to the house and is squatting to untie his trainers on the lawn when he sees his father crossing to the shed with a big white rubbish bag for the bin. Alex realises suddenly that he is going to do it. After last night he feels superhuman. He waits for his father to return then steps onto the path.

Dominic stops and raises his eyebrows because the body language is unequivocal. *What's this about?*

Benjy read the message on your phone.

What message?

You know which message.

No, I don't know which message. So it wasn't Angela. Thank God for that.

The message from Amy.

And what about it?

331

Who's Amy?

Amy is an old friend of mine and I really don't see what this has got to do with you.

From where? An old friend from where?

From college. Alex, what are you suggesting?

You're having an affair.

Dominic laughs. *I think you need a bit more practice in the Sherlock Holmes department.*

Alex wants to quote the text but he can't remember the words. He should have planned this better. *What was she so upset about?*

I really don't think she'd want me discussing her personal problems with my teenage son.

His father's composure, the way he is laughing. Alex had got the wrong end of the stick, hadn't he, made a twat of himself by jumping to conclusions. But that phrase, *my teenage son*, something offensive about it. He wants to punch his father for winning the argument with such bad grace. Pause, breathe . . . He has to extricate himself with some shred of dignity. *My mistake.* He starts to walk away, then stops and turns because, fuck it, he's come this far. *So it's OK if I ask Mum. About Amy.* He holds his father's eye.

That's not a good idea, Alex.

You fucking . . .

Don't talk to me like that.

I'll talk to you how the hell I like. Grabbing two fistfuls of his father's shirt and pushing him backwards. *Alex, stop this.* Winded as he slams against the wall.

You sit all around all day moaning, you get some shitty job in a bookshop while Mum goes out and works her arse off and all the time you're fucking someone else.

Alex. Keep your voice down.

You coward.

Something broken in his father's eyes. He lets go. There are things he meant to say, promises he meant to extract, but something else is demanding his attention. Crouch End. The fear has gone and will never come back, he knows this with absolute certainty, but he had not realised the price he would have to pay. His father is lazy and weak and selfish but he stands between Alex and something that is cold and vast and dark and utterly inhuman. He realises that when he dies his parents will no longer be there to hold him. He is genuinely alone for the first time in his life. He turns away. He cannot bear to look at his father's face. He steps out of his unlaced shoes, places them neatly by the door and walks into the house.

Benjy always loved packing a rucksack, the gathering and celebration of possessions, pearls running through the king's fingers. The gladius with its handguard of plaited rope, the pen that wrote in eight colours, Mr Seal and Mr Crocodile, the metal thing, the Natural History Museum notebook, a piece of sheep poo in a Ziploc freezer bag, a dog he had moulded out of candlewax last night during supper. He was eager to get going. No one made you do homework or tidy your room or be constructive on a journey because the

journey was the constructive thing and it looked after itself
so you could do what you wanted while it was happening.
But they weren't setting off for two hours so he put their
names in the guest book, adding ages for himself and Alex
and Daisy. *I liked walking up the hill and the rain strom and the
sheepherd's pie at the grannery.* He then spent twenty minutes
filling a double page spread with an intricate drawing of the
house and garden. The horse's skull, the frogspawn pond, the
letters G and F interlaced in the rusted ornamental cast iron
of the downhill gate. Everyone said what a wonderful drawing
it was, better than a proper grown-up drawing somehow, the
wonky lines, the weird scale, the eccentric detail, for this is
how they will all remember the place, nothing quite as it
was, elements added, elements removed. The stove will loom
large for Angela, the shed for Alex. Everyone will forget the
fox weathervane. And whenever Louisa thinks about the
valley she will remember looking up from the garden to see
a plane trailing smoke and flames from a burning engine,
though this is something they will see when passing an
airfield on their way home.

Angela fills a bowl with Shreddies and full-fat milk and
sprinkles three spoons of soft brown sugar over the top before
carrying it through to the dining room. That weak washed-
out feeling you get when recovering from flu. She sits down.
Alex?

There are five pieces of toast on his plate. He is shaking.
What?

Are you all right?

Yeh. He wants to tell her why he is upset. He reaches out across the table to take his mother's hand. Then he stops and picks up the marmalade instead because he remembers Daisy saying she'd had a weird turn in the middle of the night. She's the one who needs protecting now.

Richard hobbles into the dining room and unplugs his iPhone from its little white charger in the socket by the window. *Packed and ready?*

Ten minutes, says Alex, and Angela thinks how her brother is returning to a life which is so much more solid and purposeful than the lives which await them. The hospital, the apartment on Moray Place.

Richard pours himself a coffee and stands sipping. He had expected something to be resolved or mended or rediscovered over the last few days. He wants to say to Angela that she and Dominic should visit Edinburgh sometime but he finds it hard to sound enthusiastic, so he says it to Alex instead. *Good hills for running and biking.* It won't happen, of course. This makes him sadder than he expected.

Dominic walks upstairs to strip the bed and check the drawers and perform a rudimentary clean of the bathroom. When Alex grabbed hold of him he thought something would change. Revelation, turning point, but it doesn't happen, it never happens. He pictures his life as a clumsy cartwheel down a long long hill, hitting this rock and that tree, a little more bruised and scratched with each successive impact till . . . what? till the ground levels out? till he finds himself airborne over some great ravine? He takes his phone out of his pocket. It is still turned off. God knows how many messages waiting. None maybe. He is not sure which is worse.

He squirts Cif into the sink and scrubs it with the little yellow and green sponge, paying close attention to the taps, rinsing everything with clean water and drying it with a hand towel. He has no idea what Alex will do, no way of finding out and no way of stopping it. *Guests are kindly requested to leave the house in the condition they found it.* He squirts Domestos round the toilet bowl and scrubs it with the long-handled plastic brush. He lifts the thin white liner out of the flip-top bin. Tissues, disposable razor, waxy Q-tips.

Melissa swings into the dining room. Alex smiles at her, he actually fucking smiles. She pours herself a cup of coffee, stands drinking, makes herself look like Richard who is doing the same thing on the other side of the table, glances at her watch. *Twenty minutes left.* She tries to make it sound funny but no one laughs, because it's not *A Midsummer Night's Dream*, is it? More like *Doctor Faustus.* A deal with the devil. She could make people do anything she wanted, but she had no idea what she wanted. *I need some fresh air.*

Alex thinks about last night all over again and it helps compensate for the Dad thing a little. He puts butter and jam on another two slices of toast.

Louisa and Daisy sit on the bench talking about Ian, the wayward years, the civil ceremony on Skye, the Staffordshire Bull Terrier. There is a bumpy mattress of grey cloud to the

east but above the valley the sky is a flawless blue, a valedic-
tory blessing, or maybe it's just Daisy's buoyant mood. Melissa
comes out of the front door with a coffee, glances their way
and bodyswerves left.

I hope she's OK.

Louisa spins the last of her orange juice around the base
of her glass. *She's like her father. She'll be hugely successful and
make vast amounts of money and never stop being angry.*

Alex showers and packs, stuffing everything haphazardly
into his one sports bag. Dry, damp, clean, dirty.

Angela finds Richard trying to lug a suitcase downstairs
and forces him to sit down while she wheels it outside and
hoists it into the boot.

Dominic walks into the shed. Spark plugs, the horse's skull.
In the corner a tub of old paint, four litres, Dulux magnolia.
He finds a big screwdriver, jams it under the lip and heaves.
The lid squeaks and bends and finally pops open, spraying
tiny orange flakes of rust in his face. The paint separated but
still liquid, dishwater grey with snotty lumps. Hard to believe
it would turn white if you mixed it. He takes his phone out
of his pocket, touches the surface of the liquid and lets go.
He expects it to clunk faintly against the bottom of the tin
but it simply vanishes. He imagines it falling slowly down a
tube that carries on till it reaches the centre of the earth.

Dominic? Angela is calling.

Louisa puts her hand on the bumpy wall and listens. Paint
over plaster over stone. Nothing. Complete silence.

Benjy comes out of the house carrying his rucksack and

the taxi pulls into the drive simultaneously, as if this whole holiday has been his own personal arrangement and everyone else is merely tagging along.

One last photo, says Richard. So Dominic balances the camera on the wall, a wedge of flint under the lens to get the elevation right. He presses the timer release then scoots across the grass and slots himself in beside Melissa. Just before the shutter clicks Daisy catches sight of something moving up there on the hill and turns to look, so that when Alex plugs it into Photoshop later that same evening she will be a blur, unreadable, but more alive than all her frozen family. They will look at this photograph many years later and realise that the camera saw something more clearly than any of them.

It's the same Viking guy with the scar who brought them at the beginning of the week, but he's driving a people carrier this time, which strikes Richard as odd because they always seem permanently attached to one vehicle, like centaurs. Everyone apart from Benjy and Melissa turns to one another, trying to gauge the expected warmth of the parting, but it's Louisa who breaks the spell and hugs Daisy and says, *We're going to visit you, both of us, soon*. It's obvious to everyone that she hasn't mentioned this to Richard and equally obvious that she doesn't need to.

The hug takes Angela by surprise. A little jag of shame, though she is glad that Daisy and Louisa can act as deputies for each family, displaying the familiarity that she and Richard do not feel and probably never will. She shakes Richard's hand, clasping it between both of hers to prevent the gesture seeming too formal. *Thanks. It was really generous of you.* It sounds like an apology, which it is, of course.

Alex tries to catch Melissa's eye but she is staring adamantly elsewhere. He wants someone else to know what happened last night, someone who knows Melissa, someone who understands how extraordinary it was. He wonders whether he can tell Daisy.

Goodbye, Benjamin. Richard squeezes his shoulder, but he has never had children of his own and doesn't understand that vacant look in Benjy's eyes, the way he disengages while adults do their tricky dances of arrival and departure.

Benjy? Dad is looking at him with raised eyebrows.

He returns briefly to the moment. *Thank you, Uncle Richard. The vinegar rocket was really good.* Then he is gone again.

You're welcome.

So . . . Dominic blows into his hands as if he's cold.

Two, three, seconds of discomfort then some silent signal releases them. They climb in to the taxi, into the Mercedes. Doors slide and thunk shut. The taxi does a four-point turn and bumps through the gate onto the rutted stony mud of the track, the Mercedes in its wake. A single pane of glass rattles. The brief scent of exhaust, the noise of engines fading as they circle the house and head towards the main road.

So little of them left, the faintest smell of cocoa butter, dirty sheets and pillowcases, muddy towels, a purple GoGo behind the radiator in the dining room, a yellow GoGo under the fridge, the makeshift circlip behind the washing machine. *I liked walking up the hill*. The burnt and cracked head of a china doll in the ashes of the stove.

Cloud moving in from the east and thickening. Specks of rain. A red Datsun making its way up from Longtown. Joan and her daughter, Kelly, who come every Friday to clean the house during the holiday season and make it ready for the next guests who will arrive later in the afternoon, though Kelly will spend most of the time sitting in the little window seat in the kitchen, rocking gently back and forth, tapping her chin with her fist and singing a song that has no words.

Framed watercolours of mallow and campion. *Secrets of the Night*. *A Sparrow Falls*. The banknote. The brass spoons. *Brother, my Lungs are not Goode*. The pattern of ancient paths. Hay Bluff, Lord Hereford's Knob. Heather and purple moorgrass and little craters of rippling peaty water. High up, a red kite weaving its way through the holes in the wind.

www.vintage-books.co.uk